Cataloochee Man

A Novel

ISBN   978-0-9787484-3-2

Published 2009 by **Walnut Creek Press**
2970 Walnut Creek Road
Marshall NC, 28753

www.walnutcreekpress.com

Cover design by the author
Manufactured in the United States of America

*The way that you wander
is the way that you choose.
The day that you tarry
is the day that you lose.*

From Jeremiah's Song

Cataloochee Man

by
Dennis Ruane

1

With this kill, the hunter would eat well for weeks. His arrow had entered the deer's chest and ruptured the animal's heart as it passed through. The deer collapsed to the ground seconds after it was struck, struggled, and then lay still.

The man knelt beside the animal and made certain that it was dead. He eviscerated the young doe and left a steaming pile of entrails that other animals would dine upon. The hunter positioned the carcass over his shoulders and walked away.

The day was both sunny and cool, a promising spring day. The hunter was traversing Cataloochee Divide Trail, a path so named because it follows the Cataloochee Divide, the mountain crest that marks the boundary of Great Smoky Mountains National Park. A wooden rail fence separated open pasture to the south from a vast forest to the north. Sullen, grass fields were hemmed in by panoramic swaths of brilliant snow. At this high altitude, snow could linger long after it had melted in the valleys.

The hunter came this way in early spring because deer were plentiful then. He was walking downhill toward Cataloochee Valley at a slow, measured pace while surveying the landscape in all directions. He never overlooked the opportunity to acquire more game and never assumed that he, himself, was not being hunted.

Then he saw her. A woman was riding from the east on a roan horse that was stepping up the slope toward him. At this time of year, few people were up so high on Cove Creek Ranch. The property bordered Great Smoky Mountains National Park. The hunter always melted into the forest upon seeing another person, but something about this woman made him linger. He hadn't seen a woman in six months and hadn't seen a woman he thought to be so beautiful in his lifetime.

So he stood a moment longer, dressed in a hunting frock made of deerskin and ornamented with rawhide fringe down the seams. The hunter had pants of the same material that were decorated with fringe on the outside of each leg. He had the dead deer across his shoulders and a longbow positioned at his side. She hadn't seen him, and he couldn't turn his eyes from her.

The woman had brown hair that hung in rivulets from the brim of her hat. Her hair framed dark eyes and sharp, sculptured features. She was dressed in brushed denim clothing, riding boots, and leather gloves.

The hunter could see that she was talking and soon heard her voice. To him, it was a lovely, captivating sound, and he wanted to hear more.

The woman folded her cell phone and looked up. When she saw him, she raised a hand to her mouth. The hunter stared for a moment longer and then merged with the foliage.

2

"Where did you see this guy?"

"At the top of the ranch, where it borders the park, up the hill from Double Gap trail head."

"From the way you describe him, he seems to be a cross between Robin Hood and Daniel Boone."

"No, I wish he would've been like Robin Hood, but he was more like Daniel Boone, Daniel Boone with a longbow. And he had a dead deer on his shoulders."

"Oh come on, Layla, you're not allowed to hunt up there."

"Hey, I didn't imagine it, but I don't blame you for being skeptical. Right now it seems unreal to me, too." She shrugged her shoulders and smiled. Layla Turner was a tall woman with an athletic build. She had wavy, auburn-colored hair, a long, somewhat somber face, and brown eyes. Layla was a pretty woman, especially when she smiled.

Her friend and neighbor, Tracy Ogden, was the first to hear of Layla's encounter with the mysterious man on the Cataloochee Divide. Tracy had straight brown hair that draped the shoulders of her white robe. She had a dark complexion and her features were rounded and less serious than Layla's. Tracy was also two inches shorter than her friend. Both in their early thirties, they had become close soon after Layla moved to Western North Carolina. Layla walked to Tracy's house this morning to tell her tale over coffee.

"Maybe it was one of those guys that reenacts pioneer days, Buckskinners or something like that they're called. I know someone who's in to that."

"That's a little extreme, Tracy, don't you think, skulking around in Great Smoky Mountains National Park, shooting deer with a bow and arrow?"

They laughed and sipped their coffee on a beautiful spring morning. The temperature was unseasonably high so that the friends sat on Tracy's back deck. Layla and Tracy lived at Mountain Crest, a new community located ten miles west of Waynesville, North Carolina. The development was situated three thousand feet above sea level on Balsam Mountain.

"Well, let's get to the point of the matter. Was he good looking?"

"Yes, I think so. He had a beard, so I can't say a lot about his face. But overall, yes, I'd say he was good looking. He had light-colored eyes that were so mysterious, hazel-colored maybe."

"Weren't you frightened a little? After all, that's pretty bizarre to come face to face with someone dressed like that in such an isolated place."

"No I wasn't. I was surprised at first, but he didn't scare me. It was the expression on his face that put me at ease."

"What was it like?"

"It was flattering, as if he couldn't stop looking at me."

"Uh oh." Tracy grinned.

Layla laughed. "Now stop. You're bad."

"Did you tell Davis about the hunter?" Tracy asked, her grin transforming into a mischievous smile.

"Uh no, I decided not to. Actually I haven't talked to him in a few days. He wouldn't . . . Well, you know him. He would just tell me that this is another reason to quit riding alone. Of course, he would never consider coming for a ride with me."

Tracy's smile flattened. She was aware of the problematic relationship between Layla and her husband. Now she wished she hadn't asked the question.

"Well can I tell people about this guy? Maybe someone else has seen Cataloochee Man."

Layla laughed. "I like that, Cataloochee Man. No, I don't care who you tell. I'm going to ask around at the university, myself."

Moments later, as Layla walked the quarter mile distance to her house, she was thinking about how much she enjoyed talking to Tracy. She didn't know what she would do without this friend and confidant now that she was alone so often.

Tracy, her husband, and their two daughters were so typical and happy that Layla envied them. Michael Ogden was a physician who loved his profession, but he managed to budget his time so that he passed as much of it as possible with his family. Tracy worked from their home as a free-lance editor and raised the girls. Michael practiced in Waynesville, and he and Tracy had a beautiful home at Mountain Crest.

Layla and her husband, Davis Elmore, had built a second home at Mountain Crest seven years before. She and Davis soon came to like the area so much that he left his father's law firm in Raleigh, and opened his own practice on Main Street in Waynesville. Layla had a PhD in English and had taught at the University of North Carolina at Chapel Hill. After they moved, she was fortunate to get a position at Western Carolina University in the nearby town of Cullowhee.

But unlike his wife, Davis never adapted well to life in the mountains and year by year, he and Layla drifted farther apart. When his former employer decided to run for governor, Davis accepted the position of campaign manager. He now served as chief counsel to his father, Malcolm Elmore, Governor of North Carolina.

Layla walked slower than usual to enjoy the beautiful day. Many of the houses at Mountain Crest were second homes so at this time of the year the neighborhood was quiet. That was the way she liked it.

When her home came into view, she smiled. Layla devoted a good portion of the previous seven years to this building. She had always loved the forest, and her dream since she was a girl was to someday have a beautiful home high on a mountain. That dream had most certainly come true. Layla's house was a stunning, contemporary design, with low lines and multiple levels. At her request, the architect utilized the native construction materials of stone and wood. *Contemporary rustic* was how he described his creation.

When Layla entered the house, a light was blinking on the kitchen phone. She guessed that it was a message from Davis before she heard his voice.

"Hello Layla. Hey, hon, I have to stay down here another week. Something's come up, but I promise you, next week . . ."

Layla stopped the message. She had heard too many promises over the last several years.

Four years earlier, when Layla balked at the prospect of moving back to Raleigh, Davis devised a plan by which he could spend most of his time at Mountain Crest and manage his commitments to the Governor by phone and internet. He planned to travel east only when necessary. In recent years, it was necessary for him to be in Raleigh more often than not, and Layla passed most weeks and many holidays alone.

Layla was thirty years old, and her husband was four years older. They met at the University of North Carolina in Chapel Hill, while she was working on her PhD, and he was finishing law school. Layla and Davis married two months after he entered his father's law firm.

Layla started coffee and while the percolator gurgled and chugged, she moved her laptop to the deck. She had been working on a novel for over four years but had not looked at the manuscript for six months. This morning, Layla was inspired to write. However, once settled in her chair, a mug of coffee at hand, fingers poised above the keyboard, her mind wandered.

Layla looked above the computer monitor and stared into the distance at Waterrock Knob. When she went to Cove Creek Ranch, she traveled the Blue Ridge Parkway part of the way. The Parkway wound past Waterrock Knob at an elevation of nearly six thousand feet. Layla would often stop to walk a short trail that led to the mountain's summit. From there she could gaze at the great mountain ranges of Southern Appalachia. Layla especially liked to stand on Waterrock Knob in the evenings when the sun was setting over Great Smoky Mountains National Park.

Then Layla's thoughts drifted further north, toward the park, and soon she was thinking about the mysterious hunter on the Cataloochee Divide, with his hazel-colored eyes and rugged costume. *Why did he just stand there to let me see him, and then walk away like that?*

She forced herself back to the novel, which at this point consisted of an outline and a few rough chapters. The story begins with a young woman who is trapped in a domestic situation that has become intolerable. She and her husband are professors at Western Carolina University. His PhD is in mathematics and hers in English. They met while graduate students at The University of North Carolina at Chapel Hill, married shortly after graduation, and moved to western North Carolina to lead a simpler life in the mountains.

While the husband's enthusiasm grows for his chosen field to the point of obsession, the wife begins to sense that she has made a mistake by allowing herself to be steered away from an early dream of being a writer. While she struggles with this notion, her husband begins to pressure her about starting a family.

One day, the woman abandons her career, leaves her husband, and drives to Alaska. She takes up residence in a town named Chistochina, teaches in a small elementary school, and writes in the evenings.

Layla sighed. She still liked the basic idea but there were many blanks to fill in. And she knew the story needed a subplot or two.

So much time had passed since she began writing the story that it was difficult to relate to her main character as she once did. Layla never intended for the novel to be autobiographic, but it was begun at the time when she started to harbor doubts about her marriage to Davis.

Then the phone rang. She got up to answer, once again distracted from her keyboard.

"Hello, Layla speaking."

"Layla, I've got some interesting information for you."

"Oh, hi Tracy, I'd love to hear it. I'm trying to get moving on my novel again and could use a little stimulation."

Tracy laughed. She knew all about her friend's writing ambitions and was aware of the frustration she was experiencing with her novel.

"Do you remember me mentioning Jim Palmer, the author I've worked with, the one who specialized in informational books about Great Smoky Mountains National Park?"

"Yes, the former ranger, right?"

"That's right. He knows more about the park than anyone I've ever met. Well, I was thinking about your sighting of the hunter on the Cataloochee Divide and Jim came to mind. Jim has a fantastic memory. I called him at his home in Asheville and told him the story. He was able to recall that there was a similar sighting about five years ago. He read about it in the newspaper and remembers the story."

"Really? See, I wasn't imagining things."

"I guess not. According to Jim, it was a young boy, five-years old. His family was visiting Cataloochee Valley and they'd walked back to one of the old houses that is still down there, the Woody House. Have you ever been to the Woody House?"

"Yes, once on horseback; I rode down to it on a trail."

"Well, if you come in through the valley, the house is about a mile beyond where Cataloochee Road ends. It's gated there and you have to walk from then on.

This family hiked to the Woody House to have a picnic on the porch. After eating, the five-year-old and his brother and sister ran and played in the yard. When the parents realized it was too quiet, they got up to look for the children. The brother and sister came rushing out of the woods behind them, yelling and screaming. Apparently that was their plan, for the three of them to circle through the woods and come up from behind to scare their parents. But the five-year-old didn't come out of the woods."

"Oh my goodness, this is giving me goose bumps."

"Well the story has a happy ending but be ready for more goose bumps. The parents called and searched but there was no sign of the boy. Finally in desperation, the father rushed back to Cataloochee Road and drove two miles to the ranger station.

Several rangers came back with him and made a quick search, but no luck. It's already after four in late September, so they called for help. They knew it would get dark soon. Dozens of people, rangers, park personnel and volunteers fan out and search until dark, but, still no sign of him."

"I'm glad you told me this has a happy ending, because I don't like the sound of it so far."

"Okay, so overnight, a massive search is organized and readied to launch at first light. But just before dawn, the boy walks up to some rangers who were drinking coffee outside the ranger station and tells them who he is."

"That's incredible."

"Yes, and it brings me to the point of the story. When questioned about his ordeal, the boy explained that when he circled in the woods he couldn't find the Woody House again. He got scared and ran to try to find it, but everything looked the same to him. He got tired but kept walking. When it was nearly dark a man came through the woods toward him and asked if he was lost. He said the man was dressed like Daniel Boone. He had a beard and had a bow over his shoulder."

"No."

"Yes. The boy said that the man gave him water and some kind of dry meat to eat. Later, he prepared places on the ground for them to sleep and they camped for the night. Early in the morning, the man walked him through the woods until they could see the lights at the ranger station. He told him to go up to the rangers and tell them who he was."

"This is unbelievable. So this guy has been around for a while."

"It seems that way. Oh, the boy also said that the man's name was Abe and that he said he lived in the park."

"What?"

"Yes. He told the boy that he lived in the park."

"What did the rangers think about that?"

"Not much, it was too unbelievable. They thought it was extremely lucky that the boy ever found his way out. They reasoned that what he told them was his attempt to cope with a very frightening ordeal."

"Wow. This is really interesting. There has got to be a story here. How can I ever go back to my moldy old novel now?"

Tracy laughed. "Don't, give it a break. Play around with this new idea, Cataloochee Man."

"Don't laugh. I just might. Maybe I'll get lost in the woods and see if Cataloochee Man rescues me."

"Who's being bad now?"

They both laughed.

"Got to run, Layla, I've got kids to transport."

"See you, Tracy. Thanks for the info."

3

"Timber, that's what we're talking about, son, North Carolina hardwood. It's time the state reaped the benefits of its God-given resources. It's high time for more extensive logging of the national forests in our great state."

Governor Malcolm Elmore circled his enormous mahogany desk and thumped his fist on its surface for emphasis.

The Governor was of average height with a large, round head and a wide body that was getting wider with the accumulation of years. Malcolm was not handsome, but his face had a sort of charm when he smiled. He smiled often, displaying gleaming white teeth punctuated by a gold crown on his upper, left canine. His hairline ebbed, and an extended forehead was often moist with enthusiastic perspiration.

"When our campaign begins, it'll look good that you live and vote there. You're the perfect ambassador for this assignment, Davis. Why you inhabit those mountains, a resident of Western North Carolina, a mountain-man counselor. Ha ha, it's perfect, don't you agree?"

Davis shrugged his shoulders and smiled. "I guess it is."

Davis Elmore was taller than his father with brown hair that was receding. He was of average build and while not heavy, an overhang was evident above his belt, suggesting that he might follow his father in that direction. The younger Elmore took after his mother with more refined features and sleepy, brown eyes. He was not loud like Malcolm and exhibited little of his father's pomposity, even though he tried to do so at times.

"You know, Dad, from what I've been reading, commercial logging of the national forests is one of the most controversial natural resource issues in the United States. There already is opposition to the small logging operations that are in the forests now. There will be stiff resistance to any increased logging, especially if you're proposing to let the big companies in.

Besides that, the Roadless Rule that the Clinton administration put in place before leaving office restricts road construction on national forest lands. That necessarily restricts commercial logging. Environmental activists are already well entrenched behind it."

"Ah yes, we do have the legacy of King William to deal with. That's why it's fortunate we've got a president now who understands the need to look to the greater good. That's why the Bush administration put a hold on implementation of the Roadless Rule pending further review and revision, and you know what that language means. By God, I'll call the President myself. I know we'll get his support."

Malcolm paused after this bold pronouncement. He cleared his throat and spoke in a calmer tone. "Davis, I have a suggestion to make as we begin this campaign. The western counties are some of the poorest in the state. While it's true that many wealthy people are building second homes there and moving to these counties for retirement, the indigenous population remains relatively poor."

Davis stared at his father with a blank expression.

"The point is that from now on, whether it's in my discussion

13

with the President of the United States or in your interview with a small town newspaper in western North Carolina, we need to emphasize that the working-class population is what this proposal is all about."

"It is?"

"Yes, that's the route we need to go, and we need support from them first and foremost. The indigenous population of western North Carolina is poor and this initiative means jobs. And those aren't just idle words with me, son. I know the anti-logging crowd would have everyone think that it's all about big business and money and sure, it can't get done without the business end of it. But ultimately the money trickles down to where it belongs, to the people who live there."

Davis nodded but, he didn't seem quite convinced. He stood and began gathering papers and maps that he'd spread across the Governor's desk during the course of their discussion.

"I believe this is a good initiative, Davis, one that is long overdue, and one that will define my term in office. You head back west and try to get a feel for where the public stands on this issue. Write some informational articles in the newspapers to introduce the idea and emphasize how logging the national forests will directly benefit the local economies."

Davis nodded again.

Then Malcolm sat down, leaned back in his chair, and stared up at his son. A playful grin spread across his face.

Davis looked up and stopped what he was doing. "What?"

"I was just thinking that maybe while you're up there you might have that pretty wife of yours cook you a hearty meal or two."

"Well, I . . . Yes, maybe I will. Layla is a good cook actually, when she cooks."

"I know she is."

"It's just that she's busy with her profession and her gardens, and there's always the novel."

"Davis, Davis, I hear you. Believe me. But you yield too easily, son. You deserve a good home cooked meal now and again, no excuses. Why don't you and Layla cook a meal together? Your mother and I did that often. You and Layla have got to slow down and enjoy each other's company more."

Davis began to feel uncomfortable. He sensed the direction his father was going with the conversation.

"Do you and Layla ever talk about starting a family?"

Davis was looking across the room but turned when his father asked the question. "We've talked about it before but, uh, we haven't discussed it lately. You know more and more people are choosing not to have children these days." Davis had just read an article discussing this trend. He made the statement on impulse and soon wished he hadn't.

Malcolm's face clouded over. "I don't give a damn what more and more people are doing. Sit down, son, and bear with me for a moment."

The Governor paused and gazed out the window before he spoke again. When he did, it was in a controlled and calm manner.

"People such as you and Layla, people that have been blessed with a good and comfortable life, owe it to the Lord to breathe new life into the world. The Lord tested your mother and I. Norma had trouble with childbirth and had two miscarriages before we were blessed with you and your sister. But the births were hard and complicated. For that reason, we had no more babies after that."

Davis shifted in his chair.

"When Norma died, it took a toll on me. I never felt such grief before or after. We were high school sweethearts and had our whole lives together planned out before we graduated. But things happen. The Lord works in mysterious ways. I probably should have remarried for your sake and especially for Martha's sake. Your sister needed a woman's influence."

"I think you did well with us, Dad."

Malcolm smiled. "My point is that you can't keep putting some things off. Layla is thirty and you're a ripe, old thirty-four. Tomorrow may never happen and damn it, I want grandchildren." Malcolm's grin reappeared and Davis smiled.

"Now you go west, young man, as they say. Work hard on the logging initiative, son, but spend some time with your wife, too."

Davis drove home slowly, feeling somewhat dishonest. He realized that his father had no idea of the troubled state of his relationship with Layla. Malcolm would never have guessed that one reason there was no discussion about starting a family was because his son and daughter-in-law slept in separate bed.

Davis drove through an older neighborhood on the outskirts of Raleigh and pulled up the driveway of a handsome two-story, brick house. The house stood on half an acre of sloping land that supported a stand of magnificent oak and maple trees. These towered over an array of beautiful, terraced gardens. Davis and Layla had been married for only six months when Malcolm purchased the property for them.

Unlike her husband, Layla had never been fond of the design of the house. But she was grateful for her father-in-law's generosity and worked to complement the building with her gardens.

From the garage, Davis entered the kitchen, still mulling over the conversation with his father. He went to the refrigerator and removed a bottle of Heineken. A shot glass sat next to a bottle of vodka on the counter. Davis filled the glass, quickly drank the vodka, and followed with a swallow of cold beer. He repeated this procedure and then carried the remaining Heineken into his den.

Perched in a leather recliner, Davis allowed the alcohol to separate him from his work day. He also hoped it would distance him from the conversation with his father. But half an hour later, after another shot and another beer, he entertained the notion of having children. After all, he liked children and he and Layla had once considered having a family.

Maybe that's what our relationship needs now, something to focus on. Maybe having a family would pull us back together.

4

A soldier stood amongst trees and brush that bordered a small clearing in a vast forest. He was wearing a black beret, combat fatigues, a pack, and leather boots. An AK-47 assault rifle was strapped to his side. He breathed in frosty night air that was permeated with an aroma of moist sawdust. The soldier arrived just after dark and waited for an hour to complete his mission.

Now it was time to move. The clearing was a logging operation in Pisgah National Forest. The site comprised twenty acres of clear-cut woods. The soldier withdrew a flask from his shirt pocket and took several determined drinks, throwing his head back with each one. He recapped the flask and wiped his mouth on his sleeve. Stepping from the trees the soldier moved along the edge of the clearing.

In the distance, a flashlight beam was poking and slashing at the darkness. The soldier guessed that the watchman who wielded it was about two hundred yards away. He knew the man.

Good old Ira, he thought as he came up to a DC-9 Caterpillar bulldozer. *I hate to do this to you, old, buddy. But a man's got to do what a man's got to do. These are my woods too.*

The soldier had known Ira Drew for many years and had

even worked with him the summer before the war. Ira had been a logging man his entire working life. Health problems narrowed the range of his career. He was content now with his position as night watchman for High Country Logging Company. As with all the roles Ira had assumed throughout his fifty years in the logging business, he took this job seriously and did it well.

The soldier removed his pack and withdrew a bomb made up of four sticks of dynamite and a detonator, bound together and wired to a timer. With duct tape, he attached the bomb to a hose near the gas tank of the bulldozer. He set the timer, and walked away at a brisk pace. Although he had traversed thirty yards by the time the machine exploded, the soldier was pushed forward by the blast and nearly fell.

"Goddamn," he muttered, stroking his beard, "I got to give myself another three seconds next time." He chuckled about his miscalculation, tugged on his beret and drifted back to the tree line.

The flashlight jostled wildly as it moved across the field. Ira Drew materialized into the orange glow of the blazing bulldozer. He was an excitable man under any circumstance; the explosion of the DC-9 caused Ira to nearly spin in circles. His job as night watchman had been routine up until now. Ira watched the fire in disbelief, wondering what sort of malfunction could have caused this catastrophe. He dreaded the thought of telling his boss, but Ira forced himself toward the office to make the call.

Ira almost reached a trailer that served as a field office for the company, when a blast sounded on the other side of the clearing. The watchman turned to see a tower of flames rising to illuminate the night sky. The fire was near where he had been when the bulldozer exploded, so Ira knew it must be the log skidder this time. He stared in bewilderment until he saw the dark form of a person moving away from the fire. The realization that these were deliberate acts hit him like a slap in the face.

The watchman grabbed at the gun on his side until the snap on the holster came undone. He shouted for the figure to stop and then fired two shots into the air. The figure didn't stop and soon disappeared beyond the glow of the burning machine. Ira realized that he couldn't catch up to the perpetrator and also knew he wouldn't shoot even if he could overtake him. Ira fired twice more into the air and then turned back toward the office.

"You have every right to be upset, Mr. Blass," said a tall, angular policeman. "But the sooner I can gather the information we need, the sooner we can proceed with our investigation. Hopefully that will lead to the apprehension of who is responsible." Tom Morrison was a patient man with years of experience as a state police officer.

"This is going to hurt us, insurance or not. We've got a quota to fill and every day we're down hurts." Philip Blass, partner in High Country Logging Company, was a short, stout man with a prominent bald head. He was upset and glanced back and forth at the charred machines on each side of the clearing. The equipment was still smoldering as dawn filtered through the forest.

"Why us, why is someone targeting us?"

"Well Mr. Blass. I don't believe it's anything personal; it's not just you. Another operation was hit last fall, north of here, a logging operation near Waterville."

"That's great comfort. It's some sort of environment group thing, like Earth Front or whatever the hell their name is."

"You mean Earth First. Yes, like Earth First but not them. This looks to me like the work of the Panther Patrol. They've already claimed responsibility in another case, similar to this one."

"They did, to who?"

"Jim Heinbaugh of Endless Mountain Logging. His company was the one hit near Waterville. He found an arrow with a note tied to it stuck to his office door. The note read, *stay out of my forest Heinbaugh*, and it was signed Panther Patrol.

The Panther Patrol seems to operate only in Pisgah National Forest and in the area that borders Great Smoky Mountains National Park. The evidence points to a small group, maybe even someone working alone. They move in quickly and know what they're doing.

The Panther Patrol has been around for a while but up until recently the attacks were less destructive. It used to be just tree spiking to wreck chain saws and, only once in a while, vandalizing equipment. For some reason, about a year and a half ago, the destruction rose to a new level. Things started blowing up."

Philip Blass scratched the back of his neck and wagged his head. He was an honest, hard-working man, trying to run a business that spanned three generations in his family. He and his younger brother had taken over the reins from their father.

"Well, whoever the hell they are, they're gonna' ruin me, if I don't have a coronary first."

"The FBI has been notified about what happened here. This is federal land so this falls under their jurisdiction."

"Well that's good to know, and I hope they catch these crackpots quick. If this happens again, I'm pullin' out. I'll go back to loggin' private land. Loggin' the national woods is good money but not if machinery's gonna get blown up."

5

As Layla approached the spot where she saw the hunter, she grew anxious and her heartbeat quickened. She had thought about him all week and anticipated the weekend to go riding again. Layla knew that the chance of seeing him again at the same location was remote. But by coming, she committed herself to look for this mysterious man. That alone was an exciting thought.

Her plan was to enter the park at Double Gap trail head and to follow Hemphill Bald Trail down into Cataloochee Valley until she crossed Caldwell Fork Trail. By circling to the east on Caldwell Fork Trail and then to the north on Rough Fork Trail, she would arrive at the Woody House. By this route, Layla would visit the two sites where the hunter had been seen and would traverse the most direct trails between them.

The day began with frost on the ground, but now in the noon sun, Layla had to remove her jacket to be comfortable. The sky was a clear blue, promising a delightful day for a ride in Great Smoky Mountains National Park.

The Cataloochee divide is five thousand feet above sea level at Double Gap. Layla looked back in the direction from which she came. She had a spectacular view of Cove Creek Valley and the settled, agricultural areas adjacent to the park. Interstate 40 snaked off to the east, a mere ribbon from this height. The vehicles appeared the size of insects. Only hushed sounds of their passage reached Layla's ears. The raspy scolding of crows heralded her approach to the treeline and drowned out all noise of civilization that wafted up from the valley.

The man with the bow was not standing where Layla had seen him last. She led her horse, through an opening in the fence that bordered Cove Creek Ranch and entered Great Smoky Mountains National Park. As she settled in for the long downward trek into Cataloochee Valley, Layla entertained herself with the question of why someone would live in the park if this was indeed the case with the hunter named Abe.

When Layla was young, one of her favorite books was *The Merry Adventures of Robin Hood* by Howard Pyle. The book was handed down to her by an uncle who sensed that his niece would appreciate the original telling of the legend of Robin Hood. This complete and unabridged version included all the songs and poetry shared by the outlaw band and had marvelous illustrations.

Layla loved the story and was fascinated with the illustrations. As a teenager, she fantasized about what it would be like to live in the forest with Robin Hood. She hadn't looked at the book in years now and had moved on to other fantasies, but *The Merry Adventures of Robin Hood* was on a shelf in her study at Mountain Crest.

Layla began her quest for Cataloochee Man with the rationalization that she was exploring the possibility of good material for a novel. Her natural inclination was to imagine the story of the hunter as a regional version of the Robin Hood tale. Layla chuckled as she played with the possibilities.

In the days leading up to her quest, Layla researched the history of Cataloochee Valley. As she turned west onto Caldwell Fork Trail, she found it hard to imagine that in 1932, before Great Smoky Mountains National Park was established, this forest was once part of a settlement numbering over twelve hundred residents.

The valley was now so quiet and primitive that it was easier for her to envision an earlier time when Cherokee Indians inhabited the area. She read that they used it for hunting camps and small, semi-permanent settlements. It delighted Layla to know that the Cherokee had walked some of the trails that she traversed today.

It was two o'clock when Layla's horse stepped into the clearing that surrounded the Woody House. She thought it was a surreal scene, a two-story frame house with wood siding and a covered front porch, nestled into a silent, encroaching forest. Through her research, Layla knew why the Woody House was one of the few structures that remained intact after Great Smoky Mountains National Park was established. Steve Woody, the family patriarch, exercised the federal government's option that permitted inhabitants to remain on their property after it was purchased.

Layla dismounted and tethered her horse. She walked toward the house, trying to imagine the drama that unfolded here five years before. At the scene, it was easy for her to appreciate how a five year old child could become lost in the dark forest that crowded the house.

When Layla was five years old, she lived in Boston. Her father was a history professor at Harvard University and her mother was in medical school. The city parks were Layla's first experience with woods and she had many fond memories of walking through them with her father. Her mother was always busy and never walked in the woods with them.

The sound of her boot on the porch of the Woody House startled Layla, sounding somehow too intrusive against the silence. The door was open and she stepped into a musty hall of the past. Layla was uneasy as she explored the house, as if she were trespassing. This was a home once, where real people lived. Now it was an exhibit in a national park with strangers from all over the world traipsing through. She walked from room to room in silent reverence, allowing her imagination to complete the picture of a home.

Exiting through the back door, Layla surveyed the woods behind the building. She stepped over a stone retaining wall and walked a meandering path into the forest. After traversing a short distance, she turned back to look at the house. Layla was startled when she didn't see it. She walked back twenty yards in the direction she thought she had come and then spotted the Woody House out of the corner of her eye. It was situated at a ninety degree angle from where she thought it was. She circled about in the woods for another twenty minutes but now didn't let the house out of her sight.

Half an hour later, Layla sensed that it was time to start back. The mood of the day was changing. Cool air enveloped her as a light wind moved up the slope. By the time she mounted Sundance, the sun had faded behind irritable, gray clouds.

After traveling a short distance on Rough Fork Trail, Layla looked back at the Woody House. She told herself that the more details she could picture about the place the better for her writing. The truth was that she still hoped to see the hunter. It would be a chance encounter, but she needed a chance encounter at this stage in her life. She wanted Robin Hood of the Smoky

Mountains to be real.

The uphill walk on Rough Fork Trail was much slower for Sundance. By the time the horse reached the junction with Hemphill Bald Trail, it was after four o'clock. Layla knew that they still had time to get out of the woods before dark but not much room for error. The next two miles represented the steepest incline of the day's ride and Sundance slowed again.

The sun never reappeared and it was cooler at the higher elevation. Layla wished she had brought more than a jacket. A mile later, a thousand feet higher, she shuddered against the cold. She became somewhat unnerved when a heavy, wet fog closed in around her and Sundance. It seemed as if nature were conspiring to hold them back.

Upon learning of Layla's plans for an excursion into Great Smoky Mountains National Park, Tracy warned her friend against traveling alone. "A few simple mistakes in a row can be fatal," Tracy admonished. She quoted from a book by Jim Palmer that chronicled stories about people who died in the Smoky Mountains. Layla thought of that quote now.

Layla realized she had made one mistake by not being prepared for a change in the weather and another by not allowing more time for the uphill trek. The temperature continued to fall and the fog thickened. With growing unease, Layla prodded her horse. Sundance was a dependable mount but obstinate as well. Unperturbed by the circumstances, he navigated the trail at the pace he knew was best.

Layla glanced at her watch. Only five o'clock and yet it seemed so much later. "Damn it, where is that fence?" Sundance's ears twitched in response to the sound of her voice. Fog was pushed against tree limbs by the draft from the valley and then rained down in cold droplets on the hapless travelers. Layla was wet and began to shiver. She strained to see through the fog, searching for a sign that they were nearing the ranch.

Finally, a break in the trees was evident and Layla knew that Cove Creek Ranch was just ahead. Sundance sauntered up the last slope and carried Layla through the gate. They entered a field of fog, as if they had stepped into a cloud. The breeze from Cove Creek Valley rushed against wet clothes and added to her discomfort, but Layla didn't notice so much because of her overwhelming relief to be back at the ranch.

Layla stopped Sundance and leaned against the horse's neck to compose herself. It was nearly six o'clock. Had she misjudged the time by another half hour she might not have gotten out of the park.

Layla raised her head and prodded herself to move. But before she began her descent to the stables, she looked behind into the park. The trail that she and Sundance had just traversed led to a frothing, menacing ocean of swirling whiteness.

Then, the wind shifted and the fog dispersed. Layla started and half stood in her stirrups. She thought she saw someone standing on the trail. Then mist reclaimed the area, hiding the image. Another gust of wind and she could see that it was the hunter. He was staring up at her. Just as suddenly, fog enshrouded him again.

"Hey, hello," Layla shouted, "Helloooooo."

The sound of the wind rushing through the forest was the only response. Layla strained to see, but her vision couldn't penetrate the cloud. She was so excited that for the moment she forgot the cold. When she attempted to turn back toward the park, Sundance resisted. The horse knew that north was the wrong direction now.

Layla called down the trail again. "Hello. I want to talk to you." No answer came from the swirling cloud. Her hands were numb and she was shivering. Layla knew that she had to go.

Layla drove east on Route 276, traveling parallel to the Cataloochee Divide. She was four thousand feet closer to sea level now and there was no fog or wind. Looking north, she saw that the ridge she had descended from was still covered in clouds.

Why would he have been there again, just standing and staring? Could he have been following me? Layla smiled as she remembered her comment to Tracy about purposely getting lost to be found by Mr. Abe. *Maybe he knew I was in trouble and followed to make sure I got out of the park in time.* She liked that thought.

Layla turned the heat off as her Subaru Outback neared Waynesville. She was warm and secure now, far removed from the harried ordeal in the park. Layla was elated to have seen the hunter again. Although it was only a silent, fleeting glimpse, she sensed that it spoke volumes.

At the very least, Layla had garnered some interesting literary material from her experience, and she wanted to put it into writing this evening. She decided to stop in Waynesville to buy a bottle of wine for inspiration and celebration.

6

The hunter knew that she had seen him. In his heart he was glad but in his head he knew it was foolhardy to have allowed it. *The dark-haired woman tempted fate by wandering alone into the forest on such an unpredictable day.* This intrigued him all the more about her.

On the day of their first encounter, after the woman had ridden by him and was out of sight, the hunter emerged from the foliage to study her horse's print in the moist dirt. Because people that lived outside the forest run on schedules, he knew that there was a good chance she would return seven days later. That was why he looked for the print one week later and at the same time of day that he had seen her before. This afternoon, when the hunter recognized the tracks, he followed them into the park.

He caught up with horse and rider at the Woody House and watched as the woman walked in the woods behind the old building. He couldn't guess her purpose as she wandered amongst the trees, but he grew anxious as she lingered. Even after the updraft from the valley began, signaling a change in the weather, the woman remained in the woods.

The hunter planned to travel to Cosby, Tennessee this day to see a friend but forgot his plan when he decided that the rider might not make it out of the park. He spent his afternoon following her trek from the valley to be certain that she did get out. Sometimes he was so near that he could smell her soft fragrance and other times he was at a considerable distance, moving through the forest on unmarked paths, anticipating her direction.

She called to me. Hello, I want to talk to you, that's what she said.

The hunter was moving at a brisk gait but knew well that he couldn't travel far with so little daylight remaining and such heavy fog. His immediate destination was another mile to the north where there was a rock overhang that protruded from the side of a steep slope. Underneath the rock was a recess that would provide protection from the wind. With a fire at the entrance, it was adequate shelter for weather such as this.

He left the trail. The hunter rarely used the established trails in Great Smoky Mountains National Park. When he first came to the forest, he never strayed far from them. But Cataloochee Valley had been his home for ten years now, and he could move in any direction with confidence.

When the hunter reached the overhang, he glanced inside and was glad to see that no one had been there since the frosty night in November when he last used it. He always left the shelter stocked with sticks and branches that would be ready to burn when he came again. He also left a pile of leaves against the back wall to provide a dry bed.

From a yellow birch tree, the hunter peeled a handful of bark. He tore the paper-like bark into thin shreds, crossed these into a small mound on the floor of the shelter, and lit it with a paraffin-coated match. By adding leaves, followed by twigs, then larger branches, he built up a crackling fire within minutes.

Then the hunter spread the pile of leaves into a rectangular mound and covered them with a wool blanket that he carried in a roll on his back. The blanket was large enough so that he could double it back to cover himself. This was his bed and, along with the fire, completed his accommodations for the night.

The hunter leaned against the back wall of the cave and stared into the fire. Flickering tongues of orange and yellow licked at dry wood that popped and cracked in useless protest of its fate. The flames had a meditative effect on the man and his mind was focused on one image, the dark haired rider. He had been on the move all day and the warmth of the fire enveloped him in weariness. Sleep would come soon.

If the pretty woman hadn't come back, I would've stopped thinking about her. But she did come back, and she called to me. Now I can think of nothing else.

7

With a bottle of wine in one hand and her hat in the other, Layla shut an ornate metal door and stepped into the Great Room. Named for its size and central location in the house, the room featured a beautiful, twelve hundred square-foot, red oak floor. Above this was a thirty foot high cathedral ceiling, supported by massive joists, framed in black walnut.

The north wall was a bank of windows that allowed for a magnificent view of the Plott Balsam Mountain Range, highlighted by Waterrock Knob. A large fireplace dominated the opposite side of the room and boasted a fieldstone chimney that was a masonry work of art. Across from where Layla had entered, an oak stairway ascended to a mezzanine that fronted the second floor rooms.

Layla wanted a warm shower and then a cool laptop. She started upon hearing a voice.

"Is that you m'lady?"

"Davis?"

"Whom were you expecting?"

"I wasn't expecting anyone. Where are you?"

"I'm lounging on the couch, where a working man should be after a hard week on the job."

Layla crossed the room and circled the high-backed couch that faced the fireplace. And there he was, her husband, Davis Elmore. Davis' head was propped up with the denim-covered cushions Layla had selected to compliment the tan, suede upholstery of the couch. He had a brandy snifter in his hand that was filled with a dark red wine. Layla knew it was wine because a bottle was conveniently positioned on the floor beside the couch.

"Davis, this is certainly a surprise. A good surprise though, of course. I uh, thought you were busy again this weekend." She was watching his wine glass, positioned above her couch.

"Ha ha, yes, I'm busy, but from now on, never too busy to spend quality time with my wife."

"Well that's good to hear," Layla said with little enthusiasm. "Where's your car?"

"In the garage, where a car should be. Besides, I wanted to surprise you. Are you surprised?"

Layla nodded.

Davis sat up and with his free hand reached to pull his wife toward him. Layla deftly took the wine glass from him and placed it on the coffee table. Then she bent and delivered a kiss on his lips. Davis had planned a more romantic encounter, but Layla was quick. She hit her mark and moved backward to the edge of a nearby ottoman.

Davis shrugged it off and laughed. He glanced at the narrow bag in her hand. "I see wine is our drink of choice tonight," he said with a mischievous grin and a slur to his voice.

"I've always preferred wine. It's become your drink of choice for tonight. Where's your Heineken? You'd better be careful; you know how wine gives you heartburn."

"To hell with heartburn," he said and reached for his glass.

While Layla was conversing with her husband, she was trying

to interpret the situation. Davis had never come to Mountain Crest unannounced. More often, he announced he was coming and then called with some reason why he couldn't make it.

"Where have you been m'lady? My guess is that you were traipsing about the Smoky Mountains on that infernal beast of yours?"

Layla stiffened. There was no doubt that Sundance was a troublesome animal at times, and she, herself, often complained about his belligerence. But Layla didn't like to hear Davis belittling her horse. She spent more time with Sundance then she did with him. Layla was also irritated because her plans for the evening were disrupted by Davis' unannounced appearance. She was looking forward to reflecting on the day's events and writing.

"Layla, did you eat supper?"

"No, did you?"

"No."

"Why not? You were never one to miss a meal."

"Well, I forgot is all. Or I guess I planned to eat with you, hoped to dine with my wife. Is that an unreasonable notion?"

"I was planning on crackers and cheese."

"You can't cook a little something?"

"Yes, I could cook a little something. But it's after seven now, and it would be eight before we sat down. Then, at best, I would have the kitchen cleaned up around nine. I could cook a little something, but I'm tired and I have plans."

"Tired from what, riding? And what plans might you have that are so important that they can't be changed for your husband, your husband who has been working his ass off to pay for this mansion in the mountains."

Layla paused before she responded. Davis was provoking

an argument, and they had only been together for five minutes. She learned over the years that it was best to answer this type of question in a calm manner and not be drawn into a quarrel on his terms.

"Davis, had I known that you were coming this evening, I would certainly have cooked something. Or, even better, I would have taken you out to eat. A new restaurant just opened in Waynesville . . ."

"I called and left a message four hours ago."

"Well I'm sorry that I didn't guess you were going to make your monthly visit and stay home to check messages."

Davis looked angry at first and that was the reaction Layla was used to, but then he reached out and touched her hand.

"Crackers and cheese are fine." His expression changed and a smile returned. "Crackers and cheese, a little wine, my pretty wife, what more could I ask for?"

It took Layla a few seconds to adjust to this abrupt change in the flow of their conversation. Layla glanced down at the wine bottle.

"Now, don't do that. It's not the wine speaking. I'm just glad to be here. In fact, I've decided to start spending more of my time here from now on, just like we planned in the beginning."

"Really?"

"Uh huh, I want to be a mountain man again." Davis grinned wide, catlike.

"Well, in that case, I think I'll just get the crackers and cheese."

Davis grinned and nodded as he reached for the wine bottle.

The kitchen was situated in a wing that protruded from the west corner of the Great Room. By day it was lit by three skylights and now by recessed ceiling lights and track lighting. The room was a striking exhibit of black cabinets against a white background, muted by the warm wood tones of oak flooring and walnut furniture. Layla loved to cook and had designed the kitchen herself, but she never used it to the extent that she thought she would.

Around the corner and out of sight, Layla worked to regain her composure. She poured the last glass of chardonnay from a bottle in the refrigerator and drank it down. This turn in her marriage was the one that she least expected. Divorce seemed more of a possibility than Davis returning to Mountain Crest. While Layla would sometimes complain to Tracy about Davis' prolonged absences, the truth was, she had grown accustomed to their arrangement.

She couldn't understand why he surprised her like this. One possibility was that he had a falling out with his father. Layla was more suspicious than excited about her husband's appearance.

But as she prepared a plate of hors d' oeuvres, her mood lightened with the notion of a little party. Davis was certainly in a party mood. When they were younger and in love, she and Davis could sip wine and talk all night. Cheese and crackers were the standard then. Career, ambition, money, these were all inconsequential next to their time together.

Layla wanted to write this evening, but in the spirit of the past, she sliced dill pickles and microwaved pepperoni that had been in the freezer since Christmas. Layla loved cheese and from her cache, she added slices of provolone, Swiss, and smoked cheddar to the plate. She wasn't going to cook a little meal, but she could elevate hors d' oeuvres to the level of a little meal.

"So Davis, how is your work going?" Layla entered the Great

Room, carrying an attractive tray of food and an empty wine glass.

No answer; Davis was asleep.

Layla was disappointed at first, but not for long. She talked herself into a party, but now she was relieved to see her husband asleep. It all happened too fast, Davis' sudden appearance, the spirited verbal exchange, the flare-up of tension, and then his uncharacteristic acquiescence. Layla was happy for the chance to slow down and think about it.

She sat down on the hearth and placed the hors d'oeuvres at her side. The party would go on anyway. As Layla pulled the cork from Davis' bottle, she noted that he had drunk most of its contents. Layla picked at the food, sipped wine, and studied her prostrate spouse.

Davis fell asleep with his head resting on one hand. His head had slipped off and now the hand was wedged between his face and the cushion. Gravity pulled, distorting Davis' face.

"What are you doing here, Davis?" Layla asked.

She sipped wine and attempted to answer for him. The most likely possibility, that he and his father were fighting, would seem more plausible if her husband hadn't been in such a jolly mood. Davis was typically sullen and disagreeable when out of favor with his father.

In the past, Layla was somewhat heartened when this happened because it raised the possibility that he would stop working for the Governor and stay with her at Mountain Crest. Now, conflict between father and son worried her and for the same reason. She shook her head, bewildered.

Layla didn't blame Malcolm for her and Davis' marital problems. The Governor was very accommodating with his son's schedule, always mindful of Davis' marital responsibilities. She knew that Davis didn't need to be in Raleigh half as much as he was there. And if she felt wanted, she would make more of an effort to join her husband in the city.

Layla had come to the conclusion that there were basic differences between her and Davis that were insurmountable. They avoided facing them by avoiding each other.

Layla knew from experience that Davis was out of commission for the night. She smiled, realizing that her original plans for the evening were still on. A little behind schedule now, she hurried upstairs and took a shower. Davis hadn't moved much by the time she returned, but he had repositioned his face and looked more comfortable. He was snoring, but not nearly as loud as Layla knew he was capable of.

Taking her glass, Layla left Davis' bottle at his side, having concluded that the merlot was too sweet. She went to the kitchen to open her own bottle. With a glass of chardonnay, she went to her study, another wing off the Great Room, and booted up her laptop.

Cataloochee Man, where to begin? Then she thought about the hunter's face, his eyes in particular. *That's how I'll begin, describing his face and those mysterious, hazel-colored eyes.*

Layla typed into the night, checking on her husband whenever she refilled her glass. It had been years since she'd written so freely. Hours later, eight hundred words in print, she stopped. The combination of weariness and wine overcame her nervous energy, and with a series of yawns, she shut down her computer.

Now Davis was snoring with determination. Layla was going to bed and felt that she should point her husband toward his. As he stumbled up the stairs, Davis assured his wife that he was fine, even though she hadn't asked. Layla knew he would not be fine in the morning.

Layla stood in the bedroom doorway and stared at her husband. For a brief moment this evening, she saw that clumsy charm that once swayed her heart. But she knew too well that what she saw was not a picture of the future, but only a remnant of the past.

8

"Hello, Layla speaking."

"Hey stranger, want to come over for coffee and catch up on things?"

"Tracy, hi, oh, that sounds nice and I want to soon, but I can't today."

"Are you at home? The line was busy so I tried your cell phone."

"N-no, I'm riding."

"At the ranch, this early?"

"Actually, I've just crossed the boundary of Great Smoky Mountains National Park on my way into Cataloochee Valley."

"Is Davis with you?"

"No. He's at home, busying the phone line."

"Layla, I wish you wouldn't go into the park alone, especially after what happened last time."

"I know, and I don't want to worry you, but this is about my writing, Tracy. I've got to go back. I'm being careful though. I bought a survival kit from Pigeon River Outfitters in Waynesville. It's amazing, a complete survival kit that came packed inside a water bottle. It includes waterproof matches, a flashlight, a space-age survival blanket, a pen knife, water purification tablets, and a compass. I love it."

"Somehow that only makes me feel a little better."

"I'll be okay. I know what I'm doing now. I've given myself plenty of time in case of the unexpected, and I brought along extra clothing, even though it's a warm day. And now I leave a written description of where I'm going at the stable along with a timetable of where I should be. If I don't return at a reasonable hour, they'll call Davis, and he'll alert the park rangers. At least I think he will."

"Hmm, how's it going with you two?"

"Well the first week or so was pretty good, sometimes fun. But there's definite tension now. As I suspected, there's more behind Davis' return to the mountains then a desire to be with me or to live the good life."

"Let me guess, something to do with business, right."

"Of course, wait until you hear. It took a while for me to get the whole story out of . . . Hello, Tracy? The signal is breaking up. Hey, real quick, get this. Davis now has a desire to start a family."

The signal was bad. Layla heard a gasp, followed by a string of words before the connection was lost. She grinned, aware of how mean it was to drop a bomb like that on Tracy when her friend had no chance of hearing the complete story. But she didn't want to discuss the details over the phone. Layla continued down the slope into Cataloochee Valley and out of range of the signal. This was a subject that needed to be discussed over a long lunch.

Another topic Layla didn't want to talk about now was the initiative being advanced by her father-in-law and her husband that would allow for more extensive logging in North Carolina's national forests. It was too nice a day to ruin with such discourse.

Layla knew that Tracy and Michael would be even angrier than she was when she learned of the Governor's plan. Her friends were members of Forest First, an organization dedicated to ending all logging in the national forests. Layla was invited to become a member of Forest First, but never one to belong to clubs, she declined. Davis' revelation about the logging initiative caused her to reconsider.

By the time she turned onto Caldwell Fork Trail, a resolute May sun was warming the atmosphere around her, and Layla stopped to remove a layer of clothing. She didn't really have a plan for finding the hunter other than to wander about the trails and hope that he would find her again. This was her second excursion into the park since she saw him disappear into a sea of fog. Although she saw no sign of him on the previous outing, Layla had lost little enthusiasm for her quest.

Layla told no one that she saw the hunter a second time. The wave of curiosity that her first sighting generated among friends and colleagues worried her. She didn't want to expose him to the public, especially now that she had a literary stake in his anonymity. Tracy could be sworn to secrecy on any matter. But Layla also knew that her friend would think it was crazy to go into the woods alone with this strange man lurking about. She didn't want Tracy to worry about her any more than she already did.

As Sundance ambled along the trail, Layla worked on her writing. She loved to create on a laptop, but the rapid pileup of words sometimes blocked the flow of ideas. She would sometimes cut and paste herself into a corner. Here in the quiet of Cataloochee Valley, far from her word processor, she employed her thought processor to develop ideas.

Layla was excited about her new project, *Cataloochee Man*, but she hadn't abandoned her first novel. She swayed through the forest atop Sundance, alternately pondering both stories in spite of the great dissimilarity between them.

Horse and rider came to a sign that read *Big Poplars*, marking a small trail that branched to the right. Layla knew that the trail led to three, centuries-old Tulip Poplar trees. These forest giants had survived the logging that took place in the early nineteenth century, before the park was formed. She had traveled the distance from the main trail to view these magnificent trees on previous rides into the valley. Today she wanted to keep moving. She did turn to look at the poplars as Sundance carried her past them on Caldwell Fork Trail.

That's when Layla saw him. She stopped her horse. Her heart raced. The hunter was standing in a small clearing at the base of the poplars. Layla couldn't see his eyes but she knew that he was watching her. He was about eighty yards away, visible through a web of budding spring foliage. Uncertainty swept over her.

Should I be doing this? It's been mysterious and exciting to imagine meeting him, but is it wise to really do it? But he didn't harm that little boy. He may have even saved his life. Am I really going to do this? Yes, I have to talk to him. I'm a writer and sometimes I have to take risks.

With that thought, she raised her right hand. When he raised his, Layla experienced a nervous tingle along her neck and spine. She steadied herself and prodded Sundance forward. Thirty yards ahead, the other end of Big Poplars Trail rejoined Caldwell Fork Trail. Layla turned onto it and Sundance plodded toward the trees and the man.

The hunter never changed his stance while she approached.

43

From Layla's perspective he looked to be about six feet tall and possessed a muscular build. Wavy brown hair hung to his shoulders, and a brown beard masked his expression. His eyes were a hazel color, bright and inquisitive. He was dressed in the same long shirt of leather, with fringes down the seams. His pants also had fringes and he wore high leather moccasins with decorative knots.

Layla noticed that the hunter didn't have the bow, and she was relieved to see that his hands were empty and relaxed at his sides. But then she saw the end of a knife sheath below the hem of his shirt. While this caused her some alarm, Layla was now resigned to her fate. She had to trust him.

"Hello," she said when she was within thirty yards, in a voice that was louder than necessary.

"Hello," he answered.

Layla could see a smile within his beard and this put her at ease. She stopped Sundance six feet from the man and then struggled to remember the line of questioning she had prepared. In her nervousness, Layla skipped the introductory lines and stumbled right to the point of the interview.

"C-could I ask you what you're doing here?"

"You said you wanted to talk to me."

Layla hesitated and then smiled. "That's right, of course. I do want to talk to you. What I meant is what are you doing here in the park?"

"That's a long story. What's your name?"

"Oh, I'm sorry. How rude of me. I'm Layla Turner."

"That's a nice name. My name is Abe, Abe Carol Ramsey."

"Well, Mr. Ramsey, I'm pleased to meet you."

"Please call me Abe."

"I'm pleased to meet you, Abe."

Nervous silence overcame them for a few moments. Layla struggled again to remember the questions she had planned to ask. She found his gaze unsettling but in a pleasant way. He would look deep into her eyes as if he were trying to read her thoughts and then glance past her, studying each visible end of Caldwell Fork Trail. She was fascinated by his clothing, so primitive and yet well suited to the man and the surroundings. When their eyes met again, she forced herself to talk.

"Well, I, I'm a writer, a novelist, and seeing you here in Cataloochee Valley gave me an idea for a story."

He smiled at that statement but then glanced past her and looked up and down the trail again. "Layla, there's a level spot not far from here, close to the stream. Could we talk there? I don't like to stay near a trail for too long."

"Why?"

"I don't want to be seen."

"But when I came by, you were standing in the open."

"I knew you were coming; I wanted you to see me. You said you wanted to talk to me."

"How did you know I was coming?"

"Because of noises I heard, a different scent in the wind."

"Really, you're kidding?"

"Well, that's how I knew you were coming up the trail. But I had a feeling you might come into the park today so I was watching. It's because I know that most people from the outside run on schedules. What day is today?"

"It's Saturday."

"Then it was a Saturday that I last saw you last and Saturday when I first saw you."

"Yes, Saturday, two weeks ago and a Saturday three weeks

ago."

"I expected you on each seventh day. Last week, I wasn't in the area but I knew that you had come again from your horse's tracks."

Layla was incredulous. "Well, let's move away from the trail if it makes you feel better."

She prodded Sundance to follow as the hunter moved through the woods. Soon she heard the sound of rushing water and saw Caldwell Fork. The level spot was a small, natural amphitheater in a stand of hemlock trees. Smaller trees and undergrowth filled the spaces between the hemlocks except for an opening that faced Caldwell Fork.

Layla saw some items on the ground against a fallen tree: a rolled up blanket, a leather pouch, a longbow, and a quiver of arrows. She tethered Sundance to a hemlock branch as Abe rubbed the horse's nose. Layla was surprised to see how agreeable her headstrong horse had become.

Layla turned in a circle, inhaling the spring fragrance, smiling at the notion of how uncharacteristic it was for her to be in a situation like this. She stopped when she saw the hunter's hazel eyes watching her.

"It must be a fun to be an author," he said. "I never was good at writing, so it's hard for me to imagine writing a book."

"Y-yes, it is fun. I . . ." Layla hesitated. He was looking at her with such innocence and honesty that she almost told the truth. But she didn't. For some reason Layla didn't want to tell him that she was actually an English professor and had never written a novel. Instead, she directed the discussion back to him.

"It must be fun to live, to, uh, be here. You seem to be here often is what I mean. It seems to me that, well to have the time to . . ."

"I live here."

"You do, you live in the park?"

"Yes."

"Do you have a cabin somewhere?"

"No, no cabin for me. A cabin means housekeeping and upkeep and I don't have time for that."

"Well, do you live here?" Layla nodded toward the objects on the ground.

"Sometimes I stay here. I move around, mostly in Cataloochee Valley, and camp wherever I am at night. I do have a more permanent camp on Spruce Mountain."

"Then you don't have a home?"

"Well, y-yes, the place on Spruce Mountain is my home, I guess. I've had that camp for eight years and I'm there the most. I stay there during the worst weather."

"Eight years, how long have you been in the park?"

"Nearly ten years now."

Layla stared at him, wanting to know more but not sure how to ask. But she was enjoying the conversation, so unlike any she had ever had. She liked this strange man, too. Layla was fascinated by his unusual appearance and found his frankness to be refreshing.

"I'd rather you didn't write a book about me. I really don't want people to know about me."

"Oh I wouldn't do that. If I do write a novel, it would be based on you but not about you. A novelist often uses a particular person or event as a basis for a story, but it evolves into a work of fiction. I only got the idea because you seem to be an interesting person, somebody who evokes a story. But I would never tell anybody, who you are."

"And who am I?" Abe smiled

Layla was caught off guard by the question but was charmed by his teasing. She hesitated, but then grinned as she answered. "You're Cataloochee Man."

"Who?"

"Cataloochee Man, that's what we call you, my friend Tracy and I."

"Tracy?"

Layla proceeded to tell Abe about Tracy and of how his nickname was coined. She assured him that she had told no one about seeing him the second time and also that no one knew of her quest for the conversation they were now having. Abe seemed to appreciate that revelation as well as the fact that Tracy could be trusted to keep any secret.

Layla was surprised at how easy it was to converse with Abe and she felt that he hung on her every word. She proceeded to tell the story that Jim Palmer, the former ranger, had related to Tracy. Abe was smiling and shaking his head before she finished.

"Why that little bugger, he promised that he wouldn't tell anyone about me."

"Well, he sure did."

"The rangers didn't believe him, right?"

"No, they didn't."

"I knew they wouldn't. That's why I took him right to their doorstep, to make it even more unbelievable."

She was impressed with this revelation and his forthrightness emboldened her. "Abe, I have to ask, what exactly do you do, here in the park? You said you're too busy to bother with a cabin. What are you busy with?"

"For one thing, I have to hunt and fish to eat, that takes a lot of time. I travel on foot and that takes time, too. If I have any spare time, I work on the trails, clearing them of brush and shoring up wash-outs. That's one way I figure I earn my keep. It's also the best way to keep people on the trails and out of the woods."

"So you work for Great Smoky Mountains National Park?"

"In a way I do, only they don't know it. Or if they do know it, they don't admit it. I'm not on the payroll, if that's what you mean. I take a deer now and then, a wild pig, some fish, fruit and berries in season, that's my pay."

Now she *did* understand and a smile spread across her face. Her hunch was correct. There was definitely a story here. Layla decided to go slow with her questioning and to allow Abe to talk and explain at his own pace. For his part, the hunter never questioned why she was here or who she was besides Layla Turner, the author. A half hour of conversation passed before she spoke of Mountain Crest and another half hour went by before Layla mentioned Davis.

"Do you love him?"

Layla was surprised by such a blunt question. The only other person to ask it was her father and that was before she and Davis were married. "In a way I do. He's my husband. We've been married ten years. That should say something."

Abe smiled but looked puzzled.

"Were you ever married?"

"Yes," Abe answered. The smile faded and he looked at the ground. "My wife left me and took our daughter with her. And she had every reason to do it."

They were seated close together, Layla had her back against a Hemlock tree and Abe was sitting on the rolled up blanket. She was sorry she had asked the question when she saw his reaction. Now she realized that Abe's story was more complicated than it seemed on the surface. Layla didn't want the pleasant tone of their conversation to change, so she asked a question that would return their discussion to the present.

"Abe, do you live here alone?"

He nodded.

"Do you ever get lonely?"

His head bobbed up and after a few seconds, wagged from side to side. "Nah, early on I was, but it wore off. The forest is my company. It's one huge, living, creature to hang out with. Once you learn its ways, the forest will never let you down."

"Do you ever get lonely for another human being?"

He turned his eyes away from her and nodded. "Sometimes I do. Seems I do more often, lately. I guess I'm getting old and soft."

Layla smiled.

"Do you ever get lonely for another human being?"

Layla blushed but had no trouble answering. "Yes, I do," she said, looking into his eyes.

She wanted to continue this line of conversation but knew she had to go. At his invitation, Davis and she were eating out tonight, and even now, she would be hard-pressed to make it home in time. Layla knew that Davis would be mad at her tardiness and probably be silent through another dinner.

"I have to go now," she said in a hushed voice.

"Will you be coming back? Do you have everything you need for your book?"

"Well, I, uh, no not really, I could use a bit more material," she answered, smiling.

He smiled back and untied Sundance, holding the horse as Layla mounted.

"As a matter of fact, I was thinking of coming back in seven days."

"I'll be here."

9

"Of course he's for it. I talked to the president this morning and we have his blessing. This is something he's wanted for a long time, too. In fact, he told me that he plans on rewriting Clinton's Roadless Area Rule. Later this year, President Bush is going to propose a rule that requires the governors to petition the Forestry Service if they want to block road building on federal lands in their state. He threw the ball right into our court. What timing, eh Davis?

What? Oh, the blown up equipment. Yes, I mentioned that problem to him and he was incensed, as you might expect. In fact, when I used your term, eco-terrorism, he corrected me. He said, 'terrorism is terrorism and wherever it rears its ugly head, I'll cut it off.' I like him. He's a straight shooter."

Malcolm Elmore was leaning back in his chair, cradling the phone receiver between his chin and shoulder while he lit a cigar. He had his shoes off and the tips of his toes, his stomach, a scotch on the rocks, and his perspiring brow, were all at the same level.

"The ball is rolling now, son. I'm proud of you for seizing this opportunity." Malcolm took a sip of his drink while Davis briefed him on newspaper articles he had been writing that extolled the logging initiative. The Governor listened for a quarter of an hour, commending his son's efforts while weaving advice into the discussion. Then, he changed the subject.

"So Davis, how's home life? What are you and Layla up to these days, huh, ha, ha, ha? What's cooking? Huh, what? You know what I mean. No, I do understand. I told you what the problem is, you yield too easily.

She's mad at you, about what? Good Lord in heaven, she belongs to Forest First now? She wants you to pull the plug on the logging deal? Oh my, Davis, I have to go. My pressure's up, I can feel it. No, no, don't call me, I need time to think. You're coming this weekend for the reception, right? Okay, we'll talk about it then, bye."

Malcolm laid the receiver on the desk. He let go a long sigh and wiped a handkerchief across his brow. *Damn her anyway. My daughter-in-law, a member of Forest First, that's just wonderful. The media will have a field day when they get wind of this. Why the hell did Davis marry that woman?*

A few more sips of his drink and Malcolm began to relax. He shook his head and smiled. As aggravating as Layla could be, he had always liked his daughter-in-law. He especially enjoyed arguing with her. The Governor sometimes wished that Davis had more of her grit. Malcolm harbored doubts about their union from the beginning but he had still done his best to make their marriage work.

And he *did* want grandchildren. Malcolm would be out of office in two years, and he wanted to ease into retirement with grandchildren. The Governor also believed that the biggest part of Davis and Layla's domestic problem was that their marriage lacked a common goal such as raising a family.

Malcolm gazed across the surface of his desk and stopped at a framed photograph of Davis, his sister, Martha, and their mother. The Governor missed his daughter and worried about her being so far away in San Francisco.

Malcolm and his daughter had clashed on just about every issue since her mother died. The truth was that Martha was much like her father in personality and temperament, while Davis took after his mother. Malcolm shook his head and sighed.

The Lord works in mysterious ways. I wish He would have left you here with me, Norma, to help sort all this out.

10

"Kenny boy," Malcolm bellowed as he entered the ballroom. The Governor clasped Kenneth Leyman's hand and the two men grinned like school boys.

Kenneth Leyman had been a friend of Malcolm Elmore since their college days at Vanderbilt University where they were fraternity brothers. Ken was tall and lean with gray hair and a neat mustache. His impeccable dress, his mannerisms, and his slow, pleasant drawl, made one feel that Kenneth Leyman was always in control of any situation.

Malcolm was hosting a reception at the Governor's mansion for representatives of the major logging companies in the Southeastern United States. He wanted to hear opinions from people in the industry, concerning the logging of North Carolina's national forests. The Governor's friend was present this evening as owner of Southern Highlands Logging Company.

"Malcolm, this place is you."

"Now Ken, I'm merely an instrument of the populace, and it is by them and for them that I darken these halls."

"I hear you, Malcolm, I hear you. So Governor, are we finally going to do a little logging in your fair state?"

"We are indeed, Ken. And I thank you for your suggestion

that we pursue this course. The national forests were established to be managed for multiple uses and that includes timber harvesting. Yet most of this land is idle, not benefiting anyone."

"Malcolm, you have always had a way with words."

"That was nearly a direct quote from the letter you sent me."

"I know. But you quoted me so well."

Both men smiled and sipped their wine as Davis approached.

"Mr. Leyman?"

"Why, Davis is that you? You look so serious and distinguished in this setting. Must be the strain from keeping your father here out of trouble."

Uncertain as to whether he had been complimented or not, Davis smiled and half-nodded.

"Watch it," Malcolm intervened, "that's a trick question; they're a trademark of his."

An expression of mock hurt came over Ken's face and then the two friends laughed, both aware of the truth of the statement.

"Davis is our mountain ambassador," the Governor exclaimed. "He's out there in western North Carolina, in the trenches, winning popular support for the logging initiative."

Ken turned toward Davis with a benevolent smile. "Is that true, son?"

"Y-yes it is Mr. Leyman."

"Wonderful, that's wonderful." He prodded the Governor in the ribs with his elbow. "Why Malcolm, he is indeed the proverbial chip off the old block."

Malcolm smiled and waved him off.

"Not everyone is popularly supporting the initiative. What's this I hear about armed opposition out there in the wild west? What's this Panther Patrol I've been hearing about this evening?"

"A rogue band, Ken, they'll be stopped soon. That's federal land and the FBI is moving into the area."

"The Federal Bureau of Investigation is on our side? Now that is mighty reassuring. I have a low tolerance for saboteurs, and I would have zero tolerance in the case of my own equipment being blown up."

Davis detected a hard edge to Ken Leyman's eloquence, something he hadn't noticed before. Not that it detracted from his long-held admiration for this man or his desire to emulate him.

"Now Malcolm, if you want to circumvent the obtrusiveness of federalists running about in your woods, I could simply have some of my men address this matter."

"Ha ha, I only wish it were that simple, but no thanks. I can't. My hands are tied on some issues and the binds go back to Washington. But we have a good man in the White House now. He cleared the path for the logging to go forward. I believe he's working for our better . . ."

"No, he's not," Ken interrupted, his smile disappearing. "He's out for himself, just like the rest of us. The only difference is that he's president of the United States right now, and we're not." Ken's smile reappeared as he turned toward Davis.

"Son, you ever consider running for public office?"

"Why no sir, well, no, not yet."

"Well consider it. We can't all be in business, letting others make the rules. Why, Malcolm, I can see the makings of a political dynasty here."

The Governor laughed and shook his head. "So what have you been up to, Ken, speaking of business?"

"We're growing, Malcolm. The real estate and development side of the coin is starting to shine now and tying in nicely with the logging. If things keep up as they are, I may be able to retire by age seventy."

"Retire? You'll never retire as long as there's another doubloon that might be added to the hoard."

"Don't you be too cynical now, Governor. I'll have you know that I plan to air out my place on Balsam Mountain and spend more time there."

"Really?"

"Yes indeed, old man, and you should do the same with yours. When was the last time you stayed at your place on the mountain?"

"Hmm, I guess it was last Thanksgiving."

"See. You need to rejuvenate yourself in the mountains, Malcolm. Hug a tree, as they say."

"Hug a tree, you? You mean one that's cut down right? I know what you're up to, Ken. You just want to be closer to Pisgah National Forest when the cutting starts."

Ken looked at Davis and shrugged his shoulders with an expression that implied he was being picked on, but he didn't deny the Governor's allegation. Then he looked back to his friend with a sly smile. "Now how can you make such a statement when I don't even have a timber contract yet?" Ken turned and winked at Davis after he said this.

"It's just a feeling I have, Ken."

The Governor glanced at his watch. "Speaking of timber contracts, let's get this discussion started, shall we?"

"By all means, Malcolm, I'm anxious to see what the competition brings to the table."

11

Something was wrong. The night was too still. The soldier wondered why the bulldozers were sitting in the open like ducks in a row. They were usually parked on the edge of the clearing, where they were last operated. He was told at the reconnaissance briefing that there was a night watchman, but he saw no sign of one. The office trailer was dark and he was told there would be a light on.

The soldier's instincts told him to abandon this mission, to remain within the forest. But a sense of duty, a penchant for taking risks, and several hearty swallows from the flask in his coat pocket, prodded him into the clearing.

A small company, based in Newport, Tennessee, High Point Lumber Company started this logging operation only three months before. The fact that they were from another state and logging in the forests of North Carolina infuriated the soldier and made him all the more determined to strike now.

The moon was shrouded in clouds and he could see only a silhouette of the two bulldozers, massive and cold, parked side by side. These machines were his target.

He approached without a sound and slipped between them. When he saw how neatly they were spaced and aligned toward another cluster of machinery, he was certain of a trap. The soldier crouched low and was moving away from the bulldozers when searchlights snapped on from all directions, bathing the area in light. An amplified voice commanded him.

"Stand where you are. You're surrounded. Put your hands in the . . ."

The soldier swung the AK-47 off his side and sprayed bullets in an arc above the lights. The beams jostled and lost focus, and the soldier dove for the ground. When the area was once again illuminated, only the machines were visible. Another spray of bullets caused the lights to dance and cross each other. The FBI agents had underestimated their adversary.

"Get in there fast," boomed the voice from a megaphone.
By the time the agents reached the equipment, they heard rustling sounds, alerting them that the soldier had entered the forest.

"Fan out and follow. Try to get lights on him. If he shoots again, return fire."

Agent Miles Harding put down the megaphone and smoothed thinning brown hair back over his head. He didn't really expect someone who had just demonstrated such stunning elusiveness in a circle of would be captors to be apprehended in an open forest. The chase would at least serve to familiarize his men with the terrain and help them better understand the adversary they were up against.

In his mid-forties, Miles was reaching the point in his career with the FBI when a field operation such as this should be delegated to a younger agent. He received the assignment with some irritation. After the first briefing, Agent Harding had concluded that the Panther Patrol was a small, rogue group, intent on discouraging logging in Pisgah National Forests. Not the sort of challenge that should command his expertise. However, in closed consultation with the FBI director, he learned that the scope of his assignment went beyond protecting the local logging companies from the Panther Patrol.

Younger, less-experienced agents were placed under him whose only focus would be on the Panther Patrol. On paper, Agent Harding's skills were needed to work these men through this task, training them on the job. This was true to a great extent, but the operation was also a viable reason to bring Miles into the area for his larger role. Ironically, the fact that the saboteur eluded capture this evening was a positive development for the overall assignment.

But Miles hadn't planned it that way. Agent Harding had every intention of bringing the Panther Patrol era to a close this evening. He had calculated correctly on every aspect of this operation except the last.

Based on his analysis of the other companies that had been hit by the Panther Patrol, Miles chose this particular logging site to lay his trap. He also predicted that one person was carrying out these attacks. But he was wrong in assuming that this individual would be taken by surprise and offer little resistance. Instead the man was cool-headed and well-armed.

Miles was already revising his tactics as he walked around the bulldozers. He had requested that they be placed in the center of the clearing. He was a seasoned agent and never dwelt for long on what didn't work. Miles harbored no doubts that the saboteur would be apprehended soon. This first encounter demonstrated that it would take a little more time and be more interesting than he had predicted.

Seventy yards into the forest, the soldier paused to listen. When he heard no dogs, he turned north and moved at a slower pace. He stopped often, listening for noise of pursuit. When he could hear only forest sounds, he knew that he had evaded his pursuers.

The soldier turned west and soon intersected Route 284, a dirt highway that ran along the boundary of Great Smoky Mountains National Park and Pisgah National Forest. He would followed this road north toward his cabin at Waterville.

The soldier fell into an easy walking pace and began to consider his surprise encounter at the logging operation. He stroked his beard and rethought the scene until he grinned with satisfaction at how he had eluded the ambush. He was disappointed that he couldn't carry out his mission but not discouraged. On the contrary, the soldier was more determined then ever to see the next mission through.

They were waiting for me. Those weren't state cops. FBI, ATF, maybe. The game is changing. They were ready for me. I had to run. Just like Robert E. Lee said, "I must retreat so that I can fight another day.

12

The domestic situation between Layla and Davis continued to deteriorate through the month of May. The pace accelerated after Layla joined Forest First. Never one to belong to clubs, she was attracted to this one because of her love of the forest and because Tracy and Michael Ogden had been members for years. When she learned of her father-in-law's logging initiative, she attended the next meeting.

Davis turned her membership to his advantage by complaining to his father that much of their marital trouble, including lack of progress toward grandchildren, now stemmed from her affiliation with Forest First.

Among the topics the couple argued about, the subject of logging in the national forests led to the sharpest exchanges. This controversial environmental issue was emblematic of the differences between them. As Layla became more knowledgeable of the national forests and the arguments against logging them, Davis had a difficult time defending his father's position. More often, he would just repeat the party line: *logging meant jobs, and people came before trees.*

Toward the end of May, another fight was on the horizon and Davis drank beer in anticipation. An article in the morning newspaper detailed the distribution of the timber contracts under the Governor's logging initiative. Davis knew that Layla would learn the details before she came home from work. He also knew that the information would infuriate her.

Davis heard his wife's car pull up to the house. He steeled himself. Layla had the newspaper in hand when she walked in the door.

"Well, what a surprise. Southern Highlands Logging Company was handed the biggest timber contract and the owner is none other than Kenneth Leyman, your father's old fraternity brother."

"The fact that Mr. Leyman and Dad are friends was a small factor in the final decision, more coincidence than anything else. Besides, the national forests are managed by the United States Forest Service, not Dad."

"Oh please, Davis. You're not talking to the local newspaper here. I've been in this family long enough to know all about coincidence. And I know enough about Ken Leyman's wheeling and dealing to bet that he orchestrated this whole thing, from putting the idea into your father's head to pulling strings in Washington to get the contract."

Davis hesitated. He knew that Layla was right. No one had put it in those exact terms, but he suspected that this was the case since the night of the logging reception. He was coming to realize that Ken Leyman wielded a great deal of power. To Davis this was somewhat awe-inspiring. He took a determined drink from his Heineken. This bottle was his fourth and he was slightly drunk. Davis didn't want to argue with Layla anymore.

"Layla, why can't you just be a wife?" Davis sighed. He was picturing Ken Leyman's wife as he spoke. After the reception in Raleigh, Davis and his father went to dinner with Ken and Laura

Leyman. Davis thought that Laura was not only beautiful but also the ideal complement to her husband. She and Ken seemed to mesh in conversation, paraphrasing each other, finishing the other's sentence, and smiling as the other spoke.

"What do you mean, just be a wife? What you mean is, go along with everything you say with a smile and a kiss. You want me to support the plan your father and his cronies have for the national forests even when I'm opposed to it? That's it, isn't it? And you want me at the parties in a fancy outfit, charming the men and endorsing your political agenda, whatever it might be, right? You don't have to answer, Davis. I know I'm right."

Davis didn't answer. Layla *was* right. He knew he wasn't exactly a Ken Leyman, but that was the sort of man he aspired to be. In his mind, that's what he was working toward: that sort of confidence, that sort of calm command, and that sort of domestic stability. Layla could never appreciate this and thus would only hold him back from achieving these goals.

"Davis, why can't you just be a husband?" She mimicked his sigh. Layla was thinking of Michael Ogden, Tracy's husband. Michael was strong, handsome, athletic, and at the same time, soft-spoken, gentle, and always attentive to Tracy. When together, they were a perfect team whether it was an outing with their daughters, working in the garden, or at a formal dance at the country club.

"What do you mean, just be a husband? I work ten hours a day in the city so that we can have a comfortable life in the country. What do you think pays for this damn place? What you want is for me to follow you around the trails every weekend on some stinking horse and then in the evening eat sushi with chopsticks at Tracy and Mike's house, right? You don't have to answer, dear, I know I'm right."

Layla didn't answer. Davis *was* right. She knew she wasn't exactly a Tracy Ogden but in some corner of her mind was a picture of a simple, happy situation with a man who loved her without conditions, a man who loved her *because* of the way she was. Layla wanted a partner, but one who appreciated her desire to be a writer, understood her love of the forest and one who never expected her to play any role for any reason. Davis couldn't understand this and thus would never be that person.

Silence ensued; half a minute passed. Then Davis couldn't help but gloat at how he had turned Layla's argument back on her. "Am I right or am I right?"

Layla paused, gathering her wits, trying to choose the right words. She didn't want to hurt Davis or incite him to anger.

"Am I right or am I right?" He asked again, staring at her with glazed eyes.

"Davis." Layla hesitated, looked at the ground and then back at her husband.

"Yes m'lady?" He had the makings of a triumphant grin, twitching at the corners of his mouth

That made it easier for her. She looked into his eyes. "Davis, I want a divorce."

13

"Divorce, she just came out and said it, and he never saw it coming?"

"That's what he told me, Ken. But then, there are a lot of things that Davis doesn't see coming. I never did understand how those two got together in the first place."

"They were young, Malcolm, young and impetuous, full of ideas. We were like that once."

"Were we?"

"Oh yes, especially you."

Malcolm laughed and then grew serious again. "What bothers me now is that I was against the match from the beginning."

"I know, I remember."

"Not that I didn't like Layla, and I still like Layla, but I just knew she was not the right girl for Davis. She's, well, she's uh . . ."

"Too cerebral."

"Y-yes, that's a good way to put it. Her father wasn't happy about the marriage either"

"Really, now that's interesting. Did he tell you that, himself?"

"No, he didn't have to. I could see it in his eyes. I could tell by the way he sighed throughout the ceremony. Yeah, he was a funny man, a professor at Harvard then. From what Davis has told me, he pretty much raised Layla. Her mother was a medical doctor and a lot younger than the professor. She was his second wife and they divorced when Layla was still young. We got along well enough, the professor and me, considering the man was a rabid liberal.

Henry is his name. Davis told me that Henry was so angry about the invasion of Iraq that he denounced his citizenship and moved to Canada with his third wife. That's where he is now."

"My word, one can excuse Layla if she tends to be a bit eccentric, considering all that."

On Saturday of Memorial Day weekend, Governor Elmore and his friend, Ken Leyman, were sitting on the south deck of the Leyman's summer home on Balsam Mountain. Ken and Laura referred to the house they built in 1975 as the *cabin*, but it would more aptly be described as the *lodge*. Built of massive cedar logs and cut stone, it was contemporary in design and decor. The house had large windows on all sides to allow the occupants to appreciate the stunning views afforded by its elevation. The cabin was located at four thousand feet above sea level.

The Governor also had a house on Balsam Mountain. He and his wife built it five years before the Leyman's built theirs. It was located half a mile away, and the Governor's fifty acres bordered the seventy owned by Ken and Laura. Malcolm had traveled to dinner tonight by golf cart on a path that connected their properties. Decades before, Malcolm and Ken owned several square miles of Balsam Mountain. Most of it was developed into gated communities such as Mountain Crest at a huge profit.

Malcolm seldom used the house on Balsam Mountain after his children left home and hardly at all since he became Governor. Norma Elmore had a hand in every detail of the construction and décor. She had loved the house. At her request, when all hope of recovery from cancer was gone, she was brought there to die. The house made Norma's absence more poignant, especially when Malcolm was there alone. He would have given it to Layla and Davis, but Layla was determined to build a house of her own design.

"Wait until you taste Gerard's cooking, Malcolm."

"That's a little extravagant even for you, isn't it, Kenny?"

"What's that Governor?"

"Employing a famous gourmet chef at your summer home."

"Ha ha, you've always had a tendency toward exaggeration, old man. Gerard is a friend of ours as you well know. He looks forward to these working vacations away from Miami. And it's only recently that he's been appearing on the Cooking Channel."

Malcolm grinned. "I hear you, Kenny, I hear you."

Laura Leyman moved to the edge of the deck with a look of concern. "Where are those two? I hope they haven't lost track of the time."

"I'm sure they'll be along soon, dear. I've never known an Elmore that was tardy for dinner."

Malcolm laughed and sipped his margarita. Then he nodded across the lawn, ninety degrees east of Laura Leyman's gaze. "There they are. Would you look at those two?"

Laura turned and smiled. "My goodness, just like when they were children."

Davis Elmore emerged from the woods onto the manicured lawn that surrounded the Leyman's summer home. He was laughing and chatting with Carolyn Leyman, daughter of Ken and Laura. Carolyn and Davis were the same age and had known each other since they were infants.

"How is Carolyn adjusting to life in the mountains?"

"Real well, Malcolm, peace and quiet is just what she needs to get over Stradivarius."

"Now Ken. Don't start on Antoine. He's a nice man," Laura interjected. "Carolyn and he were very happy together for many years. The life of a musician is demanding and he's very devoted to his art. He tried to be a husband too."

Ken looked over at Malcolm like a little boy who had been scolded. He spoke softly. "He was too old for her, plain and simple, too set in his ways. Besides that, they weren't really married."

"Ten years is not that much of an age difference. After all you're six years older than I am." Laura added.

Ken was working on his second margarita and feeling good. "Yes, but I'm young and feisty for my age; he's old and stodgy for his."

Laura rolled her eyes and waved him off. "And they were together for almost ten years. That's longer than many real marriages last these days. By law, they were married."

"I don't buy that common law business, you know that Laura."

Laura smiled. Her husband was teasing her and after years of experience, she wasn't going to take the bait. "Whatever you say dear, I'm going back to help Gerard. Don't let the kids wander off again." She went back to the kitchen.

"Who is divorcing whom?" Malcolm asked

"Carolyn chose to leave Antoine. She wants to have children now and he told her that he absolutely didn't want children. But the decision to separate was mutual in the end, and it's being done quietly and civilly."

"Well divorce doesn't get much better than that," Malcolm said as he watched Davis and Carolyn approach the porch. He knew that in his son's case, that would probably be an unlikely scenario.

After dinner they lingered at the table, laughing, talking, and filling each other's wine glasses. Gerard joined them when he concluded that there was nothing more he could do to enhance the meal.

In the midst of the merriment, Malcolm grew melancholic. He looked at the face of his friend and saw that Ken was getting old, too. They were both approaching sixty years of age and a point where one could no longer deny the accumulation of years.

He gazed across the table at Davis and Carolyn who were no longer young themselves. They had all sat at this same table several decades before and then Malcolm's wife, Norma, was amongst them. They were young, then, and the spaces between the adults were filled with children, happy, carefree children, the promise of the next generation.

Out of the corner of his eye Malcolm saw a bottle edging toward him. Ken had recognized the look in his friend's eyes.

"Refresh your glass there, old man. Leave the past where it is for tonight, and let us drink to the future."

Malcolm smiled and took the bottle. Laura and Gerard were deep in conversation. She was an accomplished chef, herself, and the two of them never tired of talking about their craft. Malcolm raised his glass toward Ken. Ken raised his own, took a sip, and then nodded toward Davis and Carolyn. When Malcolm observed their children this time, he saw them from a different perspective. He noticed how closely they sat, how they smiled, and how they attended only to each other. He looked back at Ken. His friend raised his glass again and grinned.

14

From the angle of the sun, the hunter knew that two hours of daylight remained. For the final two miles, he was guided by the rumble and clanking of heavy machinery. Nearing the logging site, he slowed his gait and scanned the woods. Abe Ramsey was methodical and cautious on these reconnaissance missions. He left nothing to chance. When he saw unnatural breaks in the tree pattern, he stopped. The clearing for the logging operation was just ahead.

Abe moved back in the direction he had come for about one hundred yards and found a suitable spot to camp. He hid his bow and arrows, and supplies there. From this base camp he would have quick access to and from the clearing, and if necessary, enough forest cover to confound and delay pursuit. Not that he expected it. The hunter's formal training in stealth tactics had been augmented by a decade of practical use in Great Smoky Mountains National Park. In these situations, Abe always assumed that he was being searched for from all directions at once and conducted himself accordingly.

From within the wool blanket, he procured a pair of field binoculars and secured them inside his shirt. The binoculars were given to Abe by his father. The hunter crouched low and moved toward the logging operation.

Abe approached a clearing that was the first footprint of the Southern Highlands Logging Company in Pisgah National Forest. Many more prints were to follow while Ken Leyman and Malcolm Elmore had their way. The hunter knew nothing of the politics behind this operation. He only knew his mission, and that was to observe.

When Abe could see moving objects through the trees, he stopped his forward progress and began to circle, always keeping well within the forest. The hunter found a good vantage point and moved in close to scrutinize the humans and their machines. He was familiar with all of the equipment, although what he saw today was larger and present in greater numbers than he had ever seen before. Part of the mission was to determine what machines were most vital to the operation.

Abe also noted that there were six housing trailers spread across the clearing. The field office of a logging operation was typically a trailer and they were sometimes used for storage, but it was unusual to see so many on one site. During his watch, Abe would determine the purpose of each of these, even if it required that he move in close enough to peep in the windows.

He timed his arrival to observe the operation as it shut down for the evening and thus learn where equipment was parked for the night. When darkness came, he would learn how well the site was guarded. In the past, he considered one evening of reconnaissance to be sufficient for a logging operation. After what happened at the High Point Lumber Company logging site, Abe planned to observe here for two days. He didn't want another surprise on the night the equipment was hit.

As the operation shut down for the evening, most of the

73

equipment was parked in the center of the clearing and spaced widely. A smaller collection of machines was situated at one end of the operation, near the forest. Abe had observed in most logging operations that the machinery was left in small clusters near where it last operated. What he saw now was a larger version of the arrangement at the High Point Lumber Company operation on the night of the ambush.

The next day at dawn, the area was filled with the sound of heavy machinery interspersed with the whine of chain saws. The Southern Highlands Logging Company had been in Pisgah National Forest for only three weeks but had already made a considerable impact. The hunter estimated that the area of forest cleared was as large as several football fields. He was astounded at the number of machines in operation and had never seen such an army of workers at any ten logging operations combined.

At mid-morning he saw pale men wearing black clothing, and dark glasses. One, who seemed older than the others, wore a black dress suit. His father had told him about these men. His father warned him of their coming since Abe was a child. With these men was a tall, well-built man who was dressed in camouflage military fatigues, black boots and a green beret that was fringed in red.

An hour later, two black, Chevy Suburbans pulled into the clearing. Eight men in camouflage fatigues got out of the vehicles, stretched, and studied the surroundings. These men were dressed in garb that was similar to that worn by the soldier Abe saw earlier. All wore the unusual beret. They were soon greeted by that same soldier, and Abe was certain that he was their leader. Abe learned what two of the housing trailers were for as he watched the soldiers carry luggage and guns into them.

For another day the hunter observed the Southern Highlands Logging Company. He departed under the cover of darkness after the second day. Late that night, back in Great Smoky Mountains National Park, Abe stared at the stars and thought about what he had observed in Pisgah National Forest. For the first time, he worried that the Panther Patrol was out of its league in aiming at such a large target.

Abe eased his troubled mind by allowing thoughts of Layla to seep in. During the day, he focused on his mission, not permitting himself to be distracted by the recurrent daydream of holding her in his arms. But now, mission completed, he allowed such thoughts to envelop him like a warm blanket.

Abe turned onto his side and tried to sleep. He needed to go to Waterville the next day, but by the following evening, he would be back on Spruce Mountain. The next day, the seventh day, he would keep a date with the woman he was in love with.

15

As Layla approached Big Poplars, she tried to convince herself that the main purpose in coming was still literary, but her nervousness indicated otherwise. Because the first meeting had gone so well, she worried that this one might not for some reason. She wondered if she and Abe would have as much to talk about, or if she could think of more questions to ask.

Layla had fussed with her wardrobe as if it were a bona fide date. She finally chose an older, faded pair of jeans, a stone-washed denim jacket, high leather boots, and a wide-brimmed felt hat. The hat she bought on a whim three years before and then never wore. Layla did her best to appear a bit more rugged. But now she felt silly, especially about the hat. She was about to take it off and hide it in her saddle bag when she saw Abe standing near the big poplars, watching her.

Abe didn't think she looked silly. He thought Layla looked wonderful, and he loved the hat. He was glad now that he wore the new hunting frock that he had just finished. In fact he hurried to finish it for this meeting.

"Hello, Abe. Is that new?"

"This? Oh, yes. The old shirt was getting pretty rough and well, so, I, uh, wore this one today."

"Did you make it?"

"Yes, it's made from the hide of the deer I shot on the divide the day we first saw each other."

"Really? That's so interesting."

"Is that hat new?"

"Uh, well, sort of. Why?"

"It just looks new. I really like it."

"Oh, thank you. It's my favorite."

Layla was flattered that Abe wore a new shirt for this occasion and she thought he looked magnificent in it, like a prince of the forest. She also noticed that his hair and beard were trimmed.

Layla need not have worried about a shortage of conversation. When she asked about the process of creating a garment from a deer hide, they had a lively, thirty minute discussion of Abe's technique. His life was so strange and primitive to her and yet at the same time, simple and appealing. She wanted to know more and with every answer he gave Layla seemed to have another question.

Abe began to feel that he was talking too much, so before Layla could ask another question, he posed one of his own.

"Where are you from, Layla?"

"Do you mean, where was I born?"

"Yes, I know you're not from Haywood County."

"No, I'm not. I was born in Newton, Massachusetts, near Boston. My father was a history professor at Harvard, and my mother was in medical school. She lives in Texas now and my father lives in Canada. My parents divorced when I was twelve. But I've lived here for seven years, so I'm from Haywood County now. Are you from Haywood County?"

"Yes, I'm from Cruso, a little town south of Waynesville."

"Oh yes, I know where it is. I've driven through there."

"My parents had a little farm. Dad grew tobacco and did some logging on the property."

"Do they still have the farm?"

"Oh no, my mother left my father when I was fourteen. She and my sister and kid brother moved to Newport, Tennessee, where mom's from. Dad sold the farm and moved out to Montana five years later, right after I joined the army. I hate to say this Layla, but my father's kind of an odd person."

"Mine is too, Abe. After my parents divorced, I lived with him in an apartment in Boston. He wasn't stingy with me but he was very frugal. Dad didn't believe in accumulating anything that wasn't functional or necessary.

I love my father and those years with him were fun, but I'm not like him. Even as a child, I knew that someday I wanted more than we had. I don't want a lot of unnecessary things, but at least a nice house with a yard, some good furniture, and a big kitchen."

"It sounds to me like you got all that."

"Yes I got all that, but I also wanted a happy marriage and I didn't get that. My husband and I are getting divorced."

"What? That's too bad. Has this happened since you were here last week?"

"This past Wednesday I told Davis that I want a divorce. But the trouble that led to this has been going on for years."

"I'm sorry to hear that, Layla, I really am."

Abe was sincere. He had heartrending memories of the fights between his parents that led to the dissolution of the family. He also harbored painful recollections of his own divorce.

Yet, because of his feelings for Layla, he couldn't help but be somewhat heartened that she would be free from her marriage.

As remote as the possibility seemed that he and this wonderful woman could ever be a couple in a romantic sense, he dreamed of that possibility every day.

"Well thank you, Abe. I appreciate your concern. But it's for the better. Davis and I were a bad match from the beginning; we probably should have done this years ago. And I'm sorry for bringing something like this up. You shouldn't have to hear my problems."

Yet even as she said this, Layla couldn't help but be glad to be informing Abe that her marriage was ending. As remote as the possibility seemed that she and this mysterious man could ever be a couple in a romantic sense, the thought had crossed her mind more than once.

"I like talking to you, Layla, and I like listening to you talk. It doesn't matter what you're talking about."

Layla blushed. Then Abe felt warm and embarrassed. He tried to rephrase the statement. They both began to speak at once and then laughed. Abe decided to let his words stand and he allowed Layla to speak first.

"I like talking to you, too, Abe. You're such an easy person to have a conversation with and you seem to like to talk. It surprises me that you choose to live so far away from people." She saw an uncomfortable expression cloud his features. He looked toward the ground for a few seconds and then back into her eyes.

"Layla, there's a reason why I live here. I, I would rather not talk about it, not now anyway. You're the type of person who would understand. I don't think it would change your opinion of me. But I don't want to tell you now. I want you to know me better first."

"Of course, Abe, I wasn't trying to probe. I meant it as a

compliment. If you don't want to talk about it, that's fine, and if someday you do, that's fine too. I like listening to you talk, too." Layla smiled a warm and caring smile and Abe felt comfortable again.

"When you say someday, does that mean that we'll talk again, even when you have enough for your book?"

"I want to."

Abe smiled. "I do, too."

They looked into each others eyes, both pleased with this first measure of commitment.

Abe looked toward Caldwell Fork. "Would you like to go for a walk along the stream?"

Layla nodded and started to get up, but after sitting on the ground for two hours, she was unsteady and lost her balance. Abe was quick to help her stand. They held hands a few seconds longer than was necessary.

Layla and Abe wandered for over an hour along Caldwell Fork, their path dictated by the undergrowth. Conversation came easily. Abe was most at ease, talking about his life in the forest and Layla was glad to accommodate him. But he did inform her that he was not as much of a hermit as she thought. He told her that he had a good friend who lived in Cosby, Tennessee, a small town north of the park.

When it was time for Layla to begin her ascent from Cataloochee Valley, she was in a happy, meditative mood. For half a day she had forgotten the many problems, swirling about in the world outside the park: her own domestic tribulations, the controversy surrounding the logging of Pisgah National Forest, overpopulation, global warming, the war in Iraq. Instead she thought only about the rugged gentleman in her company who attended to her every word and who had a look in his eyes that made her feel like she was all that mattered in the world.

Just before mounting Sundance, Layla hugged Abe. Not expecting this, he only half reciprocated but he was pleased. Emboldened, he asked Layla if the following week she would come earlier, so that they could have more time together.

16

"Davis, your game has lost none of its punch. You hit the ball like you did in college."

"Well, Mr. Leyman, I think I'm a little off that pace, but I try to keep my game in tune. Work has a way of interfering with golf."

"Tell me about it. And Davis, let's not be so formal now, call me Ken."

Davis smiled and nodded.

Ken had invited Davis and his father to breakfast at the Balsam Mountain Country Club. The Country Club bordered Ken's property such that they could ride to breakfast by golf cart. Breakfast was followed by a round of golf.

Ken turned to the left as he walked up the fairway, looking to see if Malcolm had located his ball. The ball had been sliced out of play into thick brush. Ken knew from experience that the Governor was irritable after such a shot.

"What are your long-term plans, son? I'm talking about when your father's term in office is over. Do you plan to stay in Raleigh and practice law?"

"I don't know. I've been so busy, I haven't thought that far ahead."

"Well you must think ahead, son, and the farther ahead, the

better. There's no other way for a businessman to think. Have you thought about staying here in the mountains? Caroline tells me that the area is beginning to grow on you again."

"Y-yes, that's true. But I didn't expect the trouble between Layla and me."

"I thought she wanted a divorce? Agree to one and move on with your life."

"Well, it's just that she would be in the area then, here on the mountain and . . ."

"Tell her you want the house and make a generous offer, one she can't refuse. Offer her enough money so that she can get away from here, enough so that she can build another house, anywhere. If she'll settle for a lump sum like that, you'll be better off in the long run."

"H-how much do you think that would have to be?"

"Well now, I can only guess at her financial situation, but I would think that a million dollars would do the trick. Just the word 'million', impresses most people."

"A million dollars? Mr. Leyman, I don't have that kind . . ."

"Yes you do. In the course of your life, you'll have many millions, so it's worth giving up one now, however you have to come up with it. Believe me, if she gets a good attorney and drags you into court, a million dollars will seem cheap. And call me Ken."

Davis smiled and nodded. "I suppose you're right, Ken."

"Of course I'm right." Ken grinned and patted Davis on the shoulder."

Ken stopped and turned to see that Malcolm was still searching for his ball. "Come on up out of there, old man," he yelled through cupped hands. "I'll kindly grant you a drop on the fairway if you bring the cart up here and give me a ride."

Malcolm was thrashing at the brush with his five iron and not having much luck locating his ball. He glanced over his shoulder at his friend's offer and turned back to thrash the weeds a bit longer. A minute later, Malcolm climbed into the golf cart.

Ken turned back to Davis. "Davis, let me tell you something that a wise old gentleman once told me. He said that life is like a merry-go-round, the years keep turning around and every now and then, you have your chance to grab the ring. He likened the ring to life's big opportunities."

"The ring?"

"Yes, in my youth, merry-go-rounds were common and the challenge was to grab a ring that was suspended just within reach. I believe the practice is some throwback to ancient days and the training of knights or gladiators. The ring was made of gold then.

But this man's point was that you only get so many chances at the ring. When the ring is there, son, you have to grab it, or you'll just turn on the carousel and have nothing but accumulated years to show for the ride. When opportunity comes, seize it."

Davis nodded but didn't quite understand the point.

"There's opportunity here in the mountains, son. Things are changing fast. Don't let the small, irritating details of your life distract you from the big picture."

Davis was still uncertain about what Ken was getting at. He opted to change the subject rather than say something that would make him appear naïve. "Are you really going to award Dad a drop on the fairway?"

Ken smiled and shook his head. "Nah, he wouldn't take it anyway, but I knew that a remark like that would get him up out of there. He'll come up now to harass me. But at least I'll get the cart. My hip's bothering me again."

"I'm sorry, Mr. Leyman or, uh, Ken."

"Nothing new, it's been bothering me for years. I don't want to deal with replacement surgery yet, so I live with it." Ken looked back toward Malcolm who was approaching in the golf cart. The Governor had a sullen expression on his face.

"Davis, you know it does my old heart good to see you and Carolyn laughing and talking again, like when you were children."

Davis smiled and nodded, but when he saw a sparkle in Ken's eyes and a benevolent smile playing on his lips, he realized that this was more than a casual statement.

The golf cart pulled up with a hot and red-faced driver.

"Curse the luck, I pulled it again and can't find it."

"You pulled it all right, Governor. The way that ball was hooking, it may have crossed the border into Tennessee."

"That's very funny, Ken, very funny."

Ken eased himself into the cart as Malcolm stepped out.

"I don't want a free drop, either."

Ken winked at Davis as Malcolm positioned his ball. The governor's next strike was much better and his humor returned as he and his friend drove off.

They waved to Davis as they went by. He was on foot, taking the opportunity to burn some calories. Davis had been playing tennis with Caroline Leyman and he wanted to shed a few pounds and improve his stamina.

Davis was enjoying life in the mountains this time around, and much of the reason was Carolyn. He felt young and happy again when he was with her. He was thinking of Carolyn when her father passed by and waved. Then he thought he realized the point of Ken's advice. *The merry-go-round is turning, the ring is there, and this is a ring of gold.*

17

"This is unbelievable. He's staying?"

"It seems that way, Tracy. Isn't it ironic? Before I could never get Davis to come and now my problem is that he won't leave."

"Is he just not accepting the fact that it's over and thinks that by staying you'll eventually come around?"

"Oh no, he's accepted the fact all right. He's made it clear that he wants the house and he thinks that I should go."

"Well that's odd. He never seemed too thrilled with the house before. I thought it was too contemporary for him. What are you going to do?"

"Well, my attorney's advice is that if I want the house in the end I should stay put throughout the divorce no matter how unpleasant it gets. She said that unless I feel physically threatened, I should remain in the house."

"*Do you* feel physically threatened?"

Layla rolled her eyes in Tracy's direction and smiled.

Her friend laughed. She had asked the question on impulse but knew well that Davis was harmless in that way. She also knew that Layla was tougher than her husband in many ways.

Layla and Tracy had finally gotten together and they had

volumes to talk about. They met at a popular bistro located just off Main Street in Waynesville. It was a warm spring day, and they were eating outside in the restaurant courtyard.

"So why do you suppose he wants to stay now, even though you want a divorce? Is it because of the logging project?"

"I think that's the main reason. That's why he showed up in the first place. Not because of me or of any real desire to start a family."

"What ever came of that?"

"Davis eventually came right out and told me that his father was pressuring him about grandchildren. That's what it was all about. I think he was almost relieved when I told him it was out of the question."

"So what exactly is Davis' role in the logging effort?"

"His job is to educate the public about the many benefits of logging the national forests. He writes informational articles for the papers, speak to various groups, and as much as possible, he points out that logging means jobs for local people. 'I'm the perfect ambassador for this initiative, a mountain-man counselor', to quote Sir Davis."

"But I still don't understand why he wants the house. Couldn't he just stay at his father's place to work on the logging initiative?"

"Yes, that's what I say, Tracy. And as far as the divorce is concerned, Davis will be getting off easy if I only ask for the house. Considering our other assets, the place in Raleigh alone would be worth more."

"Do you think he's just doing it for spite?"

"I don't think so. He' not being mean or petty about it; he's very casual and definite."

"Do you think you'll stay?"

"You know how I love that house and what I've put into it. I think I have to take my attorney's advice."

Tracy nodded. She knew well how Layla worked and fretted over the house for years. Over the same period, she watched her friend become accustomed to an absentee husband. Tracy became angry with Davis.

"Well, Mike and I will back you, whatever happens, as references, witnesses, whatever. Mike was furious when he heard about the logging initiative. He said that had he known about it when you guys were over for dinner last month, he would have hit Davis over the head with a chopstick."

Layla laughed. Michael Ogden was a passive person and slow to anger. He would never hit Davis with anything But like his wife, he was devoted to the cause of preserving the forests. Michael was particularly opposed to logging in the national forests.

"You're tough, Layla. I think you can wait him out."

"I'm going to give it a good try. Surprisingly, our domestic arrangement is not that different. Sleeping in separate bedrooms is nothing new and, like before, he spends most of his time at the computer in his study. If anything it's to my advantage because now I come and go and eat at my leisure and without guilt. There is one interesting development that I never would have guessed."

Tracy leaned forward, knowing from her friend's tone of voice that this would be good.

"Did I ever mention Ken Leyman's daughter, Carolyn?"

"I knew he had children but not much more than that."

"Yes, the man does have children, two sons and a daughter and the daughter's name is Carolyn. I've only gotten to know Carolyn, and she's very nice. But anyway, Carolyn is Davis' age and they were playmates when they were growing up. He practically lived with the Leyman's during the summers. Recently, Carolyn split up with her longtime boyfriend, a really cute violinist who I met once. She's now living at her parent's house on Balsam."

Tracy had been following intently and jumped a step ahead. "No, there isn't something going on between Carolyn and Davis?"

Layla smiled. "There might be."

Tracy shook her head. "That's weird."

Layla nodded and grinned. "Well that's what I get for marrying a lady's man like Davis."

Tracy had just sipped her coffee and had to cover her mouth with her hand to keep from laughing and spitting it out.

When her friend regained control, Layla continued. "Lately, after a ten year hiatus, Davis has taken up tennis again."

"Really?" Tracy asked, wiping her eyes and still giggling.

"Oh yes, he and Carolyn will often play a set before lunch and then dine on the deck overlooking the Leyman's tennis court."

"And Davis tells you this?"

"Yes, sitting there in his tennis outfit, which is a little snug these days, I might add. He was happy to tell me all about it."

"Do you think he's trying to make you jealous?"

"You know, I don't really think so. He may have a crush on Carolyn, but I think this is also part of his general fascination with the Leymans. Davis used to keep it under control because he knew I disliked Ken Leyman. But since I asked for a divorce, he makes no effort to hide it anymore. He even went to church with them last Sunday and he hasn't been to church in years."

"Would it bother you if there was something between Davis and Carolyn Leyman?"

"Hmm, no, I've already thought of that. I'd rather it wasn't the next door neighbor, but it wouldn't bother me. And you know, they say that's the sure sign that you're over someone."

Tracy studied her friend's face. Although Layla spoke casually of her domestic situation, Tracy knew that there must be underlying strain and sadness. She remembered a time when Layla and Davis were in love and happy together. They were excited about building a new house in the mountains when Tracy first met them.

Although Layla could laugh at the current state of their relationship, its imminent dissolution must hurt at some level. And if there was something going on between Davis and Carolyn Leyman, it would have to be embarrassing at the least.

Layla looked into Tracy's eyes and then read her thoughts. She didn't want sympathy. She also didn't want to spend their entire afternoon talking about her domestic situation. So Layla decided to change the subject. She had something she was dying to tell, anyway.

"Tracy, promise to keep a secret?"

Tracy's head jerked to attention, and nodded.

"Tomorrow, I have a date with Cataloochee Man."

"What?"

"Cataloochee Man, the hunter on the Cataloochee Divide, I've been seeing him."

18

Sundance knew the way now. The horse plodded down Hemphill Bald Trail while his rider was lost in thought. Layla thought about the domestic predicament at Mountain Crest and then about the wilderness experience that awaited her. She was beginning to find life with Davis unbearable and wondered if she had the mental stamina to adhere to her attorney's advice. The deeper she descended into Cataloochee Valley, the more her thoughts shifted toward wilderness.

By the time Layla approached Big Poplars she was uneasy. *Will Abe be there? Will he be happy to see me again?*

Compared to the routine events of her work week, memories of her Saturdays with Abe became almost unreal by comparison. By the time Layla was approaching Big Poplars she was worried that maybe it wasn't real.

How can it be possible that Layla Turner, a professor of English at Western Carolina University and a mysterious man who lives in Great Smoky Mountains National park have met and are falling in love? I could never make up a story like this.

Layla enjoyed the last visit so much that she didn't want to leave and it was obvious that Abe would have liked for her to stay. She had come earlier as Abe requested and they passed most of the day together. They went for another walk, and he talked more about the fantastic forest where he lived. During the course of that marvelous day, Layla gained more of a yearning for undisturbed wilderness than she had from any Forest First meeting.

Layla passed the massive poplar trees, hardly noticing them. She maneuvered down the slope, dodging branches, straining her eyes to see the clearing. Her heart palpitated and she smiled with relief when she saw Abe, standing in the center of the clearing, smiling at her.

The week before, Abe was ready for the hug when she departed. They held each other for several minutes, breathing hard, and then she kissed him on the lips, promising to be back. Over the ensuing week, Layla developed a wild, romantic yearning to pick up where she left off.

Abe held Sundance, rubbing the horse's neck as Layla dismounted and alighted to the ground close to him. When she looked into his eyes, Abe's smile widened into a beaming testament of how happy he was to see her. Worn down by the domestic standoff at Mountain Crest, his smile was a beacon of hope and she was drawn toward it. Layla put her arms around his neck and Abe encircled her with his.

"Oh Abe, I'm so happy to see you."

He didn't speak but pulled her close and rubbed his cheek gently against hers. The feeling of her body pressed against his was strange and wonderful. Her fragrance was exhilarating. Abe could feel that she was trembling, which helped to ease his own nervousness. He didn't remember feeling such excitement and happiness at the same time ever in his life. It was something like the feeling he got from waking in the forest on a glorious spring morning but many times more intense.

Layla moved her cheek along his beard, following the contour of a hidden jaw until her mouth found his. They kissed softly at first, unsure, lips barely touching. Abe had not been with a woman in ten years and she had known no man but Davis over the same period. But this didn't hold them back; they moved on to the next decade. Their feelings for each other were expressed in long passionate kisses that forced them to pause for air.

Once the dam was broken, all caution washed away in a flood of emotion. Each was what the other had been longing for although from different social perspectives. Layla and Abe sank to the ground as one and scattered their clothing as they helped each other undress.

The weather was warm on this June day, but a breeze from the direction of Caldwell Fork caused goose bumps on their naked skin. Not that they noticed; they were only aware of each other. The rhythmic sounds of breathing and sighing blended with the swishing of foliage, undulating in the breeze.

For having reached this level of intimacy, Layla knew little about Abe's life, and he only knew a little more about hers. Layla was cautious with her questions now that she knew Abe was uncomfortable with talking about his life before he entered the park. He spoke with enthusiasm about the last decade, and so Layla confined her conversation to that time frame. For his part, Abe never questioned Layla's past or present circumstances beyond the information she offered.

Layla rarely revealed to anyone that she was the daughter-in-law of the governor of North Carolina, but she never purposely omitted that she was an English Professor. Layla liked the fact that Abe only knew her as Layla Turner the author. Just as she could shut out the problems of the world when she was in Cataloochee Valley, Layla could imagine herself as an author when she was here with him. When Abe asked about her writing and listened with an expression of absolute belief in her abilities, she was inspired to make it be true.

Layla did continue to discuss the situation between her and Davis. From the first time she mentioned their problems, Layla came to appreciate Abe's quiet, objective opinion, a judgment not clouded by legal or financial considerations.

Abe had more dramatic reasons to prefer that their conversation not drift into the past. He didn't want to talk about the war that still haunted him with memories of black nights and silent movement, of knives and guns, of brilliant flashes and thunderous retorts, of blood and death. He didn't want to tell her about the desperate fight in the alley, the fallen police officer and the stolen police car. Abe didn't want this woman that he was so in love with to know why the police and FBI searched for him still.

Layla had dozed off, but stirred when a sudden rush of wind thrashed the rhododendron, causing the leaves to clap and chatter. Abe was lying on his back and Layla's head was on his chest, nestled under his chin. They were partially covered by Abe's blanket

"Layla, stay here with me.

"Oh, I have time yet; I don't have to hurry to. . ."

"No, I mean stay tonight. Stay for a couple of days."

Layla paused and opened her eyes wide. The proposal surprised her at first, but when she thought about it, she liked the idea.

"I can't tonight, Abe. I would be missed at Cove Creek Ranch. If I don't come back in, they would call the park rangers."

"Stay for good, then. Your husband doesn't want you at the house. The rangers will never find you in here."

"It's not that easy, Abe. I-I couldn't do that. I don't think so."

As much as Layla enjoyed these visits to the park and being with him, she couldn't imagine living here. But Layla liked the idea of staying with Abe for a longer period of time. She smiled and kissed him.

"I'll tell you what I'll do. Next week I'll get a back country permit and I'll stay the night. We'll see how it goes from there."

He smiled and nodded.

Then she looked at him with a grave expression. "Abe you do have a back country permit, don't you?"

"No Layla, you see I . . ."

She prodded him in the ribs and laughed.

Realizing the tease, he smiled, closed his eyes, and pulled her close again.

"What should I bring?" Layla asked.

"What do you mean?"

"What should I bring to stay overnight?"

"Oh, just bring the basics, a change of underwear and a toothbrush."

"What, where do you get underwear and a toothbrush?"

"I don't wear underwear but I know you do. My friend in Cosby supplies me with toothbrushes. I may be a mountain man, but I'm not a barbarian."

19

To Layla, it seemed like a huge sum of money. Although she had been a member of the Elmore family for over a decade now and knew that Malcolm's net worth was well into the millions, when it came to finances, she still thought in terms of hundreds and thousands. Davis had just offered her one million dollars as settlement in the divorce.

She was stunned. Layla loved her house but with that kind of money she could extricate herself from this domestic entanglement and start again, anywhere she wanted to.

Layla had felt certain that her husband would leave Mountain Crest when she asked for a divorce. Then she planned to concede all of their other assets in return for the house as her part of the settlement.

Davis was standing across the room smiling as if he knew she would say yes. He was inebriated, and his voice had that cavalier tone that often accompanied his drinking. Layla detected it as soon as he asked her to come into the Great Room to speak with him. Experience cautioned her that she should get away from her husband or else risk another argument. But before she managed to escape, he made his offer.

While Layla could not help but to be enticed by the money,

Davis' haughty demeanor and the startling size of his offer caused a discordant note to sound in her mind. She had been faintly hearing it ever since Davis announced that he wanted the house, and now it was sounding loudly.

A million dollars, why is he offering so much? Why is he so anxious to have this house when for years he has shown so little interest? Layla needed time to think over his offer and for some reason, she needed to know what was motivating him to make it.

"That's a generous offer, Davis, and I'll think it over."

"What's there to think over? A million bucks is a chunk of change. It would take a long time to save that kind of money teaching English."

"I don't want to discuss it now, Davis."

"Well, we need to get going on this divorce and uh, well, move on with our lives. It's a good offer. I want to be fair. There's no reason for us to be petty or drag this out."

"I agree. But could I ask you one question?"

He nodded.

"Why?"

Davis stared at her for a moment. He expected a wordier question. Yet as the seconds ticked by, and he struggled to answer, he realized that his wife had asked several difficult questions with one word.

"Layla, I uh, I want to stay here in the mountains, now. I'm not so sure I want to be counsel to the Governor, anymore. I want to start over, have a new life, here, maybe." He could hardly look at her as he spoke.

Layla considered his words in silence

Davis shuffled. He felt somewhat vulnerable under her gaze, especially so, standing there in his tennis outfit.

Layla noticed that the clothes fit him now, the result of many hours of tennis with Carolyn Leyman. Then suddenly, the note in her head sounded loud and clear. She realized her husband's vision for a new life.

Davis read his wife's expression and averted his eyes.

"Layla, I know what you're thinking and that is not the only. . ."

"Oh, I understand now, Davis. Why didn't I see this sooner? In your new life you want to be a Leyman. First 'Mr. Leyman' became 'Ken', and if all goes according to plan, and Carolyn's tennis game keeps improving, 'Ken' becomes 'Dad'."

Davis remained silent. In her own sarcastic terms Layla had outlined his expectations.

"And how very convenient, you already have a nice little house right here on Leyman Mountain with Mom and Dad only a stones throw away. And what's this I've heard about Carolyn wanting to have children?" Layla opened her eyes wide in mock surprise. "What a coincidence, so do you."

By his silence, Davis knew he was justifying her words. As his embarrassment gave way to anger, he no longer cared. He straightened up and met her stare.

"What a brilliant plan, and it makes good business sense, too. It's the perfect merger. Tell me, who came up with it first, you, your father, or was it . . . ?"

"You're so damn clever aren't you Layla? Well you're the one who asked for a divorce. I'm just getting on with my life. And beside, why should I just move away and hand you the house? It was hardly paid for with your salary. And my father gave us this land."

Layla braced herself. Most arguments with her husband came

to this point. Eventually, he saw the need to remind her that she married into privilege and that his salary was the bulk of their income. For him, the house at Mountain Crest had become symbolic of all this.

But Layla *was* clever and knew Davis well. She could deal with his invective. She also had an exceptional memory that held many facts and figures concerning the Elmore family, many of which Davis forgot that he told her.

"That's right he did. He gave us ten acres of the eight hundred that he owned in partnership with his good buddy Kenneth Leyman. Wait, where have I heard that name before? And speaking of money, isn't that how the family fortune was made, wheeling and dealing with Mr. Ken in real estate and logging? Logging, now that sounds familiar, too."

Davis became silent again. He was starting to feel warm and uncomfortable in the face of Layla's maneuver. She had used this tactic in previous arguments whenever he brought up money. She was implying that the family fortune was a bit tainted.

Another time he would shrug it off and come back at her from another angle but now an alarm sounded. Layla would not be a member of the Elmore family soon, and she was now a member of Forest First. Her knowledge of his family's business affairs could be a real threat. Anticipating Layla's next statement, he recited one of the party lines.

"My father sold his shares in Balsam Mountain Logging Corporation before he ran for office."

"Oh of course he did. To none other than Kenneth Leyman who is holding them until your father leaves office. Didn't you tell me that one night, about seven years ago over too much beer?"

With that statement, Davis became unnerved. That Malcolm

Elmore, the Governor of North Carolina, had once been a share-holder in Balsam Mountain Logging Corporation was a known fact, albeit, rarely mentioned now in the Governor's second term.

Steps were taken to distance the Governor from his logging past. The name of the corporation was changed to Southern Highlands Logging Company shortly after Malcolm's exodus. Until the logging initiative was introduced, the Governor was careful not to even mention the word 'logging'. While in office, Malcolm was not seen in public with Kenneth Leyman until the reception that marked the introduction of the logging initiative.

Layla had turned the table on their discussion. From his end of the table, Davis now wondered if he should offer her more money. He would have to discuss such a move with his father, of course, and that meant the standoff would not end today, as he had hoped.

He was meeting Ken in an hour to tour the logging operation in Pisgah National Forest. Since it was Ken's suggestion that he approach Layla with a buyout offer, Davis was hoping to inform him that Layla had agreed to the terms. Instead, Davis was worried about Layla's knowledge of his family's financial relationship to Ken Leyman.

Layla could see that her last statement hit a nerve, so she remained silent, watching the growing consternation on her husband's face. She didn't love Davis, but she didn't hate him, either. She wanted to get away from him now before the argument turned bitter.

"Davis, let's not fight. Give me some time to think. I-I don't want to discuss the house right this moment."

He shook his head and turned away.

Layla moved across the room toward the stairs. The doorbell rang just as she reached the first step. She wasn't expecting anyone. At the sound of the doorbell, Davis walked into the kitchen.

To her dismay, Layla opened the door to look into the blue eyes of Dennis Galloway, the right hand man of Kenneth Leyman. Although she could never quite uncover his precise condition of employment, her joking appraisal, spoken only to Davis, that Dennis Galloway was Ken's *muscle*, was not far off the mark.

In his early fifties, Dennis was handsome in a rugged way. He had a long face, striking blue eyes, and thinning brown hair, flecked with gray. His hair had been cut crew-style since his college days. The one inch scar on the left side of his chin didn't detract from his features. From his height of six feet and two inch, he looked down at Layla and smiled.

"Mrs. Elmore, it is once again my pleasure."

"Oh, uh, Mr. Galloway, it's been a while."

"Too long, and please, call me Dennis."

Layla hadn't liked the man since she first met him a decade before. He was always polite and friendly, but she sensed condescension. She believed that whatever interest Dennis might express in conversation was disingenuous and was instead, a means to size up a person for his own dubious purposes. Although he had been corrected twice before, Dennis Galloway still referred to Layla as Mrs. Elmore.

"Is Davis ready?"

"Ready for what?"

"Your husband and I are meeting Mr. Leyman to tour the Southern Highlands Logging Company operation in Pisgah National Forest."

Layla gave him a disdainful look. "Well, I'm sure he is, Mr.

Galloway." She started up the stairs and then leaned back into the room, shouting in the direction of the kitchen. "Oh Davis, your escort is here." She gave Dennis Galloway a false smile and continued up the stairs.

Layla entered her study and shut the door with a shudder. Although she had encountered this man only a few times over the years, something about Dennis Galloway made her uneasy. In spite of the trouble between her and Davis, Layla did not like the thought of him associating with this man. She watched from her window as they got into a white pick up truck, Davis talking all the while. Layla knew that her husband was somewhat impressed with Dennis' tough deportment.

Then Layla sat down and gazed at a higher angle toward a scene of beautiful, forested slopes, lush with green shades of midsummer. She thought of Abe. *What an uncomplicated life Abe lives. He has to work hard to survive, but everything he does has a purpose. I spend so much time worrying about things that don't even exist in his life.*

Layla had come to appreciate Abe's simple, objective opinion. She decided to ask for it once again, this time concerning Davis' monetary offer on the house.

20

The soldier remained hidden within the trees and circled the clearing until he was behind a long, aluminum clad trailer. This was the largest logging operation he had ever seen and it presented him with more than the usual number of targets. While he typically targeted machinery, the soldier decided on a trailer that he knew was used for storage. He also knew from the reconnaissance report that a box of dynamite was part of the inventory.

The weather conditions were perfect and that was what determined that the strike would be carried out on this particular night. The moonlight was muted by clouds, providing just the degree of visibility that this mission required. Well aware that it would be his most daring and perilous strike, the soldier drank liberally from the flask in his coat pocket. The night air was cool and he inhaled it in long, hearty doses, preparing for the physical exertion that would soon come.

The soldier attached a bomb to an axle of the trailer, set the timer, and rushed toward the forest. He was fifty yards into the trees and circling back in the direction of the logging equipment when the blast came. Forty yards further, he heard a second detonation and felt percussion from the explosion of the stored dynamite.

The soldier glanced over his shoulder in the direction of the flames. His eyes reflected the light and seemed to flicker with excitement. This is what he lived for now, the adrenaline rush that came once the battle began. When he saw silhouettes of humans rushing toward the fiery scene, he grinned and continued to move in the opposite direction. As he had calculated, this seemingly insignificant target was now the center of attention.

Miles Harding sat straight up in bed with the sound of the first explosion. Seconds later he launched himself out the door, pulling on clothes and carrying his gun, still in the holster. He witnessed the second blast, which sent fragments of the storage trailer high into the air accompanied by a shower of sparks.

The trailer from which he exited was located midway between the site of the explosion at the north end of the clearing and the rows of logging equipment at the southern end. It was serving as Miles' home and as field office for the FBI. Because of the immense size of this operation and the documented pattern of activity from the Panther Patrol, Miles had calculated that they would strike here next.

For this reason, the machinery had been strategically arranged and, until the explosion, had been carefully watched.

Miles shouted to one of his agents that came rushing past him. "Dowling."

"Sir?"

"What the hell happened?"

"I don't know yet. I just relieved Hostetler when something exploded."

"Who we got out here?"

"Ballard and Mike are just ahead of me. The Red Berets were practically down there before debris started hitting the ground."

"Who's at the equipment?"

The young agent said nothing.

"Damn it, come with me." Agent Harding drew his gun, threw the holster on the ground and trotted toward the machinery.

Agent Dowling was confused at first but when he came alongside his superior, Miles enlightened him.

"It's a diversion and everybody went for it."

The agents circled toward the logging machines until they were at the southern end of the clearing. Then Miles led a stealthy approach toward the equipment. As they came near a log skidder with the logo of Southern Highlands Logging Company emblazoned on each door, they heard muffled sounds. Circling the machine, they saw a man with his back to them. He was working with his hands under the tread of a bulldozer and muttering to himself.

Tom Dowling was wide-eyed; Miles Harding was elated. *It doesn't get any better than this,* he thought. *Everybody took the bait and it's left to the old man to finish the job.*

"Hands up," Miles shouted.

The man stiffened but he didn't turn or stop working.

"Hands up, now," Agent Harding shouted with more volume. "I have a weapon trained on you and I will not hesitate to use it."

Still the man delayed. Then he raised one hand while the other worked.

"Both hands up now or you're a dead man." Miles fired a shot that ricocheted off the machine inches away from the soldier. At that the man turned and raised both hands above his head.

Agent Harding recognized him as the same bearded man they had surrounded a month earlier at the High Point Lumber Company logging site. Miles knew from experience that he was clever and armed. "Check him out Tom and I mean thoroughly."

Agent Dowling took the soldier's AK-47 and also relieved him of a three-fifty-seven magnum pistol and a bowie knife.

Then without a word, the soldier started to walk.

"Stop, where the hell do you think you're going?"

The soldier turned to face agent Harding. His face was partially painted black, which made his pale eyes all the more ominous as he spoke. "Machine's gonna blow up. I set the timer. Machine's gonna blow up and unless we put a little distance between it and us, we're gonna blow up with it."

Miles knew he wasn't bluffing. He motioned with his gun toward the center of the clearing. "All right, move. Walk in a straight line and don't try anything funny."

When they had progressed a short distance, Miles glanced back to see that Tom Dowling was too close behind, his own gun in one hand and the prisoner's weapons cradled in his left arm. He was looking over his shoulder. "Eyes forward, agent. Watch the prisoner."

When Miles turned forward, he became uneasy. The prisoner was too close as well. He began to sense that the soldier was directing the flow of events. He was moving too slowly for someone who had just warned of an imminent explosion.

Agent Harding had reason to be uneasy. The soldier had been counting the seconds and measuring his steps since his finger left the bomb. So skilled was he at this sort of work that he knew how far away he should be to escape harm and how close he should stay to keep his captors in harm's way. The fact that there were two human bodies between him and the coming blast was a factor in his calculation.

As far as escape was concerned, he scarcely considered Agent

Dowling, so young and excited; the older man had to be outwitted if he were to get away.

When the bomb detonated, the soldier felt a body hit his legs as he was hurled to the ground with the force of the blast. He rolled with the blow and then reacted, wresting the gun from Agent Harding's hand and punching him on the jaw. Already dazed by the blast, Miles collapsed to the dirt, rendered unconscious by the blow.

Agent Dowling was dancing about, yelling that he had been shot. He hadn't been, but he did have a piece of shrapnel protruding from his leg. The escaping prisoner dropped the agent to the ground with a blow across the back of the neck. He retrieved his own weapons and took the agent's assault rifle.

Then a gun fired twice from the middle of the clearing. The bearded man didn't turn but instead, ran toward the blazing machinery, scuttling around it when he was only five feet away. The fire was a sparking, popping, meandering blaze, laced with sinister blue flames, licking about the bulldozer engine. The soldier chose this route of escape because it was the least inviting trail to follow.

Harrison Coulter, commander of the Red Berets, realized that the first explosion was a ruse as soon as he viewed the fiery remains of the trailer. He then turned and ran toward the machinery, the members of his eco-terrorism strike force close behind.

The explosion among the logging equipment hadn't surprised him; the silhouettes that materialized in front of the flames did. Captain Coulter concluded that the bearded figure was a foe but fired only warning shots from side to side. He knew that the figures who were being struck were friends and he couldn't risk shooting from such a distance.

The Captain waved his gun from side to side, directing those who ran with him to fan out on each side of the wreckage.

When the Red Berets reached the tree line, Harrison Coulter raised his hand and the six men that flanked him stopped. They listened. The silence was interrupted by a faint cracking noise. The Captain used hand signals to direct his men to spread out and then to advance into the forest.

The soldier was a hundred yards ahead of them when he stopped to listen. *I'll be damned. They're in the woods, a bunch of them.* A nervous smile appeared on his face. *What the hell? Who are these guys anyway?*

Then he heard a limb break to his right and a rustling noise from behind. *Shit, they're right on my tail, trying to surround me. God damn it, they must have night goggles.*

The man moved fast now, realizing that stealth had been trumped by technology. Rather than attempting to silently elude, he tried to put some distance between himself and his pursuers. He lacked the advantage of night vision goggles, but he had often been in the forest at night. With enough light to distinguish forms, and the experience to move around them, he was able to keep ahead of his pursuers.

A skill that preserved the soldier's freedom on many occasions and saved his life on some of them was his ability to think clearly and act decisively in dire situations. When he realized that he was being surrounded, he decided on the route of escape. It would be a swollen stream at the bottom of a steep slope about two hundred yards to the west. It was a cold choice, jumping into frigid mountain water to be borne downstream and away from those who followed him, but to be apprehended was out of the question.

Of the three escape contingencies he had drawn up, the water route was the one he least expected to need and planned to use it only if the situation became desperate.

Soon the soldier could hear the sound of rushing water. He moved down the slope toward it. When he could see breaks in the foliage and knew the stream was only yards ahead, he turned and sprayed bullets in an arc above his pursuers. He wanted to give them cause to hesitate and consider the worth of their lives. Then he pushed through tangled brush to the edge of the water. The soldier had a wild look on his face but exhibited no fear. Without hesitation, he leaped into the torrent and was swept away.

21

"Huh, what?" Layla awoke to a strange noise. She raised her head and looked from side to side, disoriented at first. Then, she remembered where she was. The noise came again, this time much closer.

"Abe," she whispered, prodding the man lying beside her.

"Hmm, Layla what?"

"Shhh, listen."

He raised himself onto his elbows and listened. The noise came again.

"Did you hear that?"

The noise sounded several more times in rapid succession.

"Listen, what is that?"

Abe grinned and shook his head.

"What is it, Abe?"

"It's a deer, Layla, a deer snorting at us."

"Why is it doing that?"

"It's scared; the snorting is an alarm. Probably comes by here every night and is used to me. But now it smells you and is worried. It's warning other deer."

Abe cupped his hands on each side of his mouth. With his lips drawn as if to whistle, he exhaled forcefully.

Layla sat up when she heard the same forest noise that had startled her, emanate from the man beside her. Abe repeated the snort several times. Within seconds she heard the noise returned from the forest but louder than before. Then she heard the thumping of hooves and repeated snorting as the animal ran away.

Abe chuckled. "They don't know what to think when a creature that smells like a human snorts like a deer."

He lowered himself onto his back, and Layla positioned herself on top of him. His arms encircled her under the blanket and silence closed in.

Because she now had a back country pass, Layla was spending the weekend in Cataloochee Valley with Abe Ramsey. They were at his home on Spruce Mountain, which was not a house or even a small cabin. It was little more than an elaborate shelter with only as much floor space as the shed at Mountain Crest that Layla kept her garden tools in.

Abe simply referred to it as the *main camp*. Four thousand feet above sea level on the southern slope of the mountain, the shelter was situated in a cluster of enormous hemlock trees. It was rare level terrain on a steep slope. Abe had lived in Cataloochee Valley for two years before he decided on this location for his main camp. It was an area that no one frequented, and his shelter could not be seen from any distant vantage point, even with binoculars.

Abe's home blended so well into the setting that the day before, Layla was thirty yards away before she realized it was there. The shelter was constructed of stone, wood and deerskin. The stone was stacked two feet wide and three feet high to form the lower portion of the walls. Logs that had been flattened on two sides lay along the top of the stones and smaller logs ran vertically from these to support a roof of layered deer hide. The upper half of the walls were also constructed of deer hide that was stretched between the uprights. Within the multiple layers of hide was a system of flaps that could be opened for light or ventilation.

Layla was impressed with the ingenious design of Abe's home and loved the muted, earthy tones of the building materials. To her delight, she found the inside orderly, clean, and a model of efficiency. Certain areas of the space served the purpose of a room or even several rooms in a typical house. A fireplace for heating and cooking was built into one of the walls. The sleeping area was a loft built high against the opposite wall so that the occupant benefited from rising heat. Beneath this was an assortment of wooden pegs, supporting Abe's scant wardrobe.

Layla couldn't get back to sleep after the snorting incident. She lay still in the dark loft, inhaling the aroma of wood smoke that permeated Abe's home and listening to the gentle whir of night insects. Layla smiled as she thought about how different Abe's life was from her own. That led her to think about her own shelter.

"Abe, are you still awake?"

"Yes."

"What do you think I should do about the house? What would you do if you were me?"

He was silent for a moment and then Layla could feel him shifting his head to look at her.

"I would go."

"Take the money and go?"

"I would go with or without the money."

"But I can't do that. I need to live somewhere and that takes money. And besides, I have put a lot of hard work into that house."

"But why have you put so much work into a house? A house is a place to live not a place to work. I come here to eat or rest or sometimes just to think, but I never work here. Why do you need such a big house, anyway?"

"It's not so big, well, not in comparison to many places these days. And as nice as your place is, I couldn't live like this. I need more comfort and security. I need a place to write."

"Okay, I know that. Then how about a cabin with a desk and a lamp, you could sleep in the loft and heat it with a wood cook stove. An arm load of wood now and then would be the work required. You could spend almost all your time writing instead of keeping house."

"Abe, life isn't that simple."

"It can be."

Layla laid her head on Abe's chest and listened to slow, steady heartbeats. She had been hoping that he would advise her to keep the house, that's what she really wanted to do. She even envisioned him coming there to be with her. Sometimes, Layla fantasized that she made a living by the success of her novels. In these fantasies, she wrote every day and tended her gardens and awaited the next visit of Cataloochee Man.

But Abe's advice was to walk away from it all and not for the reasons she might have guessed. In his objective way, he pointed out that the ultimate cost of her house was the time taken away from what she really wanted to do, which was to write. Somehow in this simple, forest setting, far away from her life at Mountain Crest, she sensed that he was right.

The next day, they walked north. Layla wanted to hike and Abe said he would show her something interesting that was located three miles away. Along the way she saw many things both interesting and beautiful so that she wondered what he wanted to show her. But no matter how she asked, he wouldn't tell what it was.

As they walked Layla and Abe talked about many things but not about the house at Mountain Crest. Layla was certain that she couldn't take his advice and so didn't revive their conversation of the night before. They talked of the forest mostly, Abe's favorite subject. And eventually, he asked about her writing. So she told him the story line of her first novel, never letting on that the writing had been stalled for years.

"Why do you have her go to that town? What was the name?"

"Chistochina."

"Yes, Chistochina, have you been there?"

"No, I've never been to Alaska. When my father was in college, he and a friend took a semester off and hitchhiked to Alaska. They stayed there and worked for a few months at a campground. According to my father, it was one of the best experiences of his life. I've heard many stories about Chistochina over the years."

Abe was silent for a moment, then he looked at Layla and smiled. "If I were to leave the Smoky Mountains, it would be to go to Alaska."

"Really, you would leave the park to go to Alaska?"

He nodded. "When I was in high school, I read a book about Alaska. I've wanted to go there ever since."

They were both silent for a few minutes, trudging along Abe's unmarked trail. Layla had no idea of which direction they were going, she just followed this mysterious man that she was in love with. She stopped when he turned and gazed into her eyes.

"Now if you would do that, leave that big house and go to Alaska, I would come to visit soon after."

"Oh really?"

"Yes."

"And how would you get there?"

"Walk," he said, and as if to demonstrate, he turned and continued forward.

"And how long would that take?"

He turned again and was silent for a moment while he considered the question.

"Three months, four months, somewhere in there." Abe turned and walked again.

Layla smiled and followed. "If you took a jet, you could be there in a day."

He turned to face her, shaking his head. "That's not so; it would take longer to get there by jet. First I'd have to find a job, which could take weeks. Then I'd have to work until I earned money to buy my ticket. After that, I'd need new clothes, and luggage, and who knows what else. It would be many months before I got started toward Alaska. If I walk, I could start right now." He turned and started walking again.

Layla laughed, caught up to Abe, and pushed him on the back. "Okay wise guy, but you could at least compromise and take a bus part of the way. They're cheap and you won't need a fancy wardrobe."

Abe grinned. "I'll keep that in mind."

Layla and Abe walked for over an hour, plodding into

crevices and over knolls, roughly staying at the same elevation. They stopped for a break on a small rock outcrop overlooking a steep mountainside. They could hear the distant whine of a chain saw.

"Do you think that's coming from a logging operation?" Layla asked.

"No, we're too far inside the park. That's most likely maintenance work being done by park personnel."

"Have you ever seen a logging operation, Abe?"

"Yes, plenty of them."

"What do you think about logging?"

"Well if it's done right, I don't have anything against it. Trees grow back."

"Then you feel that as long as it's done right, logging in Pisgah National Forest is making proper use of it?"

He was surprised at such a specific question but readily offered an opinion. "No I don't think so, not in those woods. They belong to everybody. There's plenty of private land to log."

That prompted Layla to talk about her involvement with Forest First and their efforts to stop logging in Pisgah National Forest. Abe had never heard of the organization but was impressed with their numbers and fascinated by the passive, nonviolent methods they employed.

"I would never chain myself to a tree or stand in front of a bulldozer. Please don't ever do that Layla. Most of the loggers are good people but all it takes is one bad one."

"Well, I haven't gone that far yet. I'm new to the group."

"Do you think that Forest First is making a difference?"

"Honestly, sometimes it seems that at best, our efforts only slow things down a little. The politicians and corporations get their way in the end. I get so frustrated that I can understand why a group like the Panther Patrol resorts to violence."

She was looking in the direction of the chain saw noise and didn't see Abe's eyes flash toward her with that sentence.

"But even they only manage to slow things down. There are always more machines behind the ones they blow up. And in the long run, I think the government is more comfortable at dealing with violence than it is with non-violence."

She paused and sighed. "The real problem isn't the loggers or the machines or the people who oppose them. The problem is the corporations and politicians who orchestrate these things. And their motivation is always money."

"I know what you mean. We're hacking at the branches when the root needs cut."

Layla smiled and nodded. She was surprised at this profound statement and pleased that by uttering it, Abe included himself among the opposition.

They continued walking at the same elevation for a quarter mile, and then Abe turned down a slope and walked to the west for a hundred yards. He was leading toward a large stand of Catawba Rhododendron. Large pink blossoms hung in striking contrast to lush green leaves.

Layla glanced ahead and was startled to see sunlight reflected off metal in the dark interior of dense shrubbery. As they approached, she saw more reflection and soon the outline of a large object. Abe hadn't brought her to a natural forest scene but to a site where civilization had intruded upon the park.

"My God, an airplane, there's an airplane in there. When did this happen?" Layla was viewing battered remains of a small airplane that were woven into the vegetation.

Abe shrugged. "I found it eight years ago and it looked about this way even then."

"Do you suppose the passengers died?"

"Oh, I know they did. They're still on board."

"What?"

Abe nodded and then walked toward the wreckage. He worked his way to the opposite side of the plane, to an opening where a door had once been.

When Layla came to his side, she raised a hand to her mouth. A time-worn human skull with a green hue lay on remnants of a seat, among a small pile of weathered bones. The skull was tilted to one side and facing toward them. There were just bone fragments on the other seat.

"You're the only one who knows about this?"

"I'm fairly sure I am. I've never seen any sign that other people have been here. I pass by this way every year or so and it all seems the same, just slowly wearing away."

"I wonder who they were."

"I don't know. Even when I first found it there was nothing left that I could read. I think they were married though."

Abe extended his hand into the opening and pointed to a darkened wedding band on the floor. "There was another one on the pilot's seat for a few years but it disappeared. Probably some animal stole it. The bones get scattered and taken too."

"Why haven't you ever told anyone about this?"

"Who would I tell? Why would I tell?"

"So that these people can be properly buried; for the sake of the family."

"Well, the way I see it, this plane has been here for a long time. By now, the family's gotten past what happened. Finding them now would just make it sad all over again. And as far as being buried, I can't think of a better spot. They're slowly becoming part of the forest."

It was a beautiful day with sunlight filtering through the rhododendron canopy, bathing the scene in patches of light. Layla could almost see Abe's point about the burial site, but the thought of the tragedy still upset her.

"I hope they were happy together before this happened."

Layla appeared so sad as she said this that Abe put his arms around her.

She turned and looked into his eyes. "Abe, are you afraid of dying?"

"No, I don't want to die, and I'll do whatever I can to keep living, but I'm not afraid to die. It's going to happen one day and there's nothing I can do about it. I really don't think about it. Maybe it's because I'm too busy living. Are you afraid of dying?"

Layla nodded and pulled him closer.

"Do you believe in heaven and hell or some sort of an afterlife?"

Abe shook his head. "I believe we live until we die and no longer. What do you believe?"

"I, I like to think that after this, there's another life without all the worry and work of this one, a place without war and want, where we can all be together again and be happy."

Abe stared at her with a puzzled expression. "If that's what you think then why are you afraid of dying?"

She thought about this for a moment. Then she smiled and kissed him. Layla rested her head on his shoulder and gazed at the airplane. Then she felt a tingle along her spine. It seemed to her as if the skull was staring back.

Layla became panicky, overwhelmed by the notion of this vast wilderness wherein a plane and two people could vanish from civilization. And this man that she loved lived here. She put her hands on each side of Abe's head and looked into his eyes.

"Abe, please be careful."

22

"You say that Randall has decided on the University of North Carolina? Well that's good to hear. Is he going to play ball?"

"Well, Mr. Leyman, he'll be on the team, but won't play much at first. Truthfully, I would've been happy if he decided not to. He's a good basketball player, but he'll probably never get much playing time and there's no chance at the pros. He's about in the same position I was in when I played football for Kentucky. He'd probably be better off if he concentrated on the books, unlike I did."

"I can't recall, what was it you studied in school, Dennis?"

"I majored in a number of things over the years, starting with biology. I finally got a degree in history. I've never really worked in my field, though."

Ken chuckled at the truth of that statement.

Dennis Galloway had worked for Kenneth Leyman for eighteen years. They were loyal and friendly to each other, but there remained a professional space between them. Dennis always referred to his employer as Mr. Leyman, and although they were together often, it was never simply to socialize. The rest of the Leyman family hardly knew Dennis.

Dennis Galloway was the highest paid employee on Ken Leyman's payroll and yet nobody knew for certain what he did. The truth of the matter was that Ken Leyman didn't know exactly what Dennis did. But what he did know was that when he needed him, Dennis always got the job done.

They were driving on a gravel road in a white Chevrolet Silverado that Ken purchased a month before for the purpose of touring the logging sites. Dennis handled the purchase and was driving the truck now.

"How do you like your truck, Mr. Leyman?"

"I like it, Dennis. It's big. In fact, it's the biggest vehicle I've ever owned. But it has a nice feel to it. How do you like it?"

"It's nice. I like it."

"Do you want one?"

"Nah, too big for me. I like my cars."

Ken and Dennis were approaching the Southern Highlands Logging Company's main operation in Pisgah National Forest. On the way Ken didn't speak of the destruction of the bulldozer that had occurred a few days before. The fact that someone had destroyed a piece of his equipment infuriated him, but he didn't want anger to cloud his judgment when he talked with Miles Harding.

Besides he had another matter he wanted to discuss with Dennis, one of a lighter nature but also related to the logging project.

Dennis pulled into the clearing and shut off the engine. Both men stared at the charred remains of the bulldozer for a moment before Ken spoke.

"So tell me, Dennis, what's your impression of young Davis Elmore? I trust that you have established an opinion during the course of your recent travels together."

"Nice guy, but talks too much. He told me things about his marital problems that I didn't ask about and didn't need to know. He also bragged about some of the tactics he used to win public support for the logging initiative, when all he really knows about me is that I work for you."

Ken nodded. The grimace on his face was an indication that he was aware of this tendency in Davis. "He drives his father crazy, sometimes, because of that."

"He may drink too much. Both times we drove together, I smelled alcohol, and it was the middle of the day." Dennis shrugged. "Could be nothing."

Ken nodded again and had the same expression on his face.

Ken had insisted that Davis ride with Dennis to the logging operation because the rough roads at the site required the use of a four wheel drive vehicle, like the Silverado. When he reached the logging operation, Davis was certain that his car would have navigated the roads, but he never suspected that he was being transported for the purpose of interview and evaluation.

"Well, Dennis, I'm not exactly thinking CEO material here. Davis and my daughter, Carolyn, have known and liked each other since they were children. Malcolm Elmore, Davis' father, and I always thought it would be a good match or a convenient one at least. It was mostly talk and we never pushed it. In the end, Davis and Carolyn went out into the world and made their own mistakes."

Dennis looked surprised.

"Oh, didn't I mention it? Carolyn and the fiddler have parted company. That's why she's been staying at the house on Balsam."

Dennis smiled. He knew how Ken felt about Antoine.

"Now by coincidence Davis is also staying at his home on the mountain this year and, as I'm sure you've heard, his wife wants to part company with him. Consequently, Carolyn and Davis have been playing tennis and renewing their friendship. I have a feeling it may develop into a bit more. Now it's still a little early to be planning a wedding reception, but . . ." Ken raised his eyebrows and grinned.

"That *would* be convenient."

"Yes indeed. You see, I worry that my good friend, the Governor, has become a bit soft during his years in Raleigh. Happens to politicians; they tend to lose the aggressiveness that's so necessary in business. I even detect in Malcolm slight disapproval with some of my recent business endeavors. In two years, he and I will be partners again and I think if we are all one big, happy family, he'll more easily regain his focus."

"Well, I agree that Davis isn't CEO material, but he's not dumb. He's basically a nice guy. And it's always a good idea to have an extra attorney on your team."

"I agree. And besides, Carolyn and Davis have liked each other for years. It's not strictly a business move. As long as she's happy, that's what matters, too. Anyway, I appreciate your insight, Dennis. Now let's go see if the Federal Bureau of Investigation can enlighten us."

Miles Harding walked toward the white truck, muttering to himself. In spite of the fact that at the time of his arrival, Ken Leyman was twenty minutes late for their meeting, he lingered to talk in the vehicle for ten minutes more. Miles didn't have a punctual schedule to attend; he would be here all day, as he had been all week. It was a matter of principle that made him expect some measure of respect from this man whose interests Miles and his team were working to protect.

This was the second meeting between the two men and Miles had sensed little respect in the first. He could hardly expect much change, considering that the purpose of this meeting was to discuss the destruction of a bulldozer owned by Ken Leyman's Company. But Miles was a veteran of his profession, and he knew how to deal with the characters that came his way, including the Ken Leymans of the world.

Ken approached Miles with a smile and an outstretched hand while Dennis Galloway paid little attention to the FBI agent. Instead, he looked slowly from side to side, estimating distances, considering exit routes. Wherever he went, Dennis was always gathering information.

"Agent Harding, it is again my pleasure."

Miles had coached himself to remain calm and choose his lines well. "Mr. Leyman," he said with a polite smile.

"And you and Dennis have met."

Dennis Galloway looked toward Miles at this point. He briefly starred at the agent, nodded, and resumed his survey of the surroundings.

Miles had met Dennis when Davis was brought to the logging site. Intuition told him what type of man he was, and he had a background check run that day.

"It seems we've had a run-in with the enemy," Ken said, nodding toward the blackened bulldozer.

"Yes we have and unfortunately he slipped past us again."

Dennis snorted and turned at this remark.

The agent stared at him until Ken spoke again.

"So I hear. It sounds like this Panther Patrol is not to be taken lightly. Perhaps it's time to take off the kid gloves."

"I never take anybody lightly, Mr. Leyman, and I never wear gloves. They will be apprehended."

"But there, I think you've hit on my point, Agent Harding. Maybe you should not focus so much on apprehension."

"We don't use lethal force unless it's necessary."

"That's a pity. The cost of a bullet would have spared the expense of a hundred and fifty thousand dollar piece of equipment."

"I'm sure you have good insurance."

"Yes, but bad patience."

"If you ask me, the equipment should have been more centrally placed," Dennis remarked.

"Well, I didn't ask you," Miles answered, without looking at him.

Dennis glared at the agent.

"Dennis may have a point there, Agent Harding. He is . . ."

"I know what he is, Mr. Leyman. I know more about him then you realize." With that statement, Ken's smile faded and Miles thought he saw the first hint of unease in Ken Leyman's eyes. That was precisely what the agent was looking for in this interaction.

Dennis moved toward Miles and started to speak, but Ken raised a hand to silence him.

Miles spoke instead. "Now, I want you to listen. I've been at this a long time and I know what I'm doing. The information we gather with each encounter prepares us for the next, either here or at the other logging operations we're working with. The noose will tighten around these people and they *will* be captured.

We want to know who they are, how they operate, and what motivates them. The FBI is not just interested in protecting your

126

logging ambitions, Mr. Leyman. Our goal is to learn how to prevent this type of activity in general."

Ken stared at Miles for a few long seconds and the agent didn't blink. Then Ken's smile reappeared and his eyes sparkled.

"Well, Agent Harding, I'm glad we had this chance to make our positions clear. Now that we have, I see no reason to continue this conversation. Good day and good luck."

Ken started to walk away but then turned. "Oh, by the way, could I ask you a question?"

Miles nodded.

"Who are the uniformed men wearing the unusual berets?"

"It's a newly formed unit, trained to fight eco-terrorism, the Red Berets. This is their first deployment."

"Thank you, Agent Harding. Now I know who they are and also, what sort of enemy we're fighting."

Ken turned toward the truck and his employee followed in silence. When they had driven away, Dennis was the first to speak.

"What an asshole."

Ken chuckled. "No, Dennis, Agent Harding is no asshole. He's good. That's why they sent him."

"Who sent him?"

"Good old boys in Washington. They didn't like the way I worked them to gain this opportunity."

"I thought it was Governor Elmore who pulled the strings."

"He may have pulled one or two, but I'm not so sure anymore. I was working on congress from several different persuasions. And whether they liked it or not, many of them had no choice but to steer a logging contract my way. So I figure they sent Agent Harding down to let me know of their displeasure, to let me know they're watching."

"What are you going to do?"

"Stay out of his way, talk the talk. In the end, just work around him."

Dennis swallowed hard and nodded.

23

The hunter sat motionless amid a tangle of rhododendron. Abe was at the edge of the ever-growing logging operation of the Southern Highlands Logging Company. Even with the benefit of dense, June foliage, it took him over an hour to traverse the last hundred yards to his present location without being seen. So his first observation on this reconnaissance mission was the greater military presence in the woods surrounding the clearing. While moving toward his position, a member of the Red Berets passed within twenty yards of him.

As before, his mission was to observe how the equipment was arranged at the end of the work day and also to note any changes at the site now that a successful strike had been made. This was the hunter's first visit to the site since the bulldozer had been destroyed. In spite of his circumstances, he was thinking about Layla. It was not time for him to scrutinize the activities in the clearing, so for a few minutes he blocked out the scene and refreshed himself with memories of the past weekend.

They had talked about many things during the two days that she stayed with him, and the more he learned about Layla, the more he loved her. Abe believed that she loved him, and she seemed to appreciate what he had told her about himself. But he knew that she would like to know much more. While Abe was in her arms this weekend, he felt so happy and trustful that he almost overcame instinct and told everything.

During their discussion of the opposition to logging, Abe felt somewhat guilty when Layla mentioned the Panther Patrol and he remained silent. He purposely used *we're* in his remark when he stated that the root of the problem needed to be cut. Abe even considered proceeding from that point and telling her of his affiliation with the Panther Patrol. And, depending on how she reacted to that information, he might have gone on to explain how he came to live in the park.

But when he looked into her eyes and she smiled at him, Abe lost his nerve. Saying *we're* was as far as he went toward disclosure.

A few months before, he would have guessed that there was a greater chance of being hit by a falling tree then to meet and fall in love with someone like Layla. And he would have put the odds that she would love him back at the level of being hit by a falling tree and struck by lightning at the same time. Abe knew that he would never have such luck again, and so he decided to not risk telling her, yet.

It would be four days before he saw Layla but then she would stay with him for the weekend again. To help the time pass more quickly, Abe labored on the trails in the park. He cleared away branches, shored up wash-outs, and created water diversion barriers with small, half-buried logs.

He was also working for the Panther Patrol with more resolve and not only to pass time. The knowledge that Layla was also trying to stop the logging inspired him to make today's daring reconnaissance. Because of his love for her, Layla's bleak assessment for the chances of actually stopping the logging in Pisgah National Forest didn't discourage him as much as it pushed him to try harder.

Motivated by such thoughts, Abe inched forward onto his stomach and with binoculars, began to survey the activity in the clearing. The operation was winding down for the day, with only a crane left clanking and grinding at the far end of the clearing as it loaded the last trucks. Some loggers walked toward the parking area, talking and laughing, while pick-up trucks and cars began to wobble onto the gravel road and drive away.

The equipment was being parked in the same location as before, a fact that surprised Abe. Two weeks had passed since the destruction of the bulldozer and another machine had already replaced it. The logging continued unabated, and Abe guessed that the size of the clearing had nearly doubled since he was last here.

Gazing across the field to his left he saw some soldiers in a huddle, each man wearing a radio mouth piece and bearing a weapon. When he heard a faint noise from behind, Abe turned his binoculars to the forest and spotted another soldier forty yards away, moving at a tangent to the clearing. He thought that the Southern Highlands Logging Company's base camp was beginning to look more like a combat outpost than a logging operation.

Turning back to the clearing, Abe moved the binoculars slowly to the right, studying each vehicle and any person that came into view. He followed the crane operator, hard hat and lunch bucket in hand, trudging over ruts and woody debris toward the parking area. As the man neared the gravel road, he nodded to three men standing in front of a white pick up truck. Two of these men had jackets on and the third was in casual dress.

Abe was certain that one of the jackets was worn by a man he had seen before and had since assumed to be an FBI agent. This man seemed to be engaged in conversation with the casually dressed man who appeared to be older than the other two.

The other man stood apart and seemed more interested in the surroundings than the conversation. He was moving his head from side to side and then up and down, as if he was looking for something. Abe found his behavior odd and, for some reason, unsettling.

Even with the limitation of his view, Abe thought he saw aggravation in the gestures of the first man, the presumed agent. Abe guessed that he was in charge of protecting the operation and went on to speculate that the man aggravating him was the owner of the company. The longer he studied the older man, his movements, the effect of his words on the agent, the more he was convinced of this.

Could this be the root of the problem? But he's such a small man to be the cause of so much trouble.

Abe watched the older man walk away from the agent, the mysterious man following him. Then the man turned to address the agent once more before reaching his vehicle. After this exchange, the FBI agent walked away at a rapid pace. Again, he seemed agitated.

Resting on his elbows and holding the binoculars steady, the hunter focused on the two men climbing into the truck. He guessed that the strange man was a body guard or some sort of right hand man.

The vehicle pulled further into the clearing and then backed up to turn. As it pulled away, Abe saw that the truck had a South Carolina license plate. The hunter possessed excellent vision and had spent hundreds of hours gazing through binoculars. He was able to make out the license number before the vehicle entered the shade. He repeated it several times, committing the number to memory.

Abe continued to observe the activities in the clearing, counting the individuals that remained after the operation shut down and trying to discern their roles. He scrutinized the equipment and noted that it had been placed in orderly rows but with wider spaces between each piece. This was obviously for ease of observation. Even from where he watched, Abe could easily follow a person walking amongst the machines.

When the light grew dim, Abe began his slow retreat into the forest, stopping often to listen. After a decade of living in the forest, he relied on his hearing as much as his sight. He heard no human sound while crossing the first fifty yards and so began to move more quickly.

About the time he decided it was safe to rise to an upright position, he heard the distinctive sound of human footsteps, crackling the underbrush. He turned to see lights flickering through the foliage and advancing toward him.

Abe was surprised that he had been detected but not concerned about apprehension. He knew that no one could outrun him in the forest. Trotting fifty yards to the trunk of a large oak tree he peered back toward the lights. To his surprise, there was no pursuit, instead the lights were converging on an area along the line that he had traversed. There they crossed each other, apparently searching for him.

Then Abe realized what happened. He had passed through some sort of beam that alerted the soldiers to his whereabouts. It was probably set when the last workers left. When the disruption of the beam tripped the alarm, the Red Berets assumed that someone had entered at that point, never guessing that an intruder had exited instead. Knowledge of this security system was the most important information he had garnered all day.

The hunter continued west into the woods toward Great Smoky Mountains National Park. He was about seven miles away and planned to camp within the park. In the morning he would start out for Waterville and by the time he returned to his main camp on Spruce Mountain, it would be only two days until Layla arrived.

24

"When do you plan to head back, Dad?"

"Tomorrow about noon. That will get me into Raleigh about quitting time."

Davis grinned. He knew better than anyone that his father loved his job and would never connive to get out of a days work. The truth was that Malcolm never really quit working, not even when he was at his Balsam Mountain home. Regardless of how one regarded the Governor's politics, no one could deny that he worked hard at his job.

Davis was drinking a beer with the Governor on the back porch of his father's home. The porch was located at the west corner of the house and was flanked on each side by a stand of holly trees. Malcolm and Davis gazed down a gentle slope across a manicured lawn that merged with a dark forest.

A balmy Sunday afternoon in June, Malcolm lay on a sturdy chaise lounge made of teak wood. He was wearing baggy shorts of a colorful flower pattern and an unbuttoned white shirt. Davis wore his tennis outfit. He had ample time to change after the noon match with Caroline, but Davis was proud of his trim physique. Malcolm didn't seem to notice.

"So when are you heading back, son?"

Davis had anticipated this question and knew that his father asked it in the broadest sense.

"Well, I, uh, I still have some work here. I still have some articles to write, some loose ends to tie up. There's the divorce . . ."

"And there's Carolyn Leyman," Malcolm interrupted, leveling a penetrating gaze at his son.

"Yes, why yes, there's Carolyn, of course. We seem to be getting along well after all these years. We're not serious, Carolyn and I or not yet. Well, it's not that I don't take it . . ."

"Is that why you want the house at Mountain Crest? You often referred to it as Layla's house, and you just as often mentioned that you didn't really care for it. I know you're not a spiteful person, so that's not your motive for wanting it. And the truth is, if Layla would take the house as settlement in the divorce, you would be getting off easy."

Davis sighed and looked toward the forest. He didn't want to have this conversation right now, but he knew that it was pointless to try to evade his father's questions.

"Dad, Carolyn and I are just friends, I mean that. What's to come of it, I can't say. Y-you see, in spite of how strange our marriage was in the end, it was still a shock to me when Layla asked for a divorce. I don't love her now, but for some reason, it hurts to think that she doesn't love me anymore. I was hardly ever with her and yet it bothered me to find out that she didn't want me with her ever again."

"Son, you don't have to go into all that now. The point I . . ."

"No wait Dad, I want to explain this. Layla's request for a divorce put an end to a decade long mistake and here I am now, in my mid-thirties. If things would work out with Carolyn, maybe it's a chance to get it right, to have the kind of life I've always

136

wanted. I'm still young enough to have a family, and I want to have a family now. Carolyn wants to have children, too. Did you know that? And besides, I have roots here. Why should I just give Layla the house when Carolyn and I . . .?"

Davis stopped, shrugged, and looked back across the lawn. He had begun well enough but knew his explanation was spinning out of control. Now he was saying too much.

"Son, I would never tell you what to do, but it's my duty as a father to at least give you my opinion. You know that I've always loved Carolyn and I'm delighted to see you two together again after all these years. I just think you should cool your jets a little. You get your divorce over with and let Carolyn get used to the idea that she's single again."

"We're not going to rush into anything, Dad. Marriage has never even come up."

"Well that's good. Marriage is a complicated affair, even when it's a good one. If you and Carolyn fall in love and one day decide to wed, no one would be happier than me. But I would hate to see you rush into another marriage to make up for the mistakes of your first or because of some notion that time is running out. And, as much as I would like to have grandchildren, I would rather see you happy first."

"Okay, Dad. I understand what you're saying." Davis smiled and sipped his beer.

"Now, I have to say one last thing and then I'll quit picking on you." Malcolm wore a troubled look on his face. He stared across the lawn as he began to speak.

Davis shuffled in his chair.

"Ken Leyman and I have been friends for over forty years now and I know him about as well as one person could know another.

I know him better than he thinks I know him. We're alike in some ways but in many others we're so different that I wonder how we ever became friends in the first place. Friendships are mysterious. That's what makes them special, I guess.

Ken is by nature a controlling person, always has been. I think that's what I found so fascinating about him in the beginning. Back then, I was the opposite. I was easily swayed, always ready to back off and let someone else give the orders.

Over the years we were in business together, some of Ken's ways rubbed off on me. I have to admit, it was for the better. A person can't be passive in business or in life for that matter. But in recent years, Ken's need to be in control has become almost pathological."

Davis waited for his father to grin, thinking that he was exaggerating to add a bit of humor to the conversation. Malcolm continued to look at him with a sober expression.

"And what was once a love of business and a desire to attain a comfortable lifestyle is now a drive to dominate the competition to the point of ruination. Ken would amass fortune upon fortune by whatever means necessary, short of time in federal prison. The man is incredibly wealthy. He needs nothing, nor will anyone in his immediate family for generations. It's just growth for the sake of growth now."

"But you and Mr. Leyman are going to be partners in a couple years."

"Hmm, I don't think so anymore, son."

"You're not?"

"No, I like Raleigh and I think after my term is up I may practice law again. I'm in good shape financially, so I could pick fights I believe in and maybe even donate my services. It's just an idea right now, Davis, so don't spread it around.

The chances of Ken and me working together again are just about nil. Those were plans Ken and I made over a decade ago and a lot has changed since then. The years in government have opened my eyes in some ways. Believe me, he'll get over it."

"But why did you push the logging initiative if this is how you feel?"

"I didn't back that initiative solely for Southern Highlands Logging Company, despite what Ken Leyman might think. I reviewed the arguments carefully and in the end, I came to believe that the national forests should be utilized. That's why they were established. It didn't surprise me at all that Ken's company got the big contract the way he operates behind the scenes, but I had little to do with that."

"So, Dad, why are you telling me all this now?"

"Because I worry that Ken is weaving a web around you, a picture of financial security and domestic tranquility that you may not want to get stuck in. You hang around him too long, and sooner or later you'll get stuck."

"Dad, I think you're overstating the case a little here. Mr. Leyman has never . . ."

"I'm not overstating the case at all. Now let's stop talking about this; I've said enough. Ken is my friend and it's not easy for me to talk about him like this. I never would except that my first concern is for you. But remember this one last thing, there's almost nothing he does or says anymore that isn't designed to ultimately benefit Ken Leyman, Incorporated."

As Davis drove home that evening, he was irritable and slightly inebriated. He and his father didn't talk any more about Ken, but their conversation grew awkward, and Davis filled in the gaps with drinks from his beer bottle. When he went to the kitchen for another, he would drink one bottle down quickly and bring a full one to the porch. He had suspected some of what his father told him but had hardly seen it in such a devious light.

Now that he knew of his father's misgivings, Davis was glad that he hadn't spoken of a recent conversation between him and Ken. After dinner with the Leymans one evening, Ken invited Davis into his study to show him an abstract wood sculpture he had purchased at a gallery in Waynesville. Davis wasn't nearly as impressed with the piece as he let on. But he soon realized that the request for his opinion was an excuse for them to retire to the den and talk alone.

Although Davis mostly listened, it was the first time that Ken discussed business with him. He explained that it was the intertwining of the various aspects of the company: logging, real estate sales, and development that keyed the success of the Southern Highlands Mountain Guild.

"By the way, that was my idea," Ken had stated, "to use the word 'guild'. I was thinking in terms of a coming together of related companies. It may not be exactly the proper use of the term, but it does have a warm and friendly sound to it, don't you think?"

Davis had laughed and nodded.

Ken then alluded to the many possibilities that were open to Davis if he chose to remain in the area, although he never mentioned a specific position. Considering whose son he was and whose daughter he was seeing, Davis assumed it would be high on the ladder. Ironically, he had planned to discuss the possibilities with his father this evening, never expecting to receive such doleful counseling instead.

By the time he pulled into the driveway, Davis decided that his father was wrong about Ken Leyman or at least not entirely right. And later, after his third beer and fourth shot of vodka, his head flopped onto the back of the couch and he laughed out loud. *Perhaps the reason Dad is so worried is because I'm taking an ambitious step on my own, without his overbearing advice.*

And then an even more ambitious thought came to him. *Whoa, with dad not coming back on board, that makes it even more interesting for me. Would Ken make me a partner? If I were to marry Carolyn and become full partner, my life would be set up in one fell-swoop. I won't be just the Governor's son anymore. Is that what's bothering Dad, that I might have a life of my own?*

After getting another Heineken from the refrigerator, and pouring himself a shot of vodka, Davis began to weigh the domestic side of a union with the Leymans. He was falling in love with Carolyn; he was almost sure of it. It wasn't the same as when he fell in love with Layla, not as intense and uncontrollable. But he reasoned that this was to be expected at his age. He wished Carolyn was beside him now, sipping a glass of wine, although he knew she didn't drink.

One day we'll go over to the Cabin for brunch and our children, Ken and Laura's grandchildren, will crowd around the big table with us.

Davis closed his eyes and he could imagine Ken smiling at him from across the table. He was sure his father was wrong about this man.

The golden ring is there, and I'd be a fool not to grab for it.

25

Layla pulled into the driveway at ten o'clock. She had attended another meeting of Forest First and was happy and invigorated as a result. The ranks of the club were swelling in response to the Governor's logging initiative. The spirited voices she heard that evening rekindled Layla's hope that they might be able to confront the logging threat.

When familiar names such as Kenneth Leyman and Malcolm Elmore were mentioned, Layla shuffled in her seat. Tracy and Michael Ogden respected her wish to not reveal that she was the Governor's daughter-in-law, although they knew that fact would help their cause. At the least, it would embarrass the Governor when the media learned of it.

Whatever the effect might be, Layla knew that it would be paltry compared to the political damage that could be inflicted if she shared the many stories she knew, concerning the business dealings of the Governor and Kenneth Leyman.

If the focus was only on Kenneth Leyman, she might have rushed to the podium and shouted out all that she knew, but she still felt some loyalty to Malcolm. She knew now that he hadn't wanted her and Davis to marry, but Malcolm had never shown resentment to her afterwards. And he had always been kind to her and generous with her and Davis.

Layla also remained silent for Davis' sake. He was the source of her information, and if it appeared in the papers, the onus would be on him. In spite of her anger about his plans for the house, she didn't want to hurt Davis. She pitied her husband sometimes, watching him struggle to fit into a world of power and money that was contrary to his nature. Also, she didn't want additional animosity to spice the divorce proceedings.

Layla opened the door quietly, hoping to slip upstairs and into her room without conversation about the house. She hadn't made her mind up on his monetary offer and she knew that Davis was impatient for an answer. Her attorney's response to the offer was a flat no. "You're entitled to half of everything," she said. "Don't let him buy you off on the cheap." Layla had a feeling that her attorney was itching to slug it out in court with the Elmore family. Layla closed the door and listened for Davis.

Just then, the kitchen door swung open and he appeared. Davis had a beer in one hand, a glass of vodka in the other and an unruly expression on his face.

"Just the person I want to see," he said with a noticeable slur.

"Hello, Davis."

"Hello, yes hello indeed. How very rude of me. Would you care for some wine?"

She smiled. "I'll get it, Davis. Wait here."

Layla brushed past him and into the kitchen. She was glad that he didn't follow. She poured herself a glass of wine and took a few sips. Then she refilled the glass. Before she reentered the hall, Layla coached herself to remain calm and above all else to not get angry. Davis was on the couch when she returned. Layla sat across the room and spoke first.

"Davis, I need more time to think about the house; it's a tough decision for me. I know that Balsam Mountain is . . ."

"Don't listen to that old battle axe, Weingold. She's wanted to fight with my family for years."

"Attorney Weingold has advised me to not accept, but I'm making my own decision here."

"Well what's the problem? It's a good offer."

"Money isn't everything. I put a lot of myself into this house, something that you wouldn't appreciate since you were hardly ever here."

"Money may not be everything, but a lot was spent building this damn place. I know because I was paying most of the bills. And I wasn't here because I was working to pay those bills."

What he said was not entirely true but Layla stopped. She didn't want this to escalate. "Davis I'm considering the offer, but I just want more time. I'm tired, too. Let's continue this another time." She stood and moved toward the stairs.

"Rough meeting tonight?"

"Pardon me?" Layla turned.

"Did you have a rough meeting? That's where you were tonight, wasn't it, at one of your meetings? What's the name Ken calls your little club? Uh, Forest, uh, Forest, Forest Fuss, that's it, Forest Fuss." Davis cackled.

Layla paused for a moment as Davis' words registered. When they did, she came back toward her husband, suddenly reinvigorated and unmindful of her rules of engagement.

Davis snickered into his glass as he finished his vodka.

"Well that Mr. Ken certainly is a funny guy. What a coincidence that he should mention our humble little organization because at the meeting tonight, we mentioned him."

"You did?"

"Yes we did, and your father's name came up too."

Davis wasn't snickering now. He knew Layla was on the offensive and he had an uneasy feeling about where she was going with this. Now he wished he hadn't drank so much.

"Imagine my surprise. I almost raised my hand and said, hey I know them. But I'm still new to the group, so I decided to wait. Can you believe that the members of Forest First think that Governor Elmore served this project up on a silver platter to his old fraternity brother, Ken Leyman?"

"That's not true. I just spoke to Dad, and he assured me that he only pushed the logging initiative because he truly believed in it. He had no hand in Southern Highlands getting the contract."

"That may well be, but isn't it interesting that Forest First should make such a presumption, and they don't know half the things I know."

Nervous anxiety caused the alcohol to course more rapidly to Davis' brain and he grew angry. He had begun this day with what he thought was a solid foundation upon which to rebuild his life. Now, between his father's admonition and this veiled threat from Layla, the foundation was crumbling. Davis stood and approached his wife with a menacing stare. When he spoke there was rage in his voice.

"Why the hell don't you just get out of my life? I want you out of this house and soon or I'll drag your ass into court and make you wish you never stepped foot in North Carolina."

"Oh please, Davis. I know my rights and I know what you can and can't do."

"Well, I'll tell you one thing, you mess with Ken, you'll be sorry. You and your whole goddamn pack of tree huggers will be run out of these mountains."

"Are you Leyman's spokesman now?"

"Maybe I am. I may soon be a partner in Southern Mountains, uh, I mean Southern Highlands Logging Guild."

Layla didn't know what to make of that information but she was angry now and took him at his word. "Well than an important man like you deserves a prompt response to your generous offer on the house. Not only do I say no, but hell no. If for no other reason, I'm going to stay right here to do everything I can to fight the logging, and I mean everything. Before long, Leyman may not think Forest *Fuss* is such a joke." She turned, stormed across the room, and stomped up the stairs.

This could not have gone much worse for Davis. He felt warm and drunk. He wished he could start the conversation over, leaving out the mention of Forest Fuss.

The truth of the matter was that Davis would have conceded the house to Layla by now if Ken hadn't been so against it. Ken pointed out that it wasn't so much the value of the house that was at stake or even the principle of the matter, it was the inconvenience of having bad blood in the neighborhood. Although Ken hadn't come out and said it, Davis knew that he wanted Layla off Balsam Mountain.

Davis considered more vodka but instead, he sat on the couch and stared at his empty glass. He thought about how happy and confident he felt this morning at the Leyman's house. Now he was depressed and worried that his golden opportunity was in jeopardy. He could hear Layla moving about in her room above him, and anger flared again. He stood, grabbed his glass, and threw it against the fireplace. Shards shot in all direction to the accompaniment of the sound of breaking glass.

"Damn you, Layla, I'm not going to let you ruin this for me," he murmured in a low, hateful voice. But the truth was that he didn't really know how he could stop his wife if she decided to reveal what she knew.

Then a thought occurred that calmed him down. Davis reminded himself of how Ken had been treating him in recent weeks, almost like a second father.

And why not? After all, I could be his son-in-law if things go right, the father of his grandchildren. I should simply approach Ken about Layla's threat and tell him what she knows about him and Dad. He would probably respect me for being so honest about it, and he would know how to deal with her. He knows how to deal with everything.

26

Ken Leyman shuffled the newspaper. He had the Miami Herald mailed to Balsam Mountain and liked to sit on the terrace after dinner and peruse it. But he was distracted this evening, thinking about the Governor of North Carolina and the Governor's son. No article was able to hold his attention for long, and he was growing more irritable with each false start.

In a telephone conversation the day before, Malcolm seemed distant and business-like, even a bit anxious to get off the phone.

I just wanted to talk, I wasn't digging for information. Why did he bore me with all that talk about his downstate projects? What do I care about that? It was as if to show me that logging isn't his only concern. And then he never even asked how the logging was going.

A soft breeze was ushering in a beautiful evening on Balsam Mountain but Ken was too grumpy to notice. He got up and plodded to the house. He had been drinking tea but decided to switch to something stronger. Laura was in the kitchen, talking on the telephone. She covered the mouthpiece with her hand and looked up at her husband.

"What do you need, dear?"

"Oh, a beer, I think."

"There's Guinness on the door."

"Nope, too heavy for me at this time of day." He opened the refrigerator and grabbed a Corona from the bottom shelf. He opened the bottle and tipped it toward his wife as he left the room.

Laura listened for the sound of the back door closing and then continued her conversation.

"Hello, Antoine? Forgive me Antoine, Ken came in to get a beer. Now as I was saying, I just feel that Carolyn needs more of a commitment now, that's all. She's thirty-four and tired of being just a girlfriend."

Laura listened and then smiled. "I'm sure she would be happy to hear that from you, Antoine."

Out on the terrace, Ken repositioned himself in the chaise lounge, sipped the Corona and tried to focus on the Miami Herald. Then the younger Elmore came to mind. Ken tossed the newspaper aside and leaned back, scowling over his beer. Malcolm irritated him; Davis infuriated him.

They had played a round of golf that afternoon and Ken could tell after the first few holes that something was bothering Davis. It wasn't just that his game was erratic, so was his conversation. He was silent almost to the point of being sullen and then a string of words would burst from him as if to compensate for the lapses. On the seventh hole, when they were standing close, sizing up a shot, Ken smelled alcohol.

It was at the start of the back nine holes that Davis apologized for his behavior and began to explain what was bothering him. Ken soon found himself longing for the conversation of the front nine. He tried to focus on his game and maintain a calm demeanor, but what Davis told him concerning Layla and her threats upset him very much. He pressed Davis to learn the extent of the knowledge Layla might possess and gripped his club tighter with each revelation. By the time the round ended, he wanted to hit Davis on the head with one of his irons.

The stocks that Ken held for Malcolm were well hidden in accounting jargon, but even the suggestion that they existed would be embarrassing for the Governor and bring unfavorable publicity to Southern Highlands Mountain Guild. And apparently, the stocks were only the beginning of what Layla knew. She knew of questionable land deals going back decades, of a briefcase of money, paid under-the-table, and she knew about Dennis Galloway.

Of course Layla had no proof of anything, but for those individuals and agencies who had been observing Ken's financial dealings over the years, her information could help fill in some blanks.

Why did he tell her about Dennis? How did he know? I don't even know for certain that Dennis has mafia ties. It's probably just Malcolm speculating and Davis lapping it up. Damn it, Davis, how could you be so stupid? There are simply some things a man doesn't tell his wife.

Ken drank the last of his beer and rose to get another. He rarely drank in the middle of the day and never so fast, but he rarely felt such lack of control in a matter that closely affected him and his business.

Perhaps two million would encourage her to go away quietly? Damn her; I never did like that woman.

Ken entered the house and just as the door closed, he heard a muffled knock. Laura heard the sound, too, and came into the hall bearing a puzzled expression. She raised a hand to her mouth when her husband opened the door to find an arrow stuck in it.

The door was made of dense teak wood and the tip of the arrow was imbedded at the height of Ken's chest. He peered across the lawn to an area where the forest came close to the house.

Laura came to his side. "My God, Do you suppose this is from a hunter?"

Her husband didn't answer but continued to stare at the forest outcrop, searching for some explanation.

"Ken, look, there's something tied to the arrow." As he turned, she noticed that he was breathing hard and his face was reddening.

Ken undid a rawhide strap that bound a piece of paper around the arrow shaft. Laura leaned forward as he unrolled it and read a simple printed message that was for her husband.

Stay out of our forest Leyman.
If we come again, the arrow
will fly three seconds sooner.

Panther Patrol

Laura looked at her husband. His face was crimson now. She could see that he was trembling but knew well that it wasn't because of fear.

"Ken we should call the police."

"No we shouldn't."

"But this is a threat on your life."

"And what do you think the police can do other than get this in the newspapers. The press would love it, David versus Goliath. The locals would gobble it up."

"We should call the police."

"No."

Ken gave the arrow a tug but it held firm. He glanced across the lawn once more, shut the door and walked down the hall. Laura knew that he was headed for his office.

"What are you going to do?"

"Shoot back, damn it." Ken didn't turn to see the look of dismay on her face.

Two hours later, a black Jaguar cruised up the driveway of the Leyman house. Ken was expecting it and left the house for the first time since the arrow hit the door. He met the car at the top of the driveway. Dennis Galloway emerged from the vehicle and stood at attention while Ken paced back and forth, waving his arms and talking. He read the threatening note aloud. Dennis hadn't seen his employer this angry in many years.

"It's the worst of outrages, to attack a man's home. Who does this dirt think they are, threatening me? No holds barred, Dennis. Money's no object. I want these sons of bitches erased from the picture."

Dennis nodded. Then he walked to the door and with a forceful tug, removed the arrow.

"It's a home made shaft and it looks like real bird feathers for fletching. The arrowhead looks homemade too, looks like iron or steel."

"So what does that mean?"

"I don't know, just seems odd. I know guys who make their own arrows, but it seems like kind of primitive for the Panther Patrol. They sure didn't use an arrow on your bulldozer. Could I take this with me?"

"Of course."

"And the note?"

"Whatever you need, Dennis, and do whatever you have to do."

Dennis nodded and then walked across the lawn to a point where the arrow most likely had been shot. He peered into the forest and then looked back to the door where Ken was standing.

"Hell of a shot," Dennis called, raising the arrow to signal farewell. He walked toward his vehicle, studying the arrow.

Ken half smiled. He felt more relaxed already, knowing that Dennis would deal with the Panther Patrol. He didn't know what his man would do and in fact, he might never know. Over the years, they had both come to realize that it was better this way.

Dennis often operated autonomously. His job description in the most general sense was the removal of obstacles from his employer's path. Ken rarely even had to mention what these might be and did so in this case only because of his outrage. The truth was that Dennis had been planning to deal with the Panther Patrol, anyway.

27

Layla was in her office, unwinding after teaching Creative Writing 301. Her current students responded well to her instruction, and she came away from class invigorated and inspired. Listening to their youthful, idealistic opinions, took her back to a time when she was younger and her dreams weren't complicated by the details of life.

Layla enjoyed her job at Western Carolina University, especially at times like this. Her income paled beside that which her husband received, but at least she knew she could support herself if it came to that. And it *was* coming to that.

The standoff between Layla and Davis entered a chilly stage after their last confrontation. The few words spoken between them came in the form of a question from her husband, asking if more money would change her mind about the house. When she said no, he went to his study and shut the door. Since then, that was where Davis passed most of his time when they were in the house together.

A showdown in court was coming, and Maxine Weingold assured Layla that the house would be hers, especially if she conceded all other assets. Bolstered by the attorney's words, Layla became resolute about keeping it.

For seven years, her heart and soul had gone into her home, and she planned to stay there. She refused to let Davis buy her out and use the house as part of his new domestic plan. Balsam was a big mountain, and he and Caroline could build a home on another part of it. Layla felt that if she asked for nothing more than the house, it would surely demonstrate to friend and foe alike, that money was not her motivation.

Once separated from the Elmores, Layla planned to become more active in opposition to the logging of Pisgah National Forest. In spite of her threat to Davis, Layla couldn't bring herself to reveal what she knew about Governor Elmore's business dealings with Ken Leyman. Some loyalty remained toward this family that she had been a part of for ten years.

Also such revelations would bring her into direct conflict with Kenneth Leyman. Layla would never admit it to her husband, but she was somewhat afraid of this man. From the handful of times they had associated, she sensed that he disliked her. Over the years, she heard stories of financial ruin or worse brought upon people who crossed him. Layla had disliked Ken, as well. Because of logging in Pisgah National Forest and his wooing of Davis, she now detested the man.

Layla was confident that even without revelation from her, the history between Malcolm Elmore and Ken Leyman would come into the light. Rather than violate the trust that Malcolm and Davis had placed in her, she decided to fight against their logging plans along the lines established by Forest First. And, she planned to use her writing skills to voice her opposition.

But Layla was not thinking of any of that at the moment. She was buoyed up from teaching her favorite subject and was thinking about her own career as a writer. One happy thought led to another.

Layla began to daydream about the next day, when she would descend into Cataloochee Valley to see Abe.

Abe Carol Ramsey, what an interesting name. Then on impulse, Layla typed it into the search engine on her computer. No results appeared that related to *her* Abe Ramsey. Considering that he lived in Great Smoky Mountains National Park, unbeknownst to anyone, she didn't really expect that he would be known in cyberspace.

Then for fun, she typed the words 'Great Smoky Mountains' after his name. Near the middle of the page of results, she spotted 'Abe Carol Ramsey' and 'Smoky Mountains' in bold face. She read the description and got goose bumps. *Abe Carol Ramsey, a three-year-old boy who disappeared in the Smoky Mountains and was never found.*

Clicking on the link, Layla was directed to a page that contained promotional material for a book about people who had become lost in the Smoky Mountains and were never found. She could gain no additional information about Abe Ramsey from this page. She would have to buy the book.

Layla clicked on the purchase button and was directed to the bookstore at the website of Great Smoky Mountains National Park. Layla ordered *Lost in the Smoky Mountains.* She was happy to read that profits generated by her purchase were donated to educational, scientific, and historical projects in the park.

Layla's mood went from good to euphoric with this discovery. She hummed and thought about Abe as she packed her briefcase. *This mysterious person, Abe Carol Ramsey, has entered my life at just the right time.*

28

The owner of Endless Mountain Logging, leaned against his truck and spoke into a cell phone. Jim Heinbaugh's voice sounded of frustration and his demeanor was a picture of weariness. Since early in the morning he had been at his logging operation, located ten miles east of Waterville, North Carolina. He and his wife had planned to go to Atlanta and spend the weekend with their daughter and her family, but trouble at the job site cancelled all plans.

The night before, the oil had been drained from all of their machines and this morning, half of them were started up with disastrous results. Jim found little comfort in the fact that his crew realized the sabotage in time to spare some of the equipment. The damage was bad enough to shut the operation down indefinitely. He got off the phone when Tom Morrison of the North Carolina State Police pulled up behind him.

The officer got out of his car, and nodded.

"Sorry to have to call you back so soon, officer. Looks like the same bunch came back to finish us off. Boys just found this stuck in the door of the office ." He handed the policeman an arrow and a note.

Officer Morrison glanced at the arrow, a homemade design he

was becoming familiar with. "Lots of people been handling this?"

Jim shrugged and nodded.

"Oh well, they probably covered their prints anyway. These people seem to know what they're doing." Tom turned his attention to the note. The message read:

> Stay out of our forest Heinbaugh.
> If we come again the next arrow
> will be for you.
>   Panther Patrol

The message was similar to the one Jim Heinbaugh received a few months earlier except that it was personal and threatening this time. Tom also found it interesting that this note was printed in neat decisive letters, while the other was scrawled in a slanted, rough font.

"Why do you suppose the change in tactics? I think it was easier to stomach blown up machines than to see them sitting here, looking fine, but with their engines seized up."

"Can't say for sure. It could be a new member with different ideas or somebody using the Panther Patrol's name. Their last attack was on the Southern Highlands operation, south of here, and they're still using dynamite down there."

"Yeah, why don't these panther guys pick on the big boys with the money and leave me alone. Kenny Leyman's the one that's really eatin' up the forest, anyway, not me with my two-bit operation."

"Our hope is to stop them from picking on everybody."

"Well don't count me in that group anymore. I'm going to cut my losses and go back to loggin' private land. Money may not be as good, but I won't have to worry about this crap."

Gerald Porter and his partner, Owen Phillips, decided to have one more beer before they went to bed. Owners of the new and successful Timberline Logging Company, they were staying at Gerald's hunting cabin on Utah Mountain. Gerald's young children and Owen's adolescent son were upstairs sleeping. Gerald went out to the front porch where the beer was kept in a cooler of ice. Night insects buzzed and clicked in the dark forest as he pulled two bottles from the cooler.

Gerald had just reached the door with a bottle of Michelob in each hand when an object struck the cabin wall. He was so surprised that he dropped one of the bottles. An arrow was protruding from the wall just above the cooler. Gerald looked back toward the edge of the forest and then glanced back at the arrow. He was still staring when Owen came to the door.

"What the hell was that, Gerald?"

"Look," Gerald said, nodding toward the wall.

"Jesus, do you suppose it's some kind of joke?"

"That's no joke. I was standing there a few seconds ago."

"Look, there's a note tied to it," Owen said, walking up to the arrow. He undid the rawhide and then carried the piece of paper back to his partner who had not moved. Owen unfurled the note and the partners read a blunt message.

Stay out of our forest Porter.
If we come again the next arrow
will be for you.
Panther Patrol

Ira Drew was making a circuitous path across the logging site of High Country Logging Company. Because of the destruction of the bulldozer and log skidder in the spring, he had developed a new system for pacing over the property that ensured he would cover the entire area each hour and examine the equipment at least every thirty minutes.

Many weeks passed before he got over the destruction of the two machines that had occurred while he was on watch. But four months without incident and the implementation of his new patrol system had restored Ira's confidence. He heard of what occurred at Jim Heinbaugh's operation and so was especially watchful. But he told himself that it happened because there was no watchman such as himself on site.

A hot July day had transformed into a mild, still evening, heralded by the sound of countless insects. Ira loved to be in the woods at any time of the day. Since his wife's death, he would rather be at the job site than at home without her.

Ira had worked for High Country Logging Company since Philip Blass graduated from high school. He had been hired by Philip's grandfather. Ira was regarded as the grand uncle of the company and was treated as such.

After the attack in the spring, Philip insisted that another man share the watch. But the young man that was hired didn't show up for work after he collected his most recent paycheck. His phone had been disconnected, and he could not be reached for an explanation. So Ira was manning the post alone while a replacement was found. Such was his faith in his new system of monitoring the job site that Ira was urging Philip to forego the expense of additional help.

Ira was checking the bulldozers and log skidder that were parked in the center of the clearing, when he heard the sound of breaking glass sounding from the direction of the office. Ira hurried toward the dark, rectangular outline of the trailer. He heard more breaking glass when he was thirty yards away and drew his gun.

The watchman could see a light inside the trailer when he peered in the front window, and then he saw a man exiting the back door. Rounding the structure, he faced the intruder, standing above him on a small, plank stoop. Before Ira could speak, he received a well-placed kick to the jaw. He fell backward against the trailer, flashlight and gun, falling from his hands. Ira lay still.

His attacker turned and moved in the opposite direction. Destruction of the trailer was intended to be a diversion; the equipment was the real target. Seconds later the trailer exploded, sending wreckage in all directions and hurling Ira away amid a hail of shards.

29

"So what's the word?"

"He didn't make it."

"Goddamn it," Miles Harding exclaimed, as he handed Tom Morrison a cup of coffee. The police officer had just radioed in to learn the condition of Ira Drew.

The FBI was collaborating with the state police in this case. While Miles and his team focused on what they felt was the Panther Patrol's most likely target, the state police monitored the smaller logging jobs. After a rash of unexpected attacks on smaller companies, the FBI agent and police officer met to compare notes.

"Yeah, poor old guy. When I told his boss what happened, he started to cry. He said 'I'll tell you what, Ira's as good as they come. Worked for my family for thirty-five years. He was an everyday man'."

"That's a hell of a compliment, you know that, an everyday man," Miles said. "It tells a lot about a person. I hope somebody says that about me someday."

Tom nodded. They sipped their coffee in silence for a moment. This was their third meeting. The two men had liked each other since their first. Both in their mid-forties and veterans of their respective branches of law enforcement, they found each others observations reassuring.

"So what do you think about this new development, Tom? Why do you think the Panther Patrol has suddenly mounted such a strong offensive? It doesn't fit the pattern I've been following."

"Something's changed. My guess is that it's either a rogue element within the group or someone using the name for some reason, like maybe another anti-logging fanatic."

"What would you put your money on?"

"The Panther Patrol doesn't strike me as a big enough outfit to have a rogue element, so my bet is on someone using their name."

"Yeah, I agree."

"And you know, Miles, it's almost too obvious. It's like whoever is doing it is trying to get attention as much as make a point. In the beginning, a note claiming responsibility might be placed somewhere but now they're tied to arrows and stuck everywhere. They even shot one into the door of Ira Drew's truck."

"Right. They could copy-cat much better if that was their intention. And the attack on the owner of Timberline Logging was way out of character for the Panther Patrol. The company was awarded a contract to log but hasn't cut a single tree. Talk about a preemptive strike. Not only was someone privy to information about that contract but they knew where the owner's cabin was and when he would be there."

"Sounds like mafia stuff," Tom said.

"Could be," Miles added. "I think whoever is doing this is using the Panther Patrol's name to pursue their own agenda or maybe to make them look bad."

"But why would they want to make them look bad?"

"Could be to incite us to act more forcefully against the Panther Patrol, or, I don't know."

Miles stared straight ahead and a quizzical expression appeared on his face. He shook his head from side to side. "Maybe he's killing two birds with one stone."

"What, who?"

Miles turned toward the policeman. He trusted Tom's instincts and admired his integrity. He decided to be forthright about his overall assignment in the area. "You know who Ken Leyman is?"

"Uh huh. Who doesn't in this part of the country? He owns this operation for one thing."

"You ever meet him?"

"Never spoke to him; I've seen him at a distance. Why, you think he might be involved somehow?"

"I'll be honest with you, Tom, but it's between you and me, okay?"

"Sure, Miles."

"The FBI has been monitoring Ken Leyman's business activities for some time. Whether it's logging or development or construction, there's a disturbing tendency for the competition to wither away. That's the main reason I'm down here; someone else could've handled the Panther Patrol. Not that I'm taking the assignment lightly, mind you, especially now that I've mixed it up with them a little. But I'm here primarily to watch Leyman.

This was an ideal situation. He's entered a new arena and the Panther Patrol broke the law on federal land to give us a legitimate reason for moving in."

Tom Morrison was both surprised and impressed. But professional that he was, the policeman adjusted to this new perspective. "So you think Ken Leyman is behind this recent string of attacks?"

"Now that I've given it some thought, yeah. His style is usually more behind-the-scenes, but he probably feels he can ramp it up a little, disguised as the Panther Patrol."

"Do you think Leyman has any idea why you're here?"

"Oh yeah, he's been through it before. Plus he's probably got more contacts in Washington than I do. And I don't try to hide it. In fact, I'm in his face a little. He's such an arrogant SOB that my approach is to push him and hope that in his righteous indignation, he screws up. His fierce pride and temper are well documented. That's what I'm doing here, hanging around and hoping for a mistake.

The Panther Patrol may be playing into his hands by giving him a face to hide behind, but they're playing into my hands because of Leyman's outrage over the fact that someone would dare take a swipe at him.

And what's more, I wouldn't be surprised if Leyman tries to take out the Panther Patrol himself, as a matter of principle. Just smearing them won't be enough to settle his outrage. I recently exchanged pleasantries with the man. He didn't hide his opinion as to how the Panther Patrol should be dealt with."

"Can't get him on that."

"It's just a feeling I have, that it was more than words."

"I know that feeling."

"Yeah and he has this goon, hovering around him, Dennis Galloway. I don't like the guy. I checked him out. He's big on Leyman's payroll. He's got some history from his younger days but nobody's ever got a conviction on him. He's been working for Leyman nearly twenty years now and lives damn well as a result."

165

Miles handed Tom a folder, containing information about Dennis Galloway.

"What is he, a bodyguard?"

Miles shook his head. "Nah, moves around too much; his name turns up all over the grid. Nobody can figure out what he does. I doubt many people at Southern Highlands Mountain Guild even know he exists. Considering his resume, my guess is he's Leyman's behind-the-scenes operator."

"His muscle?"

"Among other things. Intimidation, bribery, extortion, he does whatever needs done and has the contacts and the morals to see it through. We're certain that he's got connections to the mob. Leyman never gets his hands dirty and probably never knows the gritty details."

"Sounds to me like you're profiling this Galloway fellow," Tom said, grinning."

"Hah ha, you've got to in this business, Tom. Oh did I mention that I don't like the guy?"

Tom laughed. "You want me to ask around and see what people know about him?"

"No, I don't want him to spook and change his work schedule. What you can do is anticipate him. While you investigate these new attacks, keep him in mind. And in the future, if he does show up anywhere, see what follows."

"Sure Miles, I can do that. If he comes around, we'll keep an eye on him."

Officer Morrison yawned. "And now, I got to hit the road."

"Where you live, Tom?"

"Right in Waynesville, couple blocks off Main Street, near the library."

"Hey, that's a neat little town. I had coffee there the other day, a place called The Hallowed Bean."

"My wife and I like Waynesville. We grew up around here. Where are you from, Miles?"

"New York City."

"That's a neat city."

"You've been there?"

"Yeah, couple times. Went to Times Square for New Years once when I was young. Last time, my wife and I went to see *Cats.*"

"I haven't done either of those."

"Well, I've never had coffee at The Hallowed Bean."

Miles chuckled. "See ya, Tom."

30

Abe was standing amongst the trees twenty yards beyond the big poplars. He had an anxious, happy expression on his face that was similar to the one Layla wore as she approached on Sundance. She slid down from the horse and walked into his arms. Layla nuzzled up under Abe's chin and burrowed into his beard, an act she had imagined often during the past week. The lovers held each other tight and were silent as they reassured each other that their love was genuine.

Nearly twenty minutes passed before they released their hold long enough to walk to the clearing that fronted Caldwell Fork. Over an hour passed before they released their hold the next time. It was noon of a warm, sunny day, but it was still cool underneath the hemlock trees. The foliage was lush now; the scents were intoxicating. Abe had his back against a broad tree trunk and Layla leaned against his chest. A blanket was draped over his shoulders, and covered arms that encircled her.

Layla felt like she was living in a simple dream and the myriad problems of the world could not affect her while she was in it. There were issues that she wanted to discuss with Abe during this visit, but she didn't want to risk altering the mood of this gentle moment. Then Layla heard Abe's stomach growl and she chuckled.

"Poor man, I kept you busy all morning and you didn't have time to hunt for food."

"Don't worry, I planned ahead. I have some deer jerky with me and two nice trout on a string down at the water."

"Well, Abe, I, uh, brought food this time. It's not that I don't like jerky. It's actually much better than I would have thought, and you cook fish well. But I wanted to save you the bother and maybe add a little variety to the diet, so I brought food."

"What did you bring?"

Layla grinned. "A picnic lunch. How long has it been since you were on a picnic?"

Abe seemed to be thinking about it and then amusement faded from his face and was replaced by a sad expression. "It's been about thirteen years. My wife and I and our daughter went on a picnic."

"Oh Abe, I'm sorry."

"It's not your fault, Layla, it's mine. The past is past and I shouldn't let it pull at me. There's nothing I can do about it now."

"Well, then let's have a picnic," she said, standing up and putting her clothes on.

Layla had planned her menu well. She wasn't a vegetarian but ate very little meat. Hummus and lettuce in a tortilla wrap was her lunch of choice these days. But she decided on sliced turkey with lettuce and mayonnaise for this occasion. A bun replaced the wrap, but it *was* whole wheat. She knew deviled eggs were a safe bet as were slices of cheese and fruit.

By the time she had their meal spread on the tablecloth she brought, Layla could see that Abe was delighted. He ate the simple meal with relish and made her feel like a gourmet chef with his compliments. Abe was in such a good mood by the time they finished that Layla decided it was a good time for them to talk.

"Abe, I've decided to keep the house. I—I seriously considered your advice, but I can't give up the house, r now."

"You can't or you don't want to?"

"I don't want to. I want to stay there. A home like that is something I've dreamed of since I was a little girl. In spite of the trouble, I don't want to let go of that dream yet."

"Well, then you shouldn't."

Layla paused, surprised at how easily he accepted her decision. Thus she decided to move on to the next point she wished to discuss.

"Well then, when everything is settled between Davis and me, do you think you would come to my house? Could you come and stay there with me sometimes?"

"Uh, Layla, I really can't."

She had an impish grin playing on her lips as she repeated his question. "You can't or you don't want to?"

Abe was silent for a moment staring into her brown eyes, trying as he had many times before, to understand the mystery of why she was here, of why she loved him. Now the moment had come when he must tell her about his past and why he lived in the park. He didn't want to risk spoiling the mystery by telling all at once, but he knew it was time to begin.

"Layla, I need to tell you something and I hope you won't think too badly of me because of it."

Layla shook her head and smiled.

Abe believed her. "I came into the park because I was running from the police. I messed up and was in big trouble. If they'd caught me, I'd still be in jail."

Layla was stunned. She knew that the information she found on the internet, concerning Abe Carol Ramsey, the lost child, didn't fit what she knew about her Abe. But since she first learned that he lived in the park, Layla hoped that his story was something as innocent as this.

"What kind of trouble?"

Abe heaved a mighty sigh and looked at the ground. As painful as it was, he knew he had to keep talking. When he looked up, the sympathy in Layla' eyes made it possible.

"Layla, I was a heavy drinker, on dope too. Came back from the war and never could settle back into normal life. It's what ended our marriage, Sue and me. I used to hang out at a bar in Waynesville, right there on Main Street. Never bothered anybody but I didn't go there to make friends either. The crowd and the noise and the beer drowned out my thoughts. That's why I went there.

Anyway, one night a couple punks started giving me a hard time; still don't know why. So I just left the bar and headed down that little alley that leads to Wall Street."

Layla nodded, she knew the alley he was referring to.

"But they caught up with me and started pushing me around. I don't think it was for money. They were in the mood to fight and didn't like the way I looked. But I was trained to fight, Layla. In fact, I was trained to kill anyone who attacked me."

"You didn't kill them, did you?"

Abe shook his head. "Almost, and I might have except the police came. I remember people screaming and lights flashing, than a policeman yelling at me to stop. He was calling my name even. But I couldn't stop. I hit him too, and he went down. Then other police cars pulled up on Main Street, and there were more lights. Everybody was yelling at me."

Abe bowed his head and was wringing his hands as his words conjured up memories of that fateful night.

Layla got up and sat down next to him, resting her head on his shoulder. "And then you ran?" She hoped that was how the story ended.

"I ran all right. But first I took the gun from the policeman on the ground and fired a shot at the others coming down the alley. Then I ran to Wall Street, jumped in the patrol car and took off. I was drunk and crazy. I drove across parking lots, over lawns, through red lights. I saw the lights from police cars behind me. I was flying up Route 19 toward Cherokee when I got the idea to cut across the park."

Layla lifted her head and looked at him. "That's how you got here?"

"Y-yes, but there's a more to the story."

She put her head back down.

"When I got to the top of the hill, there at Soco Gap, I turned on to the Blue Ridge Parkway. The gate was still closed for winter but I crashed it. I headed toward the park and thought I might have pulled it off, but after a mile or so, I saw lights coming.

I turned right onto Heintooga Ridge Road. It ends on a gravel road that winds through the middle of nowhere for twenty miles, all the way to Cherokee. I figured I could lose them back there. But they were coming too fast and I couldn't control the car anymore. I finally turned it sideways in the road and took off on foot. That was right about at Polls Gap Trailhead."

"Where's that?"

"At the top of Rough Fork Trail."

"Rough Fork Trail, the one that leads to the Woody House?"

"Yes, instead of going down to the Woody House, if you follow the trail up the mountain about three miles, it will end at Polls Gap Trailhead."

Layla felt a tingle on the back of her neck and got goose bumps as she realized what Abe was telling her. That was how he came to live here. Ten years ago after a terrible, violent incident, he ran from the police into Great Smoky Mountains National Park and has been here ever since. That was also why he couldn't leave.

She raised her head and looked into his eyes. "And you've been here ever since?"

Abe nodded.

"You haven't left the park in ten years?"

"I leave the park sometimes, but I never leave the forest."

"And they just stopped looking for you?"

"I think so. I know the police would still like to find me, but by now they probably figure I'm dead or out of the area."

Looking at the man beside her, Layla had to use her imagination to picture him as he would have been that first day in the park. Could this same strong and resourceful mountain man who could kill a deer with an arrow from forty yards have once been a drunk, doped-up, half-crazed and scared man, hiding in the woods from the police? Could this man who treated her so gently and who once rescued a lost child in the woods have beaten three men to the ground, one of them a police officer?

"Abe, I'm shocked at what you're telling me, but mostly because it's so unlike what I know of you. It was a bad period in your life and that was a terrible thing to have happen, but surely by now people would understand. I would help you in whatever . . ."

"No, Layla, they wouldn't understand. Not when you down a cop, take his gun and steal his car. I wouldn't expect them to understand. I would go to prison and I'd deserve to go to prison."

"But, Abe, if you do, it might only be for a short while, and then you would be free to live a normal life."

Abe paused and looked into Layla's eyes as he considered this statement. He smiled and took her hand before he responded.

"What's a normal life, Layla? I think I do live a normal life. What's so normal about life out there? It's not just prison that I worry about. I know I could survive that. What I worry about more is living out there again. I don't think I can do it. I'm afraid I would turn into the same person the police chased into Cataloochee Valley that night. I like my life here and I like who I am now."

Layla didn't know what to say. This wasn't the response she expected. From somewhere within her, she understood his reasoning. She had spent enough time in the park now to appreciate the feeling of detachment from the world that this life offered. The tribulations of society: the noise and confusion, the greed, the crowds, the laws, the deadlines, all these existed beyond the distant mountain range. Abe went about his daily affairs unaffected by such concerns.

But Layla didn't believe that if Abe left the woods, he would revert back to the person he once was. She put her arms around him and spoke softly. "Abe, I understand why you might prefer living here as opposed to a life in society, I really do. But you're not the same person you were ten years ago. The forest has changed you. I believe in you. You'll never turn back into the person the police were after. If you ever want to try to live on the outside, I'll be there for you."

Abe didn't reply but simply nuzzled his head against hers.

Layla decided that they had talked enough for now. "Abe, are we going to Spruce Mountain?"

He looked at her, smiled and nodded, relieved that the discussion had ended.

As they walked, Layla focused on the scenery. She tried to

imagine what it would be like to actually live in the forest, but she couldn't. Staying for a weekend with Abe was a wonderful experience, a sort of romantic camping trip. But as beautiful and inviting as the setting was, Layla couldn't conceive of a life apart from society or without the basic comforts of civilization. She couldn't imagine living here if she didn't have to.

Then she thought of something that she had planned to tell Abe. Although the story of Abe Carol Ramsey, the young boy who was lost in the park was obviously about someone else, she thought that Abe would find it interesting.

He walked in silence while Layla related the facts that she had learned on the internet. Then Abe turned toward her with a thoughtful expression.

"I know the story, Layla. It happened in 1919, north of here in Tennessee, Dunn's Creek Valley. I first heard the story around the campfire as a Boy Scout. I think it was told to scare us about what might happen if we wandered off or to make us afraid that the boy's ghost might be around. But the story didn't scare me. It just made me sad. It didn't seem right that he was never found."

Abe told Layla the story of the disappearance of Abe Carol Ramsey, which he remembered in detail.

"But are you related to him? Did your parents name you after him?"

Abe shook his head. "Layla, my real name is Samuel Wolford. I named myself Abe Carol Ramsey after I came here."

Layla put her arms around him. "Why?'

Abe drew her close and exhaled a melancholic sigh over her shoulder.

"I nearly died the first night. I fell down slopes, ran into trees, dragged myself through water, trying to get away from the lights coming down after me. When I couldn't go any farther, I climbed into a thicket, kicked out a place to sleep, and covered myself with leaves. I was so cold during the night that I was sure I would freeze. But as I lay there, I thought about the story of little Abe Ramsey. When I was a kid, I always hoped that he made it somehow, that he didn't die. I hoped that he learned to live in the woods.

Sometime in the morning, just as it was getting light, I heard dogs barking. I climbed out and started running again. By the time the sun was up, I was high on a mountain, sitting on a rock outcrop and finally warm. I was hungry, but I felt alert and free like I hadn't felt in a long time. It was like I was somebody else. Somehow I knew I'd gotten away from them, and it was then that the idea came to just stay here and live in the forest. I decided to call myself Abe Carol Ramsey in honor of the lost boy. As far as I'm concerned, Samuel Wolford died in the thicket that night."

Layla was so moved by his story that she had tears in her eyes when she looked up at Abe. She also felt somewhat guilty that he had been so honest with her, and yet there were still many things she hadn't told him. She was silent for a moment, staring into his eyes, trying as she had many times before, to understand the mystery of why she was here, of why this man loved her. Layla didn't want to risk spoiling the mystery by telling all at once, but she felt it was time to begin.

"Abe, I have something to tell you and I hope you don't think less of me because of it."

Abe shook his head and smiled.

Layla believed him. "I'm not really a writer. Well, I am, but that's not how I make a living. I'm actually a teacher. I teach English and creative writing at Western Carolina University. I want to be a writer, but so far it hasn't really happened."

Abe grinned.

"What's so funny?"

"I was beginning to wonder about that."

"Why?"

"I've been waiting for a month to hear what the woman does after she gets to Alaska."

"Ha ha, very funny. Just for that, I'm going to finish my novel, and you'll be shocked at what happens when she gets to Alaska."

31

Davis was irritable as he drove to the Leyman house. He talked to his father earlier and learned that the Governor needed him back in Raleigh and expected him there soon. Davis knew that he couldn't put off his father for much longer. He had lingered on Balsam Mountain, hoping that a reason to stay might still congeal. In recent weeks, that possibility seemed less and less likely.

Caroline and he continued to play tennis and they still enjoyed each other's company, but like Caroline's tennis game, their relationship seemed to have reached a plateau. They had gone out to eat several times and once to a movie, but none of these outings generated the allure to pull their relationship to the next level. Now it was hard for Davis to imagine that only three weeks before, he had contemplated a proposal of marriage to Carolyn.

Laura Leyman was more formal around Davis now and rarely joined Carolyn and him on the deck as she did earlier in the summer. A career with Southern Highlands Mountain Guild, which once seemed inevitable, was now a remote possibility at best.

Ken Leyman was polite and friendly as always, but Davis felt he was kept at a distance now. He even felt awkward saying 'Ken' and would more often say 'Mr. Leyman'. On the occasion that Davis would inquire about the business, Ken spoke only in general terms and never in a way that encouraged deeper discourse.

Davis was certain that their discussion over golf, concerning Layla's threat to divulge information to Forest First had precipitated the erosion in his standing with Ken. He had approached him like he would have his own father and hoped that, like his own father, Ken would be empathetic and assure him that the problem could be resolved. Instead, he saw flashes of anger in Ken's eyes and received few words of assurance. He and Ken carded the worst golf scores either of them had tallied in years, and they could muster little to talk about on the way home.

Davis was resigning himself to the possibility that the golden ring had been withdrawn and the merry-go-round ride was now just time going by.

Pulling into the Leyman's driveway, he saw Dennis Galloway's Jaguar. Dennis Galloway was another point of irritation for Davis. During the rides to the logging operation, Dennis listened like an older brother. Lately, he afforded Davis little more than a nod, as he ambled by on the way to or from Ken's office.

Davis walked around the house toward the tennis court and passed an open window. From within he heard the sound of Dennis' voice. Davis slowed and caught fragments of talk about the logging operation in Pisgah National Forest.

About the time Davis was considering the possibility of marriage to Caroline, he assumed that Ken would invite him into the office to join in business discussions. He had hoped to be well within the inner circle of Ken Leyman's world by this time. But that never happened and the notion seemed ridiculous now.

However, this fact didn't dampen his curiosity about what was being discussed in Ken's office. If it were not for the sound of Caroline's tennis ball on the practice wall, beckoning him to the game, Davis would have lingered to hear more. He turned away and rounded the corner of the house.

"Hi, Davis, I'm ready for you today," Caroline said. "I've been working on my serve all morning."

"Well, don't go too hard on me, I've already had a trying start to the day."

"I'm sorry, nothing serious, I hope."

"No, nothing serious, it's just that dad is pushing me to return to Raleigh. Says he can't run the state without me."

Davis saw amusement on Caroline's face, but he didn't detect concern over the possibility of his departure.

"But I've grown to like it here in the mountains, Caroline. I like the slower pace of life. I like the way social life revolves around family, don't you?"

"It is nice here, isn't it?"

Davis thought she seemed nervous.

"Let's play, Davis, so I can show you my new serve."

Davis nodded and turned. After two fault serves by Caroline, Laura Leyman appeared on the back patio. She called to her daughter and then held up a telephone receiver. Caroline appeared confused at first, but when her mother continued to stare without comment she seemed to understand.

"Will you excuse me for a minute? I was expecting a call."

"Sure, that will give me time to fine-tune my own serve."

"Ha, ha, okay, I'll be back."

Davis smiled and nodded but he felt awkward. Something was different now. For the first time in his life, he wished he hadn't come to the Leyman's house. He served a few balls off the practice wall and glanced back toward the door where Carolyn had entered the house. Then he thought about the open office window. Davis had excellent control on his serve but the next ball took a wild carom off the wall and rolled behind the house. He jogged to retrieve it where it lay, about ten feet from the office window.

Davis passed over the ball and riveted himself to the wall beneath the window. He planned to pick up the ball, jog to the court, and make light of his own poor serve when he heard the back door open. Davis raised his ear to the window sill.

"Dennis, you mustn't be so obvious in your dislike for the man."

"Hah, was I obvious?"

"Well, let me put it this way, if I wondered where the expression, 'daggers coming out of ones eyes', came from, I don't now, not after seeing the way you looked at Agent Harding."

"I don't like him."

"He doesn't like you either. But you need to develop a poker face for this type of encounter. He's not a man to be taken lightly. I wouldn't be surprised if your reaction is what he was looking for. Our fight is not with him. You need to let it go."

"All right, I'll behave."

Davis was enthralled by what he heard. *Imagine that, going toe to toe with the FBI. Dennis Galloway is one tough character.*

"Now, speaking of our fight, what about the Panther Patrol."

"Done deal."

"Oh really?"

"Yeah, I got people in place. As soon as one of them rears their head, there will be a bullet in it."

"Good. Hopefully the rest of the hooligan band will get the

message."

"If not, bullets are cheap."

"Exactly the point I was trying to make with Agent Harding. The man could use a lesson in economy from you, Dennis."

"It would be my pleasure."

Ken chuckled. "I doubt there will be many tears shed for a member of the Panther Patrol in the event of their demise, considering the reckless rampage they've been on lately."

"I know I won't shed any. You know how I hate violence."

Davis could scarcely believe what he heard. He would have stayed to hear more, but the sound of a door shutting, alerted him to the fact that Caroline was returning. He lowered his head and backed toward the tennis ball. Scooping it up, he trotted toward the court. The conversation that he'd heard thrilled him and scared him at the same time.

"Sorry, Davis," Caroline said, as she came up from behind. "I didn't mean to be gone that long."

"No problem here. I used the opportunity to sharpen my own serve to a razor edge. That one must have hit a knot on the wall."

Caroline smiled and turned toward her end of the court. Davis walked in the opposite direction, still absorbed in what he heard at the office window.

The tennis was pathetic. Caroline's serve was not so different, except a little worse than usual. Davis' shots were ill-timed and lethargic. They decided to stop after two sets.

Caroline had baked a coffee cake and after Davis complimented her on it, they ate in silence for several minutes. Davis thought that Caroline seemed uncomfortable.

She spoke first. "Davis, I have something to tell you. I'm having dinner with Antoine tomorrow night."

"At his invitation or yours?"

"At his, but I didn't discourage it. There's still a lot that isn't settled. We were together ten years, Davis. To let it go lightly is to say that all that time was for nothing."

Davis nodded and looked into Caroline's eyes. She had difficulty looking into his, and he knew that she was talking about more than just a meal. Davis struggled to say something gracious but silence was all he could muster in his embarrassment.

He could feel his face reddening with each heartbeat and he wanted to get away as soon as possible. After a few more awkward exchanges, Davis told Caroline that he was meeting friends at a bar in Waynesville to watch the British Open. He rarely watched golf on television and had no friends in Waynesville.

The once familiar landscape looked different to Davis as he drove away from the Leyman's house. Summer was ending and a chill was in the air. He wished he *was* meeting friends in Waynesville because he didn't want to go to the house at Mountain Crest. His attempt to maneuver it away from Layla seemed silly now and only added to his embarrassment.

A quarter mile down the road, Davis steered into the parking area of a scenic overlook. From the glove compartment, he withdrew a flask of vodka and took several quick drinks. Before him was a spectacular view of the Plott Balsam mountain range, punctuated by Waterrock Knob.

Davis took another drink and studied the scene. In spite of the time-consuming work on the logging initiative, the grind of domestic upheaval, and an ill-fated courtship of the Leyman family, he *had* come to enjoy living in the mountains again.

Then, in the rear view mirror, Davis noticed a vehicle pull

into the parking area. He turned to see Dennis Galloway's Jaguar pull up a few yards away. Davis capped the flask, returned it to the glove compartment, and got out of his car.

"Davis, I thought that was you," Dennis said as he stepped out of the Jaguar. He was smiling as he approached and reached inside his leather coat. He withdrew a pack of cigarettes.

"Cigarette?"

"No thanks."

"Saw your car and thought I'd catch up with you. Mr. Leyman keeps me so busy these days I don't get to socialize much. Hell of a view, isn't it?"

"Yes. I-I was just thinking that myself."

Dennis lit the cigarette, took a deep drag, and exhaled the smoke toward Waterrock Knob. "Speaking of the mountains, you might be able to give me some information. I want to bring the family up here on vacation; do some horseback riding. Mr. Leyman tells me you're the man to talk to."

"Not me, Dennis. I've done a little riding. Layla's the one to talk to, my wife, or my ex-wife I should say, soon-to-be ex-wife, I guess. She does a lot of riding in Great Smoky Mountains National Park."

"Do you ever go with her?"

"I have but not anymore."

"She rides in the park alone? That's not safe."

"Ya, I know. Try to tell her that. But, it's really not my problem anymore."

"But you know where she goes? Someone should know that."

"I sort of know. She posts an itinerary and timetable at Cove Creek Ranch where she keeps her horse. That way if she doesn't return, rescuers would know where to look for her."

"This ranch is located near the park? That sounds like what I'm looking for."

"It's right on the border, along the Cataloochee Divide. The ranch is on Hemphill Bald Road, off Route 276. They're in the phone book and they have a good website."

"I'll check it out. Hey, thanks for the information, Davis." Dennis dropped his cigarette to the ground and crushed it out with his boot. Then he picked it back up and cupped it in his hand.

"I hate creeps that throw their cigarette butts everywhere. Don't you?"

Davis nodded.

"Hey, see ya around, Davis."

Dennis turned toward his car and, on impulse, Davis walked after him.

"Dennis, could I ask you something?"

Dennis turned.

"I get the feeling that I offended Mr. Leyman in some way. I know you work for him and I don't want to put you on the spot but do you have any . . ."

"Davis, I'll give you the advice Mr. Leyman gave me years ago, after he picked me up out of the dirt. Don't dwell on what didn't work, instead, look ahead to the next opportunity."

"So, you think I should forget about Southern Highlands Mountain Guild?"

Dennis snorted, shook his head, and smiled. "There's money rolling into these mountains from all directions, Davis. You're an attorney and you have an office right on Main Street in Waynesville. That's the hub of the action. Hell, if I were you, I'd open back up and be ready to ride the wave that's coming.

Leyman's getting old and cranky. Young man like you shouldn't be so anxious to hitch your wagon to his star."

Davis was stunned. He didn't expect such blunt advice.

Dennis opened his car door and grinned. "Besides, I might need a good attorney one of these days."

32

Layla hugged Tracy when the door opened. "How is he?"
"Oh, better, He's sleeping now. Nothing's broken, but his face is badly bruised. Layla, they really hit him hard."

Tracy dropped her head and cried. Layla sat her friend down on a bench in the hallway and put an arm around her.

That morning, Michael Ogden participated in an informational rally sponsored by Forest First. It was held in front of the Haywood County Justice Center in Waynesville. The event had a festival atmosphere with live music and colorful information boards. The rally was an educational event to inform the public about the practical reasons against logging the national forests.

The aerial pictures of active logging sites in Pisgah National Forest impressed the audience. The crowd was shocked at the scale of the operation depicted in the photograph labeled *Southern Highlands Logging Company*.

An excellent speaker, Dr. Ogden was giving a speech, explaining the mission of Forest First. He spoke only a few minutes when he was interrupted by angry words.

"So what happened, Tracy? I heard at school that there was trouble and Michael was hurt, but who did it?"

"Michael said two men started the trouble, accusing Forest

First of being nothing more than a front for the Panther Patrol. Michael tried to explain that it wasn't true. He said that the men just got louder and moved closer. The worst part is that some people in the crowd started to go along with them. Someone shouted, 'it's people like you that got Ira Drew killed'."

"Oh God, how awful."

"Rita Cooley who organized the rally stepped in and asked the men . . . Well, knowing Rita, she probably ordered the men to participate peacefully or leave. Have you met Rita?"

Layla nodded. "No shrinking violet, that's for sure."

Tracy smiled for an instant. "Well one of the men was right in her face, telling her where to go and how to get there. Michael asked him to calm down and stepped between them. So the man grabbed Michael by the shirt and punched him in the face over and over until he fell to the ground. The other guy knocked the display boards off the table and told Rita that there would be a lot more trouble if Forest First didn't back off."

Tracy dropped her head and began to cry again. "He's not just hurt physically. Michael tries to be so objective and open-minded, he's in shock that someone would turn on him like this."

"What did the police do?"

"The Waynesville police came soon after, but the two men who started it had simply walked away by then. Nobody expected this kind of trouble so the police were caught off guard. The bizarre thing is that nobody really knew who the trouble makers were or had ever seen them before."

This information struck a discordant tone for Layla and sorrow gave way to anger. *Those guys were planted there to intimidate and disrupt the rally, mercenary thugs. They probably could care less about the cause of the loggers or of what logging might do for the local economy.* Layla could not help but to associate Ken Leyman with such thoughts.

"Tracy, was Forest First exposing the activity of Southern Highlands Logging Company at the rally?"

"Well yes, along with the other logging companies. But they are the biggest and their methods the most devastating. If they had their way, they would turn Pisgah National Forest into one huge tree farm. Why do you ask? You don't think that Ken Leyman would stoop to something this low, do you?"

"He wouldn't do the stooping himself, of course, but I would never presume he was innocent."

"You know, Layla, sometimes, like now, it seems that we're up against too much. We're just regular people who believe in something. We're fighting big money and our own government, both at the same time."

"Tracy, do you think Michael will give up after this?"

"Oh no, he'll bounce back and keep fighting."

"Well, damn it, it's time I quit being such a coward and told people what I know about the logging and the good-old-boys that are behind it."

"Layla, you need to be careful."

Layla smiled and hugged her friend. "No, I'm too careful. That's always been a problem with me. I'm going to head back to school now. Do you need me to do anything later? I can pick up the girls."

"Thanks, but no. They have basketball practice and then they have a ride home. Layla, what's the situation with Davis? Is he still at the house?"

"Physically, yes. He's drinking a lot now; lately it's been more vodka than beer."

"Ugh."

"Ugh is right. I called my attorney and ask her to ratchet things up because I don't think I can keep playing this game."

"What about him and Caroline Leyman?"

"Well, Davis isn't saying anything, but I get the feeling it's not going well. I do know that his father is pestering him to return to Raleigh. I've heard some pointed messages being recorded on the answering machine."

"Layla, please be careful."

"With Davis?"

"With Davis, his father, Ken Leyman. I'm scared now."

Layla hugged her friend. "I will be. Don't worry about me. You take care of Michael. See you. Call me if you need anything."

33

Layla didn't want to teach her creative writing class. While driving back to campus, she thought about the trauma inflicted on Michael and Tracy. She knew that a classroom of enthusiastic and idealistic young people would not mesh well with her mood.

Whether Ken Leyman was involved in what happened at the rally was beside the point. Layla blamed him and his far-reaching ambitions for spawning such trouble. *He's the root of the problem, as Abe would say.* She missed Abe and wished she was deep inside Great Smoky Mountains National Park with him. *I wonder what Abe would think about the attack on Michael?*

Layla bought a cup of coffee on the way to the university and wanted to pass the hour before class alone in her office. As she approached her door, she saw a package leaning against it. Layla smiled when she saw that it was from the bookstore of Great Smoky Mountains National Park.

Lost in the Smoky Mountains was just the distraction she needed. Layla locked the door to prevent interruption. She rolled her chair to a window at the back of the room. Layla was excited, and her mood improved as she opened the package.

Turning to the chapter on Abe Carol Ramsey, Layla found

that the story told in the book was the same as Abe's version of it. Then she paged through the rest of the book, reading chapter titles. She stopped when she saw the name Samuel Wolford. The chapter was titled *The Disappearance of Samuel Wolford*. A younger version of Abe was pictured on the page, clean-shaven and dressed in a military uniform.

In spite of the fact that Abe had told her about his military service, Layla was surprised to see him in such different dress. After reading several paragraphs, she found more surprises. Abe mentioned only that he had been a Boy Scout and had been in the military service, not that he was an eagle scout or that he had been an Army Ranger. She also read that he was part of a special operations unit during the Persian Gulf War.

The fight outside the bar and the flight from the police was described from a different point of view, but still fit well with the story that Abe told her. But after the stolen police car was abandoned and Samuel Wolford ran into Great Smoky Mountains National Park, the printed version of the story became speculation. Layla found it interesting reading, considering that she knew what really happened to Samuel Wolford.

She read that the search had been quite extensive, at one point numbering two hundred people. The searchers included volunteers, park rangers, state police officers and FBI agents. While Samuel Wolford was never sighted, tracking dogs picked up his scent, bits of clothing were found, and blood was discovered along the edge of a rock shelf.

As the days went by, a more complete profile of Samuel Wolford was compiled, including the state of his physical and mental health. Based on this information, many felt that his chances of survival were almost none unless he was found within days.

Layla was moved by the fact that, two days after the hunt began, the same police officer that Samuel Wolford struck to the ground was among the searchers. Officer Percy Messer counseled the others that even though Samuel Wolford had a serious substance abuse problem, he wasn't a vicious or dangerous man. The policeman was quoted as saying that Samuel Wolford had been pushed into a fight and then, under the influence of alcohol, he lost control.

Abe would be glad to know this. Maybe when he hears it, he'll consider turning himself in and begin the process of clearing his record. I'm sure Officer Messer would help him.

Layla read on to learn that Abe had guessed rightly; his death had been presumed. After five weeks, the search was ended. An FBI agent stayed in the area for another two months and police in Western North Carolina and Eastern Tennessee followed tips for the next year. But after several years had passed, most people concluded that Samuel Wolford died in Great Smoky Mountains National Park.

The chapter ended with several scenarios, postulated by rangers with search and rescue experience. Considering that the night temperatures had dropped into the thirties during the week after Samuel Wolford's flight into the park, most felt that hypothermia was the likely cause of death.

Some felt that the fugitive may have climbed into a laurel thicket for shelter and died there, hidden from the searchers by the evergreen foliage. Another possibility was that he died and his body was eaten by bears or wild pigs. None of these endings were without precedent in the course of the rangers' careers.

Layla closed the book, leaned back in her chair, and stared out the window. *They're right, in a way. Samuel Wolford did die in the park. But he was born again as Abe Carol Ramsey. He still roams Great Smoky Mountains National Park, very much alive and free. Now he's Cataloochee Man.*

Layla looked at the clock on the wall to see that she had another twenty minutes before class. On impulse, she rolled the chair back to her desk, withdrew a phone book from a bottom drawer, and searched the Haywood County white pages. She found two columns of Messers, but fortunately, only one Percy. She dialed the number without hesitation.

A woman answered.

"Hello, yes, my name is Layla Turner. I'm a writer, and I was wondering if I could speak to Percy Messer?"

"Why that's my husband, but he's not here now. This time of day he's always at the station."

"Oh, then he's still a police officer?"

"Y-yes, he's the chief of police. Are you from here?"

"No, I mean yes. Well actually, I moved here."

"I see. Percy has been chief for three years now. He's usually in his office in the afternoons."

"Thank you for your help, Mrs. Messer."

"Would you like his number?"

"Y-yes, yes, thank you." Layla wrote the number on the phone book cover and thanked the woman again.

When Layla called the station, she was greeted by another woman with a younger voice. Again Layla introduced herself as a writer.

"Do you write for one of the papers?"

"Oh, no, I write novels. Well, actually, I teach, too, at Western Carolina University. I'm working on a novel though, and I was hoping that Chief Messer could help me with some information."

"Wow, that's awesome. Let me see if he can come to the

phone now, Ms. Turner. There was someone in his office earlier, but I think they're gone now."

Layla heard the sound of a chair sliding across a wooden floor, then footsteps and voices.

"Hello, Percy Messer speaking."

"Hello, how do you do Chief Messer. I'm Layla Turner."

"I'm doing great. Trish tells me you want to write a book about me."

"Uh, well, not really, she must have misunderstood . . ."

"Ha ha, I'm just teasing. You'd have to be pretty hard up for material for that to be true."

Layla chuckled. "Actually, I was hoping to talk to you about Samuel Wolford, the man who disappeared into Great Smoky Mountains National Park about ten years ago."

"Sam Wolford? Why I thought people finally got tired of writing about him."

"I don't want to write about him per se; I'm thinking of using a character like him in a novel."

"You must like sad endings."

"N-no, not necessarily. That's what's nice about writing fiction, a story can end however an author wants it to."

"Well, I'll tell you what I know, up until he went into the park. I know a little about his family, too."

"Could we meet somewhere to talk?"

"I suppose we could. How about over lunch. You ever eat at Watson's"

"Just for coffee and pastry."

"Well, it's time you had one of their sandwiches. How about we meet there Thursday at noon?"

"Yes, I'll be there."

"Good. Look for a guy that looks like Tom Cruise in a police uniform, except for the mustache, and the bald head, and the belly."

Layla laughed and assured Chief Messer that she would know him. When she hung up the phone, it was nearly time for class. Now she was in a great mood for Creative Writing 301.

34

The hunter knew that it was the month of August. He knew because of the angle of sun rays through the trees, by the dull-green color, pervading the foliage, and because of the clicking and buzzing of countless insects. Abe was following Long Bunk Trail to the north out of Little Cataloochee Valley. This was a route he traversed once a year, usually in August.

His father told him that the path was once called Pig Pen Trail because long ago a pig pen existed at its northern end. Abe wasn't sure how his father knew this but like many things his father told him over the years, he accepted it as true. It was like the stories of pale men in suits and sunglasses, the government men whose coming Abe had been warned about since he was a child. His father was right about that; they were here now.

But Abe wasn't thinking about the government men at this moment, or the Panther Patrol, or Ken Leyman, or even Layla. He was thinking about deer. The hunter was scanning the countryside with alert, relentless eyes.

A century before Great Smoky Mountains National Park was established, farmers used this area as summer pasture. The natural meadows and bounty of acorns now provided food for the wild stock. The ground was soft from rain and Abe used this to his advantage, moving up Long Bunk Mountain without a sound.

After stepping through a thicket of hornbeam and laurel and then crossing a small stream, Abe spied three deer. They were sixty yards ahead, at a point where the trail climbed at a steep angle. The animals were near an outcrop of enormous boulders that shouldered into the branches of the surrounding trees. Two of the deer were looking at him and the other was looking up the trail. All three were alert, muscles twitching.

The hunter smiled. He knew the futility of trying to shoot one of these animals. At the same time, he realized that the area where they stood was a good location to wait for other deer to pass by. Abe walked toward them at a slow pace. He wanted these animals to move away without sounding an alarm that would alert other deer.

Moments later, he was situated atop the rock outcrop, hidden in the branches, bow in hand. An arrow was notched and pointed down at the trail.

As he looked across the landscape, Abe became distracted when the arrow in his hands came into view. He had perfected their construction to the level of an art form and he couldn't help but admire his handiwork. Then he raised his eyes and chastised himself for the lapse of concentration.

But again, his thoughts wandered. He couldn't help but think back to the first arrows he had made. Archery had been a passion of his scoutmaster, Ed Hannah, and many of the Boy Scouts in Waynesville Troop 682 received their first merit badge in archery.

Abe smiled as he pictured Mr. Hannah, a skinny little man, with thinning brown hair. The scoutmaster often had a cigarette dangling from his mouth while leading his ragged little troop along the trails in Great Smoky Mountains National Park. Abe had liked the man very much. Those childhood excursions in these very woods were some of his fondest memories.

I wonder what Mr. Hannah would think of me now. I'll bet he never guessed what a valuable lesson he was teaching.

Again, the hunter forced distraction from his thoughts and focused on this most primary of tasks, procuring food.

Thirty minutes passed. Abe heard the tick of a breaking twig to his right. He didn't move, only shifted his eyes in the direction of the sound. He saw two whitetail deer. It was obvious from their movements that they were unaware of his presence. Not expecting a predator from such heights, the two doe never turned their gaze in his direction. When the animals were within thirty yards, Abe drew the arrow.

When the lead doe was under the outcrop, she raised her head and turned it from side to side. Her nose quivered. If not for the fact that Abe lived in clothing tailored from the hide of her own species, the animal would have smelled him for what he was by now.

The second animal sensed the alarm of the leader and would have bound away alongside her. But a shaft rocketed down from above, entered the deer between the shoulders, severed its spine, and lodged in the deer's right lung. Collapsing to the ground, the doe struggled to regain its footing. Life slipped away quickly and she slid back to the earth.

Abe remained in position until the doe was still. He didn't want to scare the animal into useless and painful flight. Then Abe climbed down from the stony loft, withdrawing his knife as he approached the prostrate creature. Only a human who depends on such an act for sustenance can experience satisfaction over killing such a gentle animal. The hunter was grateful for what this deer would give him and reasoned that someday, upon his own death, he would return the favor to other forest creatures.

With the success of the hunt, Abe relaxed and let his mind wander. As he cut out the arrow and began to disembowel the animal, he recalled the first deer he killed, four months after entering the park.

It was early spring when Abe escaped the police by running into Cataloochee Valley. He survived those first weeks solely on edible plants. His father believed that no one truly knew the woods until they could find wild plants that furnish good food in the season when food is scarce, that is, in winter or early spring. He taught Abe to recognize ramps, rock tripe, duck potato, Indian cucumber, crinkle-root, and a variety of other edible plants.

When warm weather came, there was an abundance of nuts and berries, and Abe's diet grew diverse and more nutritious. During that first summer, Abe devised a method of netting fish in shallow pools, employing his threadbare tee shirt, stretched between the branches of a limb. With his father's training along with that which he received in the military, Abe knew how to survive in the forest. But in late summer when he brought down his first deer with a bow and arrow, he knew he would thrive.

The evisceration complete, Abe hoisted the deer to his shoulders, leaving a pile of warm entrails for other animals to dine upon. He could tell by the weight that this was a broad and full-bodied doe. It would provide many weeks of food. He planned to make a meal somewhere west of Little Cataloochee and then walk through the night to Spruce Mountain so he could begin smoking and drying the meat as soon as possible.

Abe reached Little Cataloochee trail just before sundown. Since he knew there was no chance that another person would be in the back country at this hour, Abe allowed himself the luxury of following the trail. Little Cataloochee Trail had once been the road that ran through the Little Cataloochee settlement. The walk through this pleasant valley would be a gentle preamble to the steep climb to Davidson Gap.

He had first walked this trail over twenty years before with his friends Neil Guthrie and Billy Queen and the rest of Boy Scout Troop 682. Ed Hannah, their scoutmaster, was walking beside them. He always let one of the senior scouts lead, while he told the troop stories about Little Cataloochee. The scoutmaster was a descendant of the Hannahs who inhabited the area before the formation of Great Smoky Mountains National Park.

Mr. Hannah told them that the settlement in Little Cataloochee Valley was a satellite community of its neighbor, Big Cataloochee. It was where the children of the first settlers of Cataloochee Valley, established their own homesteads.

An hour later, Abe set up a temporary camp in thick woods near a stream. He cooked thin slices of the deer's flank over a small fire. Abe hadn't eaten fresh venison for nearly three month. He lingered, resting after a long day, cooking more of the meat, and savoring the moment.

I wonder what Layla would think of this picnic, he thought, staring at the fire and smiling. *Knowing her, she would like it, just like she seems to like everything.*

The deer carcass was straddling a nearby boulder, and Abe rubbed the sleek fur with the back of his hand. He was planning to tan the hide and make Layla a pair of moccasins. Then he thought of her proposal, that he might leave the park one day, take the steps to clear his name, and then stay with her. When Layla first mentioned the idea, such a move seemed to be out of the question.

But each time the thought came back, more time had passed, and he missed Layla to a greater degree. So by this evening, Abe was entertaining the proposal.

He stood and snuffed out the fire with his foot. *Even if I didn't spend years in jail what would I do out there now, sell cars, work construction again? I couldn't handle that life before so why would I be able to handle it now? I guess I could live in the woods and walk to Layla's house to visit.*

Abe laughed at that thought and positioned the deer carcass over his shoulders. *The neighbors would probably wonder, when I came walking up her driveway with a dead deer on my shoulders. I would ask Layla how her creative writing class went and she would compliment me on the fine kill I brought home for dinner.*

35

The events of the preceding days inspired Layla to write. The evening after the violent incident that enveloped Michael Ogden, Layla began her literary campaign against the logging of Pisgah National Forest.

Despite her angry pronouncement to Tracy, she remained hesitant to attack the family that she was still a legal member of. Rather than start on a personal level, she decided to conduct herself as an objective journalist. Layla believed that the best way to influence the public was to present the facts about the federal logging program in a way that would affect a broad spectrum of readers.

Layla opened with the basic position of Forest First: the national forests are more valuable standing. They provide social and economic contributions to the nation, simply by existing as natural ecosystems. To her mind that was argument enough, but she wanted her article to appeal to a wide audience, from professors to loggers. She needed to be more specific.

The federal logging program creates a destructive network of clear cuts and logging roads that result in long-term damage to wildlife and fish habitat, pollutes a major source of the nation's drinking water, and results in lost recreational opportunities.

Layla liked where she was going but knew that her words had to ultimately address the monetary side of the issue. The National Forests were established to control the rampant logging and mining practices of the nineteenth century, but the United States government never intended for them to become wilderness preserves.

The land was intended to be managed for multiple uses and this included timber harvesting. Timber harvesting meant revenue for the government and jobs for local people. This was the argument she had to circumvent.

Feeling a need to offset her bias, Layla visited a variety of websites that examined the issue from different angles. She found several facts very enlightening. One of these was the belief that the federal logging program represented a giveaway to the timber industry, resulting in heavy monetary losses, ultimately borne by taxpayers. She learned that taxes provide millions in direct subsidies to the timber industry for the construction and maintenance of logging roads on federal land.

In turn, subsidized timber sales on national forest lands place small scale producers who operate on their own lands at a competitive disadvantage. It seemed to Layla that the only people who benefited from federal timber sales were the big timber companies who obtained lucrative contracts through their lobbyists in Washington. She pictured Ken Leyman's face, leering in the background as she read these words.

Another website gave her the final point that she needed. It posted that while the Forest Service takes credit for creating jobs through timber harvesting, in many cases, it is simply displacing jobs that would otherwise be available from logging on private lands. And if workers are brought into the area with a large company, as they often are, than the effect is a net loss of jobs.

Layla was delighted with her rough composition and worked on it late into the night. By the following evening she had trimmed the article to nine hundred words and fine-tuned it for publication. She smiled with satisfaction. While she never mentioned Malcolm Elmore or Ken Leyman by name, they would know that she was thinking about them.

Perhaps to offset the factual nature and weightiness of the logging article, Layla turned to her fiction. The knowledge she had gained concerning Abe's entry into Great Smoky Mountains National Park bolstered her desire to write a story based on him. In her mind, she was refashioning him as a modern-day Robin Hood, roaming the forests of North Carolina and performing good deeds of mythical proportions.

Layla knew, of course, that she would have to embellish a bit on Abe's docile mountain life to reach such dramatic heights, but that would be her job as a novelist. Before she even started typing, Layla jumped ahead many chapters and daydreamed about possible endings.

But in the end, does the forest prince leave his realm to be with the fair damsel that he has fallen in love with, or does she ride off into the forest with him?

That thought distracted Layla and caused her to think of her discussion with Abe about the possibility of him coming to Mountain Crest. He seemed to be such a natural part of the forest that it was hard for her to imagine him here, walking across the Great Room or sitting on the suede couch. As far as facing society again and returning to a normal life, she understood his misgivings.

But then she considered the other possibility. *Could the fair damsel leave her castle and ride off with the forest prince?* Layla paused and stared at her computer monitor as she considered this prospect. She shook her head. *I don't think so. I need a few basics, like a bathroom and a laptop.*

Then she thought about the simple suggestion Abe had made concerning a potential dwelling for her: a little cabin with a desk and a lamp, a loft to sleep in, and a wood cook stove for heat. *He described it so enthusiastically. Was he speaking for himself to some degree? If I could simplify my life to that point, could he complicate his a little to meet me there?*

Layla heard thumping noises from the floor below, alerting her to the fact that Davis had left his study and was making his way to either the kitchen or the bathroom. This reminder of her domestic situation was timed well to augment the appeal of Abe's cabin proposal. Davis' drinking had escalated to an alarming level, and most of the day, he confined himself to his study.

While no longer offering information about his personal life, Layla knew that Carolyn Leyman's tennis lessons had ended, and Ken Leyman was addressed as 'Mr. Leyman', again. As much as his self-isolation simplified her life, she hated to see this happening to Davis. For all he wasn't in her eyes, Layla knew he was a good and kind-hearted person. But, he was too easily manipulated by others and admired the wrong people.

From the start, Layla wanted her and Davis' relationship to be open and equal with neither of them constraining the other. But she wondered now, if a little more constraint on her part could have kept Davis out of the rut he steered his life into. She might even feel guilty for his wretched condition if it wasn't for the fact that it was he who had pressed her to marry. And, at least at the outset, she adjusted her life around his career choice.

The thumping noise came again. The sound of the study door

closing soon followed. Layla sighed and repositioned her fingers above the keyboard.

Now, where was I? Ah, yes, would the fair damsel leave her castle and live with the forest prince in a humble cottage, and would the prince abandon his magnificent forest to live there with her?

Staring at darkness outside the window, Layla imagined such an arrangement and smiled. She would see Abe in another week and hoped he could help her with the ending to the story.

36

"**G**rilled cheese? That's just the start of a sandwich," Chief Messer stated, grinning from under his walrus mustache.

Layla laughed and eyed the enormous serving on Percy Messer's plate. The fried green tomato sandwich with bacon and cheese was a specialty at Watson's Restaurant, and was the Chief's favorite. Layla wasn't hungry and ordered light, but she thought that the fried green tomato sandwich looked and smelled delicious.

She followed Chief Messer through a busy dining room and out the back onto a deck that overlooked Wall Street. He nodded toward a table in the far right corner that was shaded by two holly trees. Layla had never been on the deck at Watson's and so she looked about in all directions, studying Waynesville from this new perspective. She smiled when she realized that Chief Messer had positioned himself so that the Waynesville police station was in view.

Layla had no trouble recognizing Percy Messer when she entered the restaurant. He was a big man, over six feet tall with broad, rounded shoulders, big hands, and the makings of an overhang at his belt. But he wasn't fat and seemed quite robust for a man that Layla guessed was in his mid-fifties. The Chief removed his hat to reveal a very bald head above dark hair on each side. He had a red complexion, brown eyes, a deep dimple on his chin, and a prevailing expression that made one feel he was about to say something ornery.

"Where are you from, Layla?"

"How do you know I'm not from Waynesville?"

"Besides your accent, the unsweetened tea is a dead giveaway," he said, pointing to her glass.

She smiled. "I'm from Massachusetts originally. I lived in Raleigh for some time and I've lived here for over seven years now. How long does it take before somebody is from here?"

"Well now, let me see. I know a family that moved down here from Maryland in the late sixties. Bradley's their name. They bought a little farm and started a landscaping business out near Jonathan Creek. It's been nearly forty years now, but they're still not *from* here. So I can't say for sure. All I can tell you is that it takes longer than that."

Chief Messer grinned, but never implied that he was kidding.

Layla shook her head and laughed. She wished she had brought a tape recorder.

"So what do you know about Sam Wolford so far?" The chief took a prodigious bite of his sandwich.

"Not a lot really. Just what I've read in a book that I bought about people who have disappeared in the Smoky Mountains. I read about the fight in the alley."

"Is that the book by Tom Stamey?"

Layla nodded.

The policeman bobbed his head. "Yeah, I know Tom. He was town manager in Sylva until he retired a few years ago. That's pretty much the way it was that night, the way he tells it. He interviewed everybody that was there.

Foolish thing I did, approaching Sam like that, figuring I could calm him down. I should have stuck to protocol. But I always felt sorry for Sam, always thought he deserved better in life than what he ended up with."

"How did you know Samuel Wolford?"

Percy Messer leaned forward on his elbows.

"When I was a boy, I had a friend named Billy Hannah. His father, Ed, took over the local Boy Scout Troop when Billy and I were old enough to join. Mr. Hannah was a natural for the job and stayed on as scoutmaster long after we left the troop. In fact he was still scoutmaster twenty years later when Sam Wolford joined. That's how I first knew of Sam, through Mr. Hannah.

That's someone you might want to talk to if you want stories for a novel, Mr. Hannah. He lives up near Gatlinburg now with his daughter. I've lost touch with him, but Ed Jr. is pastor of the Presbyterian Church right across Main Street."

"Well thank you. I think I will contact him. I read that Samuel Wolford was an eagle scout."

"He sure was, one of the few that came out of old Troop 682. Ed Hannah never was one to push his scouts. He did what he could to help us get our badges, but he was more for teaching practical things, mountain skills. He wanted it to be fun, too. But, young Sam, he was a go-getter. He had something to prove."

"How old would he have been then?"

"Twelve or thirteen."

"What do you think he had to prove at that age?"

"Well, it's just an opinion, but I think the kid was out to prove that he wasn't like his old man."

"Why?"

"His old Man, Cappy Wolford, was kind of a kook."

"Cappy?"

"Only name I ever heard him called by. He always had a cap on, so that might have been the reason. I can't say I ever spoke more than a few words with the man. He was a character, though. Cappy had a little land out near Cruso. He was one of those survivalist types, anti-government, everything's-a-conspiracy. You know what I mean?"

"Yes, I do. What about Samuel's mother?"

"She left when she couldn't take Cappy anymore. From what I heard, the man ran their home like a military camp. She took their daughter and a baby boy and moved up to Tennessee, where she had family. Samuel was in high school then."

"And then, Samuel lived alone with his father?"

"Yep. Everyone knew that Cappy was hard on him, smacked him around some. Social services went out there more than once. Kids at school seen bruises on Sam. But he always stuck up for his old man."

"Really?"

"Yep. Wouldn't turn him in and wouldn't let anyone talk about him either."

"Well, what happened?"

"You mean, how did he finally get away from him?"

"Yes."

"Sam joined the service, army rangers, special ops."

"I read that. What exactly does that mean?"

"Special Operations Unit. They do the behind-the-scenes stuff: sabotage, blowing up bridges, taking out guard posts, assassination. Nobody knows for sure all that they do. He joined the service just in time for the Persian Gulf War.

Cappy had a fit when he signed up, disowned Sam, sold the property near Cruso, and moved to some isolated spot in Montana. I always expected to hear about him on the news, that the FBI or the alcohol tobacco and firearms people stormed his place and shot it out with him."

"And that was the last that Samuel saw of him?"

"Far as I know. Most thought it was just as well. Sam came back from the Gulf War a hero, Silver Star, Purple Heart. Everybody wanted to hire him. Took a job with a construction company and worked hard at it for a while. He married the boss's daughter and had a little girl with her. But a few years later, the devil began to take his due."

"What do you mean?"

"I think that the damage that was done to him by his father and the Gulf War caught up with him. He couldn't stay settled in normal life. Started drinking a lot, work suffered, marriage suffered. People that knew him said he was like another person when he got to drinking; turned into a crazy man. Eventually his wife left with the kids and moved back in with her folks. Sam got fired and for a while lived where he could, which in the end, was out of his pick-up."

Chief Messer looked into Layla's eyes and saw great sadness. He was glad now that he agreed to tell Samuel Wolford's story one more time. He believed that this woman would retell it with sympathy.

Percy shook his head. "I added up the possible charges against him for that incident in the alley and then the prison time that would follow. Them medals would have cut him some slack, but not nearly enough. I often thought that in the end it was for the best that he died in the mountains that he loved."

Layla was moved by Chief Messer's quiet ending. How she wished she could tell him the truth. She smiled. "Maybe he didn't die. Maybe he still lives in the Smoky Mountains, wild and free."

"Hah ha, now there's the novelist in you. You write a book with that ending and I'll buy the first copy. But you know if it were true and if he'd walk out of the woods today and give himself up, that would go along way toward impressing a judge. I'd go to bat for him for whatever it was worth."

"It would be worth a lot, and that's very good of you to think that way."

"Well, I thank you, but right now, I've got to get back over to the station."

"I need to get back to school, too."

They got up and went down the back steps to Wall Street.

Chief Messer shook Layla's hand. "Layla, it's been my pleasure and I hope I helped you a little."

"You've been a wonderful help. Thank you."

The policeman put on his hat and headed toward the police station.

Layla was lost in thought as she pulled onto Main Street. *Do I finally know who Abe Ramsey is? What a sad story. What judge couldn't be sympathetic?*

Then she passed the Presbyterian Church and saw the name Ed Hannah on a sign alongside Main Street. At the bottom of the sign was a phone number. Layla pulled to the side of the road and tapped it into her cell phone. A secretary answered and told her that the pastor was on another line but should be free soon. Layla drove a mile toward Cullowhee when she heard Pastor Hannah's voice. The Reverend was reluctant when he learned of her inquiry.

"Ms. Turner, my father was quite fond of Samuel Wolford. He never has gotten over what happened to him. I'm sure your intentions are good, but my father is elderly and . . ."

"Pastor Hannah, I wouldn't have called except that Police Chief Messer suggested that I do."

"Percy told you to call? Well that's different. That's a pretty strong reference. I'll warn you though, once Dad gets to talking, he'll pin your ears back."

Layla laughed. "That will be my pleasure."

37

"Abe, do you love me?"

Layla was sitting on a blanket and leaning against a huge sycamore tree. Abe was lying on the ground, his head nested in her lap. He opened his eyes, looked up at her, and nodded. She smiled.

"There's something I need to tell you, one last secret."

Abe nodded again.

"My husband's name is Davis Elmore. My name is Turner because I didn't change my name when we were married. His father is Malcolm Elmore, the governor of North Carolina and Davis works for his father as his chief counsel."

Abe continued to look up at her with no change in his expression.

"I'm the daughter-in-law of the Governor of North Carolina. Doesn't that surprise you?"

"A little. Why didn't you tell me before?"

"I don't know for sure. Maybe I was afraid it would scare you off."

"I don't scare easily. It doesn't mean much to me, really, who your father-in law is, the Governor in Raleigh or an electrician that lives down the road. It doesn't change who you are."

Abe sat up and turned toward Layla. "Do you and your father-in-law get along?"

"Y-yes, we do, actually. We never agree on too many things, especially when it comes to politics, but that never caused any serious trouble between us. Malcolm has always been nice to me even though I don't think he ever wanted Davis and me to marry."

"Why didn't he want you to marry?"

"Oh, I know now that he would have preferred that his son marry someone a bit more traditional and a lot more religious. And, considering the way things turned out, maybe he was right."

"Is this Governor a good person?"

"Hmm, yes, deep down Malcolm is. He's loud and pushy and sometimes rubs people in the wrong way, but he really does want to do what's right. It just seems that anybody who plays the power and money game too long loses touch with what is right for people in general."

"Well I'm not impressed with money or power or politicians. The Governor doesn't govern me. He doesn't affect my life anymore than an electrician down the road would."

"But your wrong there, Abe. You told me that you don't like the logging in the national forest, right?"

"Right."

"Well my father-in-law, the Governor, has worked hard to allow more logging of the national forests in North Carolina. He's a big part of the reason for the logging that's going on in Pisgah National Forest right now."

"He is?"

"Yes, he believes that the national forests should be used as they were meant to be used. His argument is that logging means revenue for the United States and jobs for the people in this area. And I'm sure that Malcolm believes this. But here's the sour note. His old college friend who just happens to own the biggest logging company in the south received a major timber contract. Ken Leyman is his friend's name and Southern Highlands Logging Company has a huge operation in Pisgah National Forest."

Abe stared through a break in the trees, down into Cataloochee Valley. Layla and he were on a level spot fifty yards downhill from Cataloochee Divide Trail and half a mile above the valley floor.

"Leyman is still logging the forest?"

Layla was surprised at how he worded the question. "Yes, in fact, he has only just begun. Forest First recently received aerial photographs showing that Southern Highlands has greatly expanded its operation just in the past two weeks." When Abe looked at her, Layla saw anger in his expression, something she had never seen before.

"Is Forest First doing anything?"

"Yes, the usual protests and we're always trying to keep the public informed about what's happening. I've started writing articles for the local newspapers to point out what an environmental disaster it is. Logging the national forests doesn't even make good economic sense."

"It isn't profitable?"

"Oh it's profitable all right, but not for the public who are the real owners of the national forests. The only ones who are making money are the Ken Leymans."

"Are people listening to you?"

"Well, sometimes, but it's not as easy to get a sympathetic ear since the Panther Patrol went on their recent rampage."

"What?"

Layla told Abe about the spate of attacks attributed to the

Panther Patrol. He became visibly agitated as she spoke and asked for as many details as she could remember. When Layla told the story of the attack on High Country Logging Company, she saw his jaw set and his expression turn grim.

"Ira Drew was killed?"

"You knew him?"

Abe hung his head. "Yes, he was a nice man, a logging man, wouldn't hurt a fly. The Panther Patrol wouldn't kill Ira."

"Actually, some people don't believe that the Panther Patrol is behind these recent attacks. It seems more likely that it's an opportunist using their name. But that doesn't matter to the general public. And why should it? Violence is violence. Violence only leads to more violence. The problem for Forest First is that people are putting us in the same category as the Panther Patrol or whoever is behind this."

Then Layla told Abe about the incident with Michael Ogden. She was still upset, and her voice broke during the narration.

Abe's eyes narrowed. He clenched a fist and tapped it against the ground. Once again, he stared into Cataloochee Valley. *How can one man cause so much trouble? Leyman is just one little man and he's hurting all these good people and destroying the forests just so he can make more money than he'll ever need.*

Layla wanted to change the subject. She moved close and leaned against him. Abe yielded, nuzzling through waves of hair, until he was behind her ear. He breathed the intoxicating fragrance of the woman that he loved. After a minute, she spoke.

"Abe, if I were to give up the house at Mountain Crest and get a simple little cabin somewhere, like you suggested, one with a wood cook stove and a loft, is there a chance that you would live there with me? You could clear your record. I would help you and Percy Messer, the chief of police in Waynesville would help."

Abe lifted his head. "Percy Messer, he's the chief of police? How do you know he would help?"

Layla told Abe the story of her conversation with the Chief and Abe listened with fascination. She worried that he might become irritated with her tactics, but instead, he was impressed with her cleverness. He stared at the ground for a moment, trying to assimilate this new information.

Abe lifted his head. "I'm not afraid of jail. I could bear that for you. But I don't know if I can live on the outside after all these years. What would I do for a living? To me it would be a prison of another kind with time clocks and deadlines and taxes and alarms and . . ."

"No, we'll keep it simple. I want you, and I want to write, and I won't let anyone or anything else intrude on our lives. You can cut firewood, grow a garden, work on our cabin and go for long walks through the woods everyday."

Abe smiled and burrowed back into her hair, his mind swirling with the thought of this new proposal. *I would be a fool not to say yes. It's time I quit the Panther Patrol. Things are spinning out of control anyway. I've done enough to stop the logging. Layla will never have to know about that part of me.*

"You'll think about it, at least?" Layla asked, gently bumping her body against his.

He held her close and nodded.

38

Layla hummed as she leafed through real estate listings. She had gathered a selection of brochures on her way through Cullowhee that morning and was perusing them over lunch. In her mind, Layla had let go of the house at Mountain Crest, and now she was anxious to physically move out of it. She was focused on finding a cabin near Cataloochee Valley.

Layla hadn't told Davis that she was no longer interested in the house because she hadn't spoken with him since her return from the park. He seldom left his study, and if it were not for the occasional noise that emanated from it, she might wonder if he was in the house at all. Layla was worried about her husband, but since he had never listened to her before, concerning his drinking, she was certain that he wouldn't now. The pall that Davis' presence cast over the house was more incentive for Layla to study the real estate listings.

However, finding a cabin to Abe's specifications was not so easy. Layla came to realize that many of the real estate channels of Haywood County led toward new and large homes, built high on mountain sides. She decided that she would do better to search local newspapers and to ask people she knew who were native to the area.

Maybe we could buy a little farm somewhere near the park. I wish I could talk this over with Abe right now. I don't want to wait until this weekend. When is that man going to get a cell phone?

She laughed at this notion and reached for her own phone. Two messages from the same phone number were in her voice mail. The number confused her for a moment and then she remembered the call she made to Ed Hannah. She didn't reach the scoutmaster before she left for the park but had left a message at the number Pastor Hannah gave her.

When Layla dialed, a woman answered and said that she was Ed Hannah's granddaughter. She chatted with Layla as she took the phone to her grandfather who was outside, working in the garden.

"Hello, hello," a cheery voice greeted.

"Hello, Mr. Hannah?"

"Yes, this is he. Are you the teacher from Western who wants to talk to me about Sam Wolford? I talked to my son this weekend and he filled me in."

"Y-yes, but I never mentioned to your son that I taught at Western Carolina University."

"Well, Percy must have told him then."

Layla chuckled. "Mr. Hannah, First of all I want you to know that my intentions are good. I want to write a novel and I'm actually quite sympathetic about the case of Samuel Wolford. I would never misuse any information you gave me."

"Well you seem like a nice lady and I trust Percy's opinion."

"Thank you, Mr. Hannah."

"Your welcome. Now, I only really knew Sam when he was a boy in my scout troop. Regardless of what happened later, he was a good kid then. He loved the woods and took to them like no boy I'd ever seen. And he became as skilled in mountain craft as any

221

man I've known, including myself. I'm not surprised that when he got into trouble, he turned to the woods."

"Well then do you think there's a chance he could have survived?"

"Oh yes, I never believed that he died in the park like most people thought. That boy was a survivor in every sense of the word. The Sam Wolford I knew wouldn't just curl up under a laurel bush and die. My guess is that he stayed in the park until the search was cut back and then moved on to somewhere else. I can't believe that he's still in the park. It takes an unusual person to live alone in the woods for any length of time.

It does surprise me though that he hasn't shown up somewhere. The FBI quit combing the woods long ago, but I'm sure they got snares laid for him anywhere he might go."

Layla decided to steer the discussion back to the Boy Scouts because she felt somewhat disingenuous allowing this kind gentleman to speculate when she knew what happened. "I read that Samuel Wolford was an eagle scout."

"He sure was. And archery was his first merit badge, I might add. That's my specialty. I not only taught the boys how to shoot but also how to make their own bow and arrows. For a lot of them, that was the only merit badge they ever got. But for Sam, that was just the start. I never pushed the boys either. I encouraged them to advance and helped where I could, but I wanted them to have fun, too. So, Sam pushed himself. He was an unusual kid."

"What was he like? Was Samuel Wolford easy to get along with? Did he have a lot of friends?"

"He was kind of quiet until you got to know him. He had two real good friends from Waynesville. They joined the troop about the same time he did, Billy Queen and Neil Guthrie. Those three were always together. I had to watch them on camping trips or they would wander off at night and be up to some mischief."

"Did Samuel's friends get their archery merit badges?"

"They sure did. Billy got a few more, but Neil stopped there. All three of them were good at anything to do with mountain skills. They always won the competitions we had. They were in the Panther Patrol and their patrol always won."

"Pardon me, Mr. Hannah, what was the last thing you said?"

"Panther Patrol, the three of them were in the Panther Patrol. A Boy Scout troop is divided into patrols made up of five to eight boys. In our troop we had the Flaming Arrow Patrol, the Eagle Patrol, the Senior Patrol for the older boys, and the Panther Patrol.

Over the years, the personalities of the patrols change, depending on the boys. With Wolford, Queen, and Guthrie together, the Panther Patrol definitely had its own personality *and* won all the competitions."

Layla struggled to keep her thoughts from racing too far ahead, but in her mind, pieces of a puzzle were falling into place, and she couldn't help but be distracted. Until now she had never suspected that Abe might be involved with the Panther Patrol that was the eco-terrorist band, but learning that he was once a member of a group called the Panther Patrol, made other associations come to mind.

"Hello, are you still there?"

"Oh, yes, I'm sorry, Mr. Hannah. It's just that I'm unfamiliar with Boy Scouts and this information is all so new to me. Do you know what became of Samuel's friends?"

"Well, far as I know, Billy still has an auto repair shop right there in Waynesville. Does good work. That's where I took my car. He married a woman from Hazelwood and has three kids.

Neil Guthrie, he was in the service with Sam. Sam and Neil were tight, like brothers. In fact, Sam stayed with the Guthries a lot when he was young, probably to get away from his father."

"Chief Messer told me about Mr. Wolford."

"Well ditto that from me. Anyway, Neil never settled back in Waynesville after he got out of the service. He was out west for a few years, working construction in Phoenix. Then he moved back this way about eight years ago. He stopped to see me then. I was still in Waynesville. Neil ended up settling over near Cosby, Tennessee. Do you know where that is?"

"I've heard of Cosby, but I can't remember exactly where it is or who mentioned it.

"It's a little town a few miles north of Great Smoky Mountains National Park, east of Gatlinburg."

Then Layla remembered. Abe said that he had a friend who lived in Cosby. Her mind began to race again. "Mr. Hannah, how far is Cosby from Cataloochee Valley?"

"By road, it's thirty miles or so, depending on where you start. By trails it would be much less, maybe even as little as twenty?"

Layla felt a prickle on the back of her neck. Abe's childhood friend and fellow soldier lives within walking distance of Cataloochee Valley. And although it was under the auspices of the Boy Scouts, both of these men once belonged to a group called the Panther Patrol. *This can't be a coincidence.*

"Why do you ask, Miss Turner?"

"Well, I just . . . I spend a lot of time in Cataloochee Valley. I like to ride there."

"Horses, so you're one of those people who tear the trails up to make it rough on us hikers?"

"I-I'm careful, Mr. Hannah. I help work on the trails too,

repairing them, I mean." Layla could say this, because she had helped Abe build water diversion barriers on Hemphill Bald Trail only days before.

As much as Layla enjoyed speaking with Ed Hannah, she was having a difficult time concentrating on their conversation. She could sense that the he was just getting started. It was another fifteen minutes before they hung up, and Layla learned many interesting facts about Great Smoky Mountains National Park. She would have attended to his every word another time, but her mind was focused on one thought, Abe as a member of the Panther Patrol.

Layla glanced at the clock. She had thirty minutes until her class. She moved to the back window and thought over her conversations with Abe. *Whenever I mention the Panther Patrol, Abe doesn't comment. One of the few times he did was when I told him about the watchman's death. I wondered then why he seemed so certain that the Panther Patrol wasn't behind it.*

The more convinced Layla became that Abe was a member of the Panther Patrol, the more anxious she became. His affiliation with this group threatened their relationship on a number of levels. At the very worst, he could be killed, and at the least, it meant he was a different sort of person than she thought he was. As much as she disapproved of the logging in Pisgah National Forest, she couldn't condone violence as a means to oppose it.

Layla stared out the window and pictured Abe's face. *Why wouldn't he tell me?* She answered her own question. *He knows I would disapprove, that's why. He seems willing to leave the forest for me, maybe he'll quit the Panther Patrol, too.*

Ten minutes until class, and Layla didn't want to go. She needed time to think. Then Tracy came to mind and she dialed her friend's number.

"Hello, Tracy?"

"Hi Layla, what's up?"

"Are you in the mood for some serious, top-secret talk?"

"Always."

"Good. I have something I need to talk about. Want to go somewhere this evening to eat?"

"I've got a better idea. Why don't you come here for dinner? Michael and the girls are visiting his parents in Georgia so we can talk all evening. I'm in the mood to cook. For that matter, why don't you bring some wine and we'll turn it into a party."

"That sounds perfect, Tracy."

"It's a date; dinner at, say, six-thirty."

"I'll be there. Thanks, Tracy. See you then."

Layla grabbed her notes on the way to the door. Knowing that she would have an entire evening to talk to Tracy enabled her to disconnect from the Panther Patrol dilemma for at least the duration of a class.

39

Tracy was stunned. She knew that Layla and Abe were romantically involved, but she never guessed the level of intimacy between them. She was enthralled with the information Layla had learned about Abe's past.

During a sumptuous meal, featuring Tracy's specialty, wild mushroom ravioli, Layla updated her about everything except her belief that Abe was a member of the Panther Patrol.

Tracy refilled their wine glasses. It seemed to her that Layla had delighted in telling about her relationship with Abe Ramsey as well as the story she had uncovered of Abe's past. And her friend was most excited about the plans she and Abe had for the future. But now Layla looked worried and seemed to struggle to get words out. When she finally did, Tracy was stunned all over again.

There were some members of Forest First who considered the Panther Patrol to be a more militant extension of their own effort. At the other end of the membership were those who denounced the Panther Patrol as little more than lawless thugs whose actions ultimately played into the hands of pro-logging interests.

Tracy stood just left of center. She believed in peaceful demonstration and also that an informed public would make the right decision. But she had been working with Forest First for six years and was frustrated with the lack of response from the public. She was often angry at politicians and logging companies and wished for a more direct way to engage them. When the Panther Patrol first emerged Tracy almost rallied behind them. In the end, however, she shared Layla's point of view that, regardless of the cause, violence only leads to more violence.

"What are you going to do?"

"I'm seeing Abe tomorrow. I've got to talk to him about it."

"Are you worried that he might get mad?"

"No, not at all. That's what surprises me most about all this. Abe is such a peaceful and gentle man that it's hard for me to imagine that he's involved with such a violent group."

"Maybe he's not. Maybe it's all coincidence, Layla. I hope so."

"Me too, but I don't think so. I better go now. Thanks for lending an ear, Tracy. Hope I didn't wear you out."

"Not a chance. Oh, by the way, I loved your last article in the Smoky Mountain News. You outlined the argument against logging in the national forests better than I've ever heard it."

"Thanks, Tracy. I'm starting to hit harder. Ken Leyman has got to be feeling the heat a little."

Tracy hugged her friend. "Good luck tomorrow."

Only the living room light was on when Layla pulled in the driveway. She unlocked the door with barely a sound. Layla expected Davis to be in his study and hoped that he would remain there. She was startled to see her husband sitting in the leather recliner in the Great Room. She bought the chair for him shortly after the house was built but he rarely used it.

Davis' eyes were half closed and although he didn't move she could tell from the reflection in his eyes that he was looking at her.

He wore a blue robe over sweat pants and a tee shirt. A bottle of Heineken was on the table beside him.

"Forest First?" His voice had an obvious slur.

"Oh no, I was at Tracy's."

"How's Mike?"

"H-he's good. Oh, the trouble at the rally, you mean. Tracy says he's fine now, back to his old self."

"That's good. I felt bad about what they did to him. Can you sit for a while? We need to talk."

Layla walked to the couch and sat down. She noticed a half-empty bottle of vodka on the floor beside her husband. She was apprehensive because Davis was obviously drunk. She didn't want to repeat the experience of their last discussion.

Assuming that he wanted an answer, concerning the house, she spoke first. "Davis, I've decided to let go of the house. My plans have changed and it's really more than I need or want now. And I don't need a million dollars. A fair settlement would . . ."

"That's good, Layla. I was hoping you'd say that. You see, I quit my job, so I'll be living here for good."

"What, you quit working for your father?"

"Yeah, how about that? I told the old man to shove it."

In spite of how drunk he seemed to be, Layla believed him. But she was shocked to hear it.

"But what are you going to do, Davis?"

"Open up my office in town. I'll be a small town lawyer and represent the common man." He dropped his head back and laughed.

"Davis, I don't think that's funny. I think that's a good move. You know for years I hoped . . ."

"What did you and Tracy talk about tonight for so long?"

"Oh, the usual, work, writing, the girls."

"All evening?"

Layla was becoming uneasy and sensed that it was time to get away from her husband. "Not all evening. We discussed other things. Um, oh yes, we talked about the Panther Patrol, of all things. We were talking about the recent . . ."

"The Panther Patrol?" Davis laughed again and lifted his head to look at her.

"Y-yes, the Panther Patrol. What's so funny about that?"

"There's nothing funny, it's just that there won't be much to talk about soon from what I hear."

"What do you mean?"

"The fix is in, is what I mean."

"What are you talking about?"

"The fix is in. My man, Dennis, says that he has people in place and the next time Mr. Panther shows his head, there will be a bullet in it."

Layla couldn't believe what she heard. She stood and took a step toward her husband. "Dennis Galloway told you that?"

"Uh, ya, more or less. In fact, those were his exact words."

"Why would he tell you that?"

"Uh, cause we're pals, I guess. Tracy tells you things when you talk all evening, like tonight, doesn't she? Well, Dennis tells me things when we, uh, talk. Besides I'm probably going to be his attorney here real soon."

"What, that's your idea of the common man?"

Davis thought for a moment before he answered and then nodded his head. He picked up the bottle on the floor and added some of its contents to the shot glass that was behind the beer bottle. He drank the vodka in one jerky motion and then followed it with a swallow of beer.

"When did Galloway tell you this?"

Davis furrowed his brow. "Last week, I think."

"And you're sure he wasn't kidding?"

"My man, Dennis, never kids."

Layla had heard enough. She moved toward the staircase. "Good night, Davis."

"Was it something I said?" Davis grinned.

Layla turned. "No, Davis, I'm tired. I'm going riding in the morning and I want to get an early start. But to be honest with you, you're too good a person to mingle with the likes of Dennis Galloway." Then she turned and marched up the stairs.

Alone in her bedroom, Layla's thoughts raced. Her intuition told her that Davis was speaking the truth. The fact that Dennis Galloway had made such a threat unnerved her. Layla had been intimidated by this man since she first met him, and everything she learned about him since had augmented her fear. But it was what she imagined he was capable of doing that frightened her the most. She could picture his cold, calculating eyes, and shuddered to think that they were focusing on Abe.

Now I've got even more reason to confront Abe about the Panther Patrol. I've got to warn him about Dennis Galloway.

40

Hemphill Bald Trail seemed longer than before, and Sundance seemed to be walking so slow that Layla wondered if something was wrong with him. But the trail hadn't lengthened and the horse always kept the same pace. She was impatient and anxious to get down into Cataloochee Valley.

After a restless night, Layla arose early and watched the Asheville news. She was relieved to learn that, during the night, there had been no incident involving the Panther Patrol. Whatever misgivings Layla had over Abe's association with this group, they were far outweighed by her fear that he was in imminent danger.

With a sigh of relief she turned onto Caldwell Fork Trail and urged Sundance onward toward Big Poplars. Layla traveled a short distance when she detected a faint odor of cigarette smoke. Because this was such a foreign scent in the back country, Layla stopped and looked in all directions. She didn't see anyone, but the scent made her uneasy. Layla continued to glance behind herself every few minutes. She was startled when she did see another rider about one hundred yards behind.

This was not so unusual, she reminded herself. Occasionally she would encounter other riders on the trails. The difference was that these riders had always been coming towards her. She glanced back again and saw that it was a man dressed in black riding gear, and wearing dark glasses. Layla had the unsettling feeling that he was staring at her. She looked ahead and tried to suppress the anxiety that was coming over her. A minute later, when she looked back, Layla saw that the rider was closer.

Who is this guy? Come on, Sundance, move. The horse lumbered forward and Layla gazed up the trail. When she saw the sign for Big Poplars, she felt a surge of relief. The feeling dissipated when she glanced back to see that the rider was only fifty yards behind her now. For some instinctive reason, she knew he was coming for her.

Dennis Galloway shifted in the saddle. An experienced rider, he sat leisurely on his horse as he attached a silencer to his semi-automatic pistol. When he learned that Layla traveled alone in Great Smoky Mountains National Park and that she even posted an itinerary, he decided to kill her himself. He rarely did the dirty work anymore, but this job was too easy to delegate. Besides, Dennis loved to ride.

After learning of her implication that he was involved with the mafia, killing Layla became an option for Dennis. Her threat to expose Ken Leyman made the idea a business decision as well.

If Layla had simply gone away, or even stayed and remained silent, then this option would probably not have been exercised. But she stayed and kept talking. Her articles in the newspapers were becoming more specific and were eagerly read by the public. Considering what Layla knew, she could cause considerable damage if she decided to take direct aim at him and his boss.

Dennis smiled when he saw Layla turn. She was only making this easier for him by taking a side trail. He had packed a camp shovel to dig a shallow grave in a rhododendron thicket. Dennis prodded his horse forward.

As Layla approached the ancient poplar trees, she glanced back to see that the rider had left the main trail and was closing the distance between them. She usually loved the steady droning and clicking of insects that was typical of late August, but today the noises were like discordant orchestral sounds, heightening the tension in a movie scene.

Just beyond the poplars, Layla looked to see that the rider had a gun in his hand. She experienced a tingling sensation along her spine, and felt like she was moving in slow motion. She could hear hoofbeats behind her.

Layla forced herself to turn again, and then she saw Abe, standing in the brush to her right. He was perfectly still, his bow pulled taut, an arrow pointed back toward the poplar trees. She called his name, but he didn't move, not even so much as to look at her.

Dennis Galloway was aiming for a spot between Layla's shoulders. He wanted to get this over with. It wasn't noon yet and he hoped to be in Atlanta by evening to dine with an acquaintance. He waited a few more steps; he wanted a clear shot.

Dennis heard Layla call out as she glanced to her right. Then he saw a man, a man dressed like an animal who stood as still as a tree. He was wondering about the strange piece of wood positioned vertically across the man's face and then felt excruciating pain. Dennis looked down to see bird feathers sticking to his chest.

The horse walked out from under him as he dropped his gun and fell backwards. When Dennis hit the ground, the rest of the arrow broke off from his back. A wheezing sound escaped from his mouth as he lay on the forest floor. Lifeless eyes were fixed on the boughs of the magnificent poplars.

Layla dismounted and went to Abe. He took her in his arms.

"Abe, that man was going to kill me. Is he dead?"

Abe nodded. "I shot him through the heart."

Layla shuddered and glanced at the prostrate figure. The horror she felt mounted as recognition dawned on her.

"Oh no, it's Dennis Galloway."

"You know him?"

"He works for Ken Leyman, and, and he's a friend of my husband."

"You're husband would have you murdered?"

"No, Davis would never do that. Galloway must have used him. That's how he knew where to find me. It was probably Ken Leyman's idea."

"Why would Leyman want you dead?"

"Because of things I know about him and my father-in-law. And the articles I write against the logging, I'm sure they're making him furious."

"He's a damn scoundrel. Well, I've got another arrow for him."

"No, Abe, you can't just kill people, not even someone like him."

"But he tried to kill you and it's . . ."

"Abe, listen to me, I know you're a member of the Panther Patrol."

"Layla, I only. . ."

"It's okay, Abe. We can talk about that later, but I have to warn you about something. Dennis Galloway told my husband that the next time anyone from the Panther Patrol raises their head, there will be a bullet in it."

"He's not going to put a bullet in anyone."

"No, but he said that he has people in place that would do it." Layla saw a look of concern come over Abe's face.

Abe looked at Dennis. "Who is this guy, anyway? Do you think he meant it?"

"He's Ken Leyman's muscle, his hired thug. Galloway does the dirty work behind the scenes. If he said he's got people in place than I'm sure he has. Some people believe he has mafia connections."

Abe became excited. He grabbed Layla's shoulders "Layla, I have to go."

"Abe, no."

"I'll be all right, but I have to warn the others. The Southern Highlands operation is going to get hit sometime soon, tonight or tomorrow, depending on the weather." Abe glanced at the sky. "I've got to go right now. Are you sure your husband had nothing to do with this?"

"Yes, I'm sure he had no idea."

"Go back to your house then, but don't say anything about this to anyone. Without being obvious, start getting ready to go, pack what you need and get away from there. Don't let anyone know where you're going."

"But where should I go?"

Abe smiled. "Find that little cabin somewhere, the one with the loft and cook stove. Wherever you go, I'll find you and stay with you there, even if I have to live in a hedge row."

Layla smiled but looked scared and uncertain. They put their arms around each other and held tight for a moment.

"Abe, promise me you'll come?"

"I promise."

Layla pulled his head to hers and they kissed. Then she went to Sundance and mounted. Layla gave the dead man wide berth as she passed, as if he could still reach out and hurt her. She looked back to see that Abe had retrieved Dennis Galloway's horse.

41

The Red Berets scrambled. Within seconds, the unit converged on the spot where the beam had been broken. They moved toward the breach with nervous enthusiasm.

The soldiers approached from assigned directions, encircling the target area and then waiting for communication from Harrison Coulter, their commander. When Captain Coulter heard from each of his men, he signaled for them to begin searching their allotted quadrants. The men fingered assault rifles and peered through night vision goggles as they searched the forest.

One of the soldiers made his way to the edge of the clearing and began to circle toward the rows of equipment. He kept close to the tree line and looked from side to side. Reaching the machinery, he worked his way down one of the rows, looking under and around each piece as if this was his particular assignment.

The soldier stopped at what was the largest log skidder he had ever seen. Then he studied the structures and objects within the clearing, trying to determine where a sniper might be positioned. It infuriated him that Kenneth Leyman would stoop to such tactics, and made him all the more determined to strike hard at this man.

Moonshine coursed through his veins, emboldening him. The soldier could not help but chuckle at how easily he had slipped into this nest of law enforcement. In the excitement of the moment, no one noticed that his camouflage was the wrong shade of green or that his night vision goggles were only goggles. He simply tripped the alarm, waited until the Red Berets arrived, and then joined in the search.

From inside his field coat the soldier withdrew a bundle of dynamite wired to a timing device. He worked fast, wrapping the explosives to the skidder with duct tape. This was many times more firepower than he usually employed, but he wanted to make a statement this time. He wanted Ken Leyman to know that this was now a war. The explosion would destroy or disable many pieces of equipment and would send a clear message that the Panther Patrol was not going to back down.

Suddenly, lights flashed on from all directions.

"Stand where you are and raise your hands," boomed the amplified voice of Miles Harding.

It wasn't because he lacked faith in the ability of the Red Berets that he maintained his men in positions around the equipment. In fact, during the weeks they had spent together, he gained great respect for Captain Coulter and his men. Miles had ordered his men not to leave the equipment for any reason because he also respected the cunning and skill of his adversary.

"Drop your weapon," Miles shouted.

The soldier held his AK-47 high and turned a slow circle. He felt helpless and exposed. He'd shaved off his beard for this mission and felt naked and vulnerable without it. His hazel-colored eyes showed cat-like in the glare and darted from side to side, looking for an escape route.

"Drop your weapon. I mean right now."

The soldier could see more lights approaching from the woods.

He knew he had no chance of escape, but would not allow himself to be captured. The soldier decided to dive beneath the closest piece of equipment and roll to the other side. Then he would spray the lights with bullets and try to reach another machine.

"This is the last time I'm going to warn you."

The soldier turned toward the voice and decided to dive as the sentence ended. But just before he did, a small red hole opened on his forehead, and his head cocked backwards. From the back of his head came a brilliant red spray, glistening in the searchlights. The soldier's central nervous system reacted, and his finger tightened on the trigger of his gun. A string of bullets rocketed toward the stars.

The agents on Miles' team had been ordered to return fire and some who were uncertain as to what was unfolding, fired upon the dying soldier. He was struck in the chest, the back, and the leg before he started to fall. He hadn't reached the ground when Miles Harding's voice was heard.

"Noooooooooo. Stop firing, damn it." When Miles reached the man on the ground, he kicked his foot at the dirt.

"Who the hell fired that first shot," he shouted, gazing about, with menace in his eyes. No answer came, only the glare of myriad lights.

The agent looked back at the dead soldier. He saw vacant eyes, glistening in the spotlights and there was no mistaking a bullet hole in the center of the man's forehead.

"Goddamn you Leyman," Miles muttered.

42

Layla awoke to a dawn chorus, hundreds of birds twittering and whistling in the trees outside the motel window. After lingering at Cove Creek Ranch for an hour, Layla drove to Waynesville and checked into the Maple Park Inn. She didn't want to risk a confrontation with Davis in her disconcerted condition.

Exhausted from lack of sleep followed by the harrowing ordeal in the Park, she slept soundly through the night. She did her best to block out thoughts of the encounter with Dennis Galloway. Abe's promise came to her and she smiled. Layla lay in bed a while longer, listening to the melody in the foliage, and considering the possibilities the future now held.

The Maple Park Inn was a cluster of cottages, characteristic of a motel left over from another era. The parking lot was a circle formed around five enormous maple trees, and many more maple trees lined the perimeter of the property behind the cottages. A night at this motel was just the sedative Layla needed to compensate for the trauma of the previous day.

A half hour later, Layla walked down Main Street to Watson's Restaurant for coffee and breakfast. She sipped a strong brew while eating warm slices of pumpkin bread. Layla smiled as she recalled the entertaining and enlightening conversation with Percy

Messer. While strolling back to the motel, she collected real estate magazines. Layla passed another hour perusing them on a bench underneath the old maple trees. She wasn't in a hurry to get home.

Layla was in a happy, optimistic mood when she entered the motel office to pay her bill. The proprietor, Bill Cathey, chatted as he poured coffee. She could hear a television through the open door of a room behind the counter. She spied an elderly Labrador retriever asleep on the floor just inside the door.

Layla smiled and vowed to herself that she was going to change her life. She was determined to eliminate the distractions that had kept her from what she really wanted to do, which was to write. Now, Layla knew that Abe was right, life could be that simple. And life would be wonderful, now that he was going to share it with her.

"Did you hear about the trouble in Pisgah Forest?" Bill asked as he tallied her bill.

"No, what trouble?"

"Guess the FBI got one of those Panther Patrol fellas."

"Th-they caught one of them?"

"Shot one of them; shot him dead. Happened late last night; news just come across. Haven't said who it is yet."

Layla put her coffee on the counter and fumbled for her credit card.

"Are you all right, ma'am, you look kind of white all of a sudden?"

"Y-yes, I'm okay, I just need to get home now."

As he checked Layla out, the innkeeper looked at her registration form and saw that she lived only fifteen miles away. He shrugged and ran her card.

"You have a nice day now," he said as Layla hurried out the door.

As she drove home, Layla tried to calm down by reminding herself that Abe went only to warn the other members of the Panther Patrol. *But why did someone get shot then? Abe had time to get there to warn them.*

She wagged her head from side to side as if she could dislodge the doubts. *No, I have to believe that he's all right. He said he will find me, wherever I go, and that's what's going to happen.*

Despite her efforts, Layla pulled into the driveway of her home with uncertainty gnawing at her. She was hoping to get to her room without encountering Davis, but upon entering the house, she found him in the leather recliner, staring at her. He had a strange, glazed look in his eyes, a bottle of beer was on the side table. Layla glanced at his feet and saw the vodka bottle at his feet. He was dressed in the same wardrobe of two days before.

"Davis, oh, hi, I didn't expect . . ."

"Where were you, Layla?"

"I, well, I stayed at Tracy's."

"No you didn't. You always tell me when you're going to be gone. I called Tracy. I was worried about you."

"You're right, I didn't. I stayed at a motel in Waynesville, the Maple Park Inn. I, I needed a break from everything, that's all."

Davis nodded and stared for a few seconds before he spoke. "Did you hear the news? It looks like Dennis Galloway is true to his word."

"Dennis Galloway is true to his word about what?"

"About what he would do to the Panther Patrol. He said that when one of them showed their head he would put a bullet in it.

243

That's what happened."

Davis' words triggered a surge of anxiety in Layla. She was terrified to learn more but had to know.

"I heard at the motel that a member of the Panther Patrol was killed by the FBI."

Davis gave her a look as if to imply that she was being naive. "The man was shot right in the center of his forehead and there is some question about who fired the first shot. Dennis Galloway did that."

"B-but they haven't identified the man, right?"

"They have now. I just saw it on the news. Some guy who lived in a little cabin up near Waterville. His name is Wolford, Samuel Wolford."

The sound of his name affected her like an electric shock. Layla felt weak on her legs. She stared at her husband with a look of horror.

"No, it can't be him."

"Y-yes it is, Samuel Wolford. I just heard it. How do you know him?"

Layla shook her head, while tears trembled down her cheeks.

Davis was alarmed at the dramatic transformation in his wife and pulled himself to his feet. "Layla, what's wrong?"

She turned away, waving him off. As she ascended the stairs, she began to cry in great, heaving sobs.

"Layla," Davis called.

She didn't answer but continued up the stairs to her bedroom.

Davis had never seen his wife so distraught. He sat back down for an instant, then stood and went to the kitchen to get a bottle of beer. His hand shook more than usual as he opened it. He crept back into the hall and listened. He could hear Layla crying and talking aloud. Davis thought he heard drawers opening and closing.

Returning to his chair, he added a measure of vodka to the shot glass and drank it down. Forty five minutes passed and Layla came down the stairs with two suitcases. She said nothing to him as she took them out to her car. When she reentered the house and started up the stairs, Davis spoke.

"Are you moving out?"

Layla looked at him and nodded.

"Do you need help?"

"No, only one more box." She hurried up the stairs.

Davis stood and lumbered across the room. He met his wife at the bottom of the stairs. He had such a confused and sad look on his face that Layla began to cry again. She put the box down and hugged him.

"Good by, Davis. I'll let you know when I land somewhere." She released him, picked up her box, and walked to the door.

"Layla is there anything I can do?" He slurred his words.

She turned and looked at him, sobbing. "Yes, Davis, please stop drinking so much." She turned and left the house.

Davis stared at the door for a moment. Then he sighed and turned toward the kitchen. When he opened the refrigerator, he realized that he was out of beer. He had planned to drive to Waynesville to restock, but forgot because of Layla's appearance. Now he was too drunk to drive.

Davis returned to the living room and reached for the vodka bottle. The tragic look in his wife's eyes haunted him and he wanted to wash it away. He felt that he was somehow responsible. Davis didn't want to be married to Layla any longer, but he hated to think that he might have hurt her.

His hand was shaking as he poured the vodka. He lost his grip and the bottle fell on his lap, dousing him and the chair. He stood up and the bottle fell to the carpet, spilling more of its contents before he could right it.

Davis sat down, wet and miserable. He hung his head, disgusted with himself. And now Layla was gone. He thought about her final words and began to cry.

43

When Layla stopped near Cincinnati for gas, it was dark. She was at an enormous gas station with rows of pumps, and tractor trailers on all sides. An area the size of a football field was lit like it was day. Layla pulled up to the outermost row and charged the gas on a credit card. She was back on the road in ten minutes.

From Cincinnati she traveled Interstate 74 into Indiana, passing through Indianapolis at three o'clock in the morning. Two hours later, Layla crossed into Illinois and weariness overcame her. She pulled into the next rest stop. With rumbling diesel engines to lull her to sleep, she tilted the seat back and closed her eyes.

Layla awoke several hours later when the big trucks started pulling out. This far north, the temperature was cooler than she was used to. She pulled a denim jacket from the back seat and draped it over herself. The dawning scenery was so unfamiliar that for a short while, it served as a welcome distraction. When she recalled the motivation for her road trip, Layla hung her head to cry some more.

How could fate be so cruel, to bring us together like that and let us fall in love, only to take you away? Oh Abe, why did you go back?

She wiped away tears and laid her head against the seat.

In the end, the house didn't matter anymore; money didn't matter. In the end you were all I wanted.

The sun was appearing through a tangle of tree limbs on the horizon when Layla got out of the car. She went to the rest room and washed her face. Gazing at her image in the mirror was like looking at a stranger. Layla nearly smiled at that notion.

Never in her life had she felt such loss and sadness. But never had she felt such freedom as she did at this moment. Layla had walked away from her old life to start a new one. The terrible void that opened with Abe's death would be filled with new dreams.

And that's what Abe would want. With that thought, Layla smiled. Even though she would do it alone now, she planned to simplify her life and devote the rest of it to writing. *What better way to preserve the memory of the wonderful time I had with Abe Carol Ramsey.*

Back in the car, she looked over the map and decided to continue north on Interstate 74 and then to travel west on Interstate 80. She checked her voice mail before resuming the journey and saw there were three messages from Tracy. Looking at the clock on the dash, Layla knew her friend would be awake. She had phoned Tracy shortly after she left Mountain Crest, but knew that whatever she said then had surely been confusing. Layla knew Tracy would be worried.

"Hello, Layla?"

"Hi Tracy, Sorry I didn't get back to you sooner."

"Where are you? Are you all right?"

"I'm somewhere in Illinois and I'm doing a little better. Sorry for the weird phone call yesterday but I was a wreck then."

"That's okay. I can imagine what you were going through. But,

248

Layla, have you listened to the news today?"

"No, I don't want to hear any news for a long time. I've kept the radio off."

"Then let me ask you something. How old did you say Abe was?"

"He told me he was thirty-three. Why?"

"I have this morning's paper in front of me and the headline article is about the shooting."

"Tracy, I don't want to hear . . ."

"Please, Layla, you've got to let me read this. The victim was identified as Samuel Wolford, fifty-seven. A veteran of the Viet Nam War, Wolford was a member of the army rangers and an expert with explosives. A native of Haywood County, he . . ."

"Viet Nam, fifty-seven years old? Oh my God, I don't believe it."

"What?"

"It was Abe's father."

44

Agent Harding switched on a flashlight and directed its beam through the door of a small cabin. The building was nestled into a grove of hardwoods and rhododendron at the end of a narrow dirt road. The neglected structure hardly suggested to Miles the headquarters of a terrorist organization.

The cabin measured twenty feet by fifteen feet and was sided with rough hemlock planks. A charred, black stovepipe protruded from a rusted metal roof. The dwelling lacked running water and electricity. The only operative outhouse that Miles had ever seen in his life was located thirty-five yards to the west in a large rhododendron bush.

The inside boasted few amenities: a sink that drained to the outside onto a pile of rocks, an old, worn easy chair, a loft with a sleeping bag, and a wood burning stove made from a steel drum. Culinary effects included some old pots and pans, rice, potatoes, and some sort of dried meat in canning jars. A three liter wine bottle was half filled with a clear liquid that the agents presumed to be moonshine.

Most of the cabin was devoted to bombs. Against one wall were shelves with the necessary materials on display: caps, fuses, timers, and detonators. A carton of dynamite rested on the floor below the shelves. On a table in the center of the room was an assembled bomb.

When the dead soldier was searched, a phone number was discovered in his wallet. It belonged to a woman from Tennessee who told the FBI that the man was leasing the building from her. The old hunting cabin was situated on a four hundred acre piece of land near Waterville, North Carolina. The woman told the FBI that she thought it was odd that the man wanted to rent such a decrepit little place. But when he offered to repair fences and look after the property, not to mention pay his rent in cash, she agreed.

All indications were that only Samuel Wolford had occupied the cabin, but a team was picking through the contents to be certain of that. The agents found evidence that someone had recently removed a considerable amount of facial hair. This suggested that the slain man was the bearded adversary Miles had encountered before.

Several arrows were discovered, leaning in a corner, thus providing a link to the Panther Patrol. Aside from a cache of weapons discovered in a hidden compartment beneath the floor, there were no surprising revelations. The evidence indicated that Samuel Wolford was the Panther Patrol and as such, a disgruntled loner, fighting his own little war.

Yet the fact that Wolford lived without television or computer suggested that he must have received information from someone. That afternoon Miles was given a file on Samuel "Cappy" Wolford and learned that his namesake was also wanted by the FBI. Samuel Wolford Jr. disappeared into Great Smoky Mountains National Park ten years before and the point of disappearance happened to be only twenty miles from this spot.

Like his father, the younger Wolford was an Army Ranger;

251

Cappy served in Viet Nam, and his son was active during the Persian Gulf War. If Samuel Jr. was still in the area, that could explain the father's source of information. The possibility seemed remote since most people involved with the case believed that the younger Wolford died in Great Smoky Mountains National Park a decade ago while his father was in Montana. The elder Wolford moved to the area only eighteen months before his own death.

Earlier that evening, in his motel room in Waterville, Miles puzzled over the new developments in the case and was not getting the rest he went there for. He decided to drive back to the cabin to think it through again. He also wanted to brief the agents who would remain at the site throughout the night. He switched off the flashlight not quite convinced that the case of the Panther Patrol ended in this little building.

Miles smiled after he briefed agents Hostetler and Ballard. The two men were excited about this assignment and incognizant of their leader's overall disappointment.

Miles maneuvered his Ford Expedition along the dirt road and away from the cabin, confident that the two young agents would have an uneventful watch. The weather had been hot during the day but it was cool now and he opened the window to savor the rich night air.

Miles believed that Ken Leyman was behind the recent spate of attacks on other logging companies and also responsible for the sniper that killed Samuel Wolford. But his superiors were reluctant to sanction an open investigation of the logging magnate on the basis of mere suspicion. That indicated to Agent Harding that Leyman was winning the behind-the-scenes battle in Washington.

Miles wasn't surprised, in fact, he anticipated it. That was the reason he tried to goad Leyman into a careless move, so that the

252

man might incriminate himself before the political winds shifted back in his favor.

Now, Agent Harding assumed he would be leaving the area as soon as his team concluded their examination of the cabin and its contents. He told himself it was just as well. As much as he would like to take down Kenneth Leyman, he sensed no good opportunity here. He knew that strong evidence was needed to outflank the legal team that Leyman would have at his disposal. Without solid backing in Washington, there was no chance of obtaining such evidence.

Just before he reached the paved road, Miles thought he heard gunshots. He stopped the vehicle and listened. Then he heard more shooting. Miles shifted into reverse and backed down the road to within forty yards of the cabin. He turned the wheel hard to the left and spun sideways across the road. The agent exited with his head low and scrambled through the brush to where agents Hostetler and Ballard were positioned.

"Ballard, it's Harding, coming in behind you. What the hell happened?"

"I don't know chief. We heard breaking glass and started to move on the cabin when someone opened fire."

"Did you return fire?"

"Yes sir, I shot a round up above the cabin. We're not sure if they're inside or out."

Miles glanced back and forth and then whispered commands. "Okay men, flank them, one of you on each side. Keep your distance and keep low. When I give the signal . . ."

His instructions were interrupted by more gunfire. Agent Ballard returned fire, this time aiming lower.

Miles wondered what the purpose of this attack could be. From what he had learned so far, the cabin contained no incriminating evidence for anyone but Samuel Wolford, and he was dead. This was the reason the site was not more heavily guarded.

Miles instructed Agent Ballard to sweep the cabin with gunfire and then motioned for the other agent to go. But just as Miles started to move, there came a tremendous explosion that caused all three men to flatten to the ground. One side of the cabin was blown away and what remained was soon engulfed in flames. Fragments of the building rained down on the agents as they looked up.

Now Miles knew the purpose. He shook his head and laughed. He didn't know what else could go wrong with this assignment. At the outset, he thought that dealing with the Panther Patrol was to be a sideshow. When the younger agents looked at him for direction he signaled for them to stay down. He wasn't going to top the night off with one of them getting killed. Miles called for backup.

The ruins of the cabin were still smouldering as day dawned. Miles leaned against his vehicle and sipped black coffee as a team of agents picked through the rubble. There wasn't much to see before the explosion, so Miles didn't join them to look now. Instead, he stood alone and pondered the possible motive behind the destruction of the cabin.

There must have been something in there that we overlooked. It must have been pretty damn important for somebody to risk coming back here.

He was so engaged in thought that Agent Dowling spoke before Miles even noticed that the young man had walked up behind him.

"Sir."

"Oh, yes, Tom, what do you have?"

"Sir we found a horse tethered to a tree about sixty yards south of here."

"A horse?"

"Yes sir. Ballard's bringing her up. No sign of the rider. We made out one set of footprints, heading this way."

Miles' sullen face transformed. "Well what the hell, that's interesting. Let's have a look at that horse."

As they walked toward the woods, the men noticed commotion at the cabin site. One of the searchers jogged toward them. At thirty yards, the agent thumbed over her shoulder and spoke in an excited voice.

"We found a body in the rubble."

Miles didn't say a word but started toward the cabin at a rapid pace. When he reached the ruins, the two men who were crouched over the charred human remains moved aside. Miles shook his head in disbelief.

If not for the blackened, skeletal hand that protruded into the air and a lower jaw bone upon which teeth were visible, it wouldn't be obvious that these were human remains. Agent Dowling came up beside Miles.

"Jesus, Chief, what do you suppose?"

"Only thing I can figure is that there was something in here that they wanted and in the firefight the place accidentally blew. Or maybe they tried to blow up the place to cover evidence and didn't get out in time. At any rate, we're back in business. Let's ID this body as soon as possible."

"Will do, Chief."

Miles stood up and rubbed his hands together. As he walked toward Agent Ballard and the Appaloosa mare that he led into the clearing, he was more animated then he had been in days.

That afternoon, Miles received a call from Tom Morrison.

"Tom, what's up?"

"Got something that might interest you. A pickup truck with a horse trailer has been parked in Cataloochee Valley for two days. Park rangers called me this morning."

"Hey, you have no idea how much that interests me, Tom."

"Well then listen to this. Truck and trailer are rentals out of South Carolina, and they were rented by a Mr. Dennis Galloway."

Agent Harding was expressionless for a moment. As this information registered, the corners of his mouth began to twitch, and then a wide grin spread across his face.

45

Kenneth Leyman sat in his study, feeling old and stodgy. He had a terrible day on the golf course that afternoon, capped off by a double bogey on the eighteenth hole. His hip was bothering him again. Laura was in Italy with Carolyn. They timed a vacation to coincide with Antoine's touring schedule. The violinist's string quartet was performing in Milan later in the week.

Dennis Galloway hadn't responded to a phone message left two days before, something that was unprecedented. It was dark but Ken had only turned on a desk lamp. The gloom of the study reflected his mood.

The shooting of Samuel Wolford was also troubling Ken. Not that he felt any remorse for this man who he considered a lawless thug who got what he deserved. But the public reaction was not favorable. Even some who were squarely in the pro-logging camp were uneasy about the violent way that this man had been dealt with.

Ken rarely questioned Dennis' judgment in his area of expertise but he didn't understand the rationale behind shooting a man who was so hopelessly surrounded.

He let Agent Harding get to him, that's what happened. That's why his plan was so rigid. Harding slighted him and Dennis wanted to hit back. He wanted to make the man look foolish.

Because of his concern over Dennis' lack of communication, Ken had activated two body guards. He glanced out the window from time to time to make certain that they were making their rounds.

He rose to pour himself another scotch, determined to alter his mood. Ken reminded himself of the pleasant conversation with the Governor of North Carolina that morning. It was just like old times. He sympathized with Malcolm's concern over Davis' erratic behavior and obvious drinking problem. Layla's sudden departure delighted Ken. He assured Malcolm that it was for the better. Ken eased back into his chair, drink in hand, his humor starting to improve.

Then he noticed a man standing a few feet from him. Before he could react, he was lifted from the chair and thrust onto his back atop the desk. The intruder crouched over Ken like a great cat and stared down with hypnotic, hazel-colored eyes. Ken's fright turned into terror when he realized that the man had a knife at his throat. The man said nothing for half a minute, only stared as a cat would, waiting for the prey to make a move.

Ken could stand it no longer. "Is, is it m-money you want? Please, I'll . . ."

"I don't want your money Leyman. I don't have any use for your damn money."

"What d-do you want then?"

"In the military we use an expression, 'decapitation strike'. It's an operation designed to take out the enemy's leader. It's usually done with rockets or bombs. This right here, this is as basic as a decapitation strike gets."

Ken shuddered but dared not move. The edge of the knife was

pressed against his throat and even swallowing caused it to crease the skin.

"Why?"

"For all the trouble you've caused that's why; for logging my forests. You killed Ira Brewer, and you killed Cappy Wolford."

"No, no, I didn't kill anyone. I have a man who works for me. He, he s-sometimes goes too far. I was just thinking about that tonight. I'll rein him in, I swear."

"You won't have to. Your man's already been reined in."

This was said with a casual certainty that sent a tremor through Ken's body. He knew that Dennis must be dead and so, felt even more helpless. He pleaded for his life.

Abe applied pressure to the knife. "Shut up and die like a man."

"No, no, please, I'll do anything you ask. I have money, lots of money. I, I'll give you whatever you want."

Abe shook his head in disgust. "Why is it that someone like you, a weak little coward, can have so much power and cause so much trouble? It's just because you have money, and it's not right. Well, Mr. Leyman, I'm not impressed with your money. You don't have any power tonight and soon you'll cause no more trouble."

"No wait, I have a wife, children . . ."

"Shut up. Did you send your man to kill Layla Turner?"

"No, no, I didn't know anything about it, I swear. Dennis must have . . . But she's not dead. She's not dead. I talked to her father-in-law this evening. She just moved away. She left her husband and drove to Alaska."

Abe eased up on the knife as he considered this information. Layla had taken his advice but he didn't expect her to go so far away. He had to force himself not to smile as he thought about

259

Layla. *She went to Alaska, just like the woman in her story.*

Abe was never certain that he would kill Kenneth Leyman, although he felt the man deserved to die. Because Layla was brought to mind, he remembered what she had said, that violence only leads to more violence. He stared at the pitiful man beneath him, quivering with fear, whimpering for his life. Abe decided just to warn him again.

He bent down close to the face of his captive. "I'm not going to kill you *now*, Leyman, but I'll be watching. I'll be in the woods at the edge of your lawn or in the rhododendron, watching you double bogey the eighteenth hole."

Ken listened in dread and spoke in a whisper. "Who are you?"

Abe stared for a moment and then answered in a low, coarse voice. "I'm Cataloochee Man. Stay out of my forest."

Abe withdrew the knife from Ken's throat, jumped from the desk, and disappeared.

46

The hunter awoke at his main camp on Spruce Mountain and stared into a web of hemlock branches. It was noon and he had slept for ten hours. Abe was recovering from days of exhausting work. Realizing the time, he rolled to his feet, stretched his body in all directions, and then ambled down the slope to the spring.

Thirty yards from Abe's dwelling, water flowed from crevices in a rock outcrop. Some of the water collected in a shallow depression on a ledge as if nature had designed a suitable wash basin for a mountain man.

While pulling the frigid water across his face, Abe heard the hoot of a Barred Owl, an unusual sound for this time of the day. He smiled; he knew that Neil Guthrie was nearby. Abe cupped hands around his mouth and returned the call. Neil would not come any closer until he heard it.

As Abe turned, he spotted his childhood friend, edging down the slope above the shelter. Neil was grinning, and Abe knew he had accomplished his mission. The two men clasped hands and patted each others shoulders.

Neil Guthrie was an inch shorter than Abe but broader than his friend and possessed a powerful, muscular frame. His eyes were hidden by dark shades underneath the bill of his cap. He had straight blonde hair, and a rough, wild beard of various blonde shades. Neil wore camouflage fatigues, leather combat boots and an AK-47.

"Mission accomplished, comrade Ramsey. Man, that guy was ripe by the time I blew him up. What did you say his name was?"

"Dennis something."

"How did it go with his boss?"

"Good. I didn't kill him. We had a talk, and I think he got the message."

Abe told Neil the details of his conversation with Ken Leyman and his friend grinned during the entire narration. He laughed aloud at the final lines. When Neil told his story about the destruction of the cabin near Waterville, Abe was also amused but even more amazed.

"No one but you could have pulled something like that off, Neil. Dad would be proud."

Neil's grin faded. "Too bad about Cappy, Abe. I'm sorry, man. Hard to believe the old cuss is dead."

"Well I tried to stop him, but he was determined to go in there, sniper or no sniper. In fact, he seemed more determined to complete the mission when he found out there was a sniper. Anyway, that's the way he would have wanted it, to go down facing the feds."

"Hah, ain't that the truth. But, he knew his time was up, too. The cancer was killing him. He was in a lot more pain than he let on."

Abe looked at the ground.

"You know, Abe, when your old man got sick, he come back lookin' for ya. He wanted to make it right. That says a lot."

Abe didn't look at Neil as he considered his remarks. Then he grinned. "Yeah, I know. Course then he decided to stay and take charge again."

They laughed and then were silent for a moment. Both men were thinking the same thought, but Abe spoke first.

"Neil, I think it's time to disband the Panther Patrol."

Neil smiled. "I have to confess, I was thinking that same thing. It won't be the same without our fearless leader, anyway."

"Actually, I was thinking of it before Dad got killed."

"Well, you won't get any argument from me this time."

Abe was surprised that Neil was so agreeable on this point since the Panther Patrol had been his idea.

"What will you do with all your free time, Neil?"

"Stay right in Cosby and do what I been doing. I've been there over eight years now. Hard to believe isn't it? In the beginning, I just wanted to see if you were still alive. I planned to go back out west. But I like my weldin' business. In fact, I'm thinking of hiring help and expanding it some. I like ridin' my Harley in the mountains. The Panther Patrol's been fun, but that's not the only thing that keeps me going."

"You forgot to mention Jen."

"I didn't forget. I was just savin' her for last 'cause that's another reason I should give up this dangerous sport. Jen and me are thinking, real serious, of moving in together."

"Getting married?"

"Hmm, maybe that, too. But hey, Abe, I'll still be around and I can bring you what you need, arrowheads, matches, toilet paper, you name it."

"Thanks, Neil. That reminds me, I have a favor to ask. Could you pick me up some clothes?"

"You mean street clothes?"

"Yes, street clothes, something other than camouflage or Harley Davidson. I want simple things. Get me some blue jeans, tee shirts, and a pair of tennis shoes, a jacket, just the basics."

Neil was bewildered. "Sure, Abe, I can do that. Do you want me to bring them here?"

"No, I'll come by your place in a few days."

"What the hell, Abe, you comin' out of the woods or what?"

"I, I think so. No, I mean, I know so. It's a long story, Neil. When I come by, I'll tell you all about it."

"Hey, sounds like a party. I got a gobbler that I shot last spring. I'll thaw him out for the occasion."

Abe and Neil shook hands. Neil held Abe's hand a moment longer and stared into his friend's eyes, thus marking the end of an era. He spoke the same parting words he had used since they were Boy Scouts. He borrowed the lines from *Jeremiah Johnson*, an old movie about a legendary mountain man. He and Abe had loved the movie when they were boys. "Keep your nose in the wind, Abe, and keep your eyes along the skyline."

"You do the same, Neil."

Abe's friend nodded, turned to the north and moved down the slope.

Abe watched Neil until he was out of sight and then stood for a few minutes longer, staring down the steep slope through a maze of foliage. It was mid September and at this elevation, many of the maple leaves were losing their green color. A cool breeze wafted up the slope, a breeze laced with autumnal melancholy.

Abe turned and surveyed the humble abode that had been his home for eight years. He looked up through the towering hemlocks that protected and hid him, buffering the elements and dissipating the smoke from his fires. The sighing of the wind through countless evergreen leaves had lulled him to sleep many nights. Everything about this place was simple and predictable. Abe felt secure and at peace when he was here.

Yet of all the hours he had lived on Spruce Mountain, those he passed with Layla were the best. Abe walked to the entryway of his shelter. He imagined himself, lying on his back in the loft and Layla lying on top of him with her head resting on his chest. Abe was overcome by an intense yearning to be with her again.

Two hours later, Abe pulled down the last of the deer hides that comprised his roof system. Then he dismantled part of the back wall until a leather bundle was uncovered. Unrolling it across his lap, Abe stared at the gun he took from Percy Messer. He hadn't looked at the firearm since it was built into the wall eight years before.

The sight of it conjured up memories of that terrible night in Waynesville and also reminded him of the man he once was. But now Abe could leave the past where it belonged. Because a person as wonderful as Layla loved him, he thought better of himself. If Layla believed in him then he could believe too.

The deerskin also contained a wallet. Abe opened it to see his own image staring back from a long ago expired driver's license. It was a beardless young man who had gotten married the year the photograph was taken. Abe also found fourteen dollars, the change from the bar that night in Waynesville. He knew that wouldn't get him far, even by bus.

Despite the argument Abe had made in favor of walking to Alaska, he knew he had to see Layla sooner than three or four months. He decided to take her advice and travel by bus.

Abe went to his quiver and removed the arrows. He reached inside and withdrew a wad of folded bills. He counted eleven hundred-dollar bills. Smiling, he tucked them inside the wallet. He could only guess why Dennis Galloway needed to carry so much cash. Whatever the reason, Abe was certain that he didn't need it anymore.

Now the hunter was excited and anxious to depart. He unstrung his bow and wrapped it in deerskin along with the quiver and arrows. The policeman's revolver was wrapped in deerskin again and Abe rebuilt the wall around both weapons. Then the entire site was covered with brush. After circling the area several times, Abe was satisfied that it wouldn't be detected.

Collecting his duffel bag and food pouch, Abe walked north. Late in the afternoon, he crossed the Appalachian Trail at Cosby Knob. The hunter continued north into Tennessee along Cosby Creek. He planned to walk for another five miles and then camp for the night. In the morning he would follow the creek out of Great Smoky Mountains National Park

47

Layla opened French doors to a spectacular view of Mount Sanford and breathed in frosty autumn air. She loved her new job at Chistochina Elementary School and was in an exuberant mood. Layla felt fortunate to have arrived just as the position opened. Her employment was all the more fortuitous, considering that the entire student body consisted of sixteen Athabaskan students, and only one teacher was necessary.

With a population of ninety-eight, Chistochina was even smaller than she had imagined it from the stories her father told her. Besides the school, the community hosted a cafe, a bar, a campground, a bed and breakfast and a gas station. Layla loved everything about her new location.

She was renting a cabin on the edge of town that had a small deck facing Mount Sanford, the highest mountain in the Wrangell St. Elias National Park. She went out on the porch, collected an arm load of kindling, and carried it inside to a wood cookstove. She fell in love with the stove at an antique shop in Juneau and had it delivered to Chistochina after she rented the cabin. With its brass fittings and ornately enameled backing, it became the centerpiece of her home.

Layla lit a fire in the stove and placed an iron pot on top of it.

The pot contained lentil soup she had prepared the night before. Her routine for this time of day was to sit in a rocking chair that was located between the stove and the open doors. With the heat at her back and the magnificent view to her front, Layla would read poetry and excerpts from her favorite novels.

This evening, however, she was opening a letter from Tracy with great anticipation. Layla had no internet access, and the two friends had been communicating in the old fashioned way. Both women had much to tell. With the dramatic upheaval in her life, everyday was a new adventure for Layla to write about. But these days, Tracy had her share of news as well.

Layla was surprised to hear about the fiery demolition of the cabin near Waterville and shocked at the discovery of Dennis Galloway's body among the ashes. She realized the genius in this development as Tracy kept her updated on the FBI investigation that was dogging Ken Leyman.

Layla was delighted to learn that Governor Elmore declared a moratorium on logging in the national forests after the latest spate of violence. It was a prudent move, considering his long-time friend, logging magnate, Kenneth Leyman, was being investigated by the FBI for possible connection to an eco-terrorist group.

Tracy heard that Kenneth Leyman was seldom seen in public anymore, and when he was, it was always with body guards. Michael Ogden had a patient who maintained the grounds at the Balsam Mountain Country Club. He said that Mr. Leyman had been a regular at the club since it was established, but now he never set foot on the course.

Layla smiled when she read that Tracy had seen Davis in Waynesville. She wrote that he looked good and behaved like his old self. Davis told Tracy that he joined Alcoholics Anonymous and stated that he hadn't had a drink in over a month. Tracy wrote that Davis was excited about his law practice on Main Street and didn't want to live in Raleigh again.

Just as Layla finished Tracy's letter, there came a rush of wind, causing the leaves on the porch to swirl in an eddy. Layla stood and stepped onto the porch. She stared at Mount Sanford, rising from the distant wilderness.

Layla felt a tingle on the back of her neck. She shuddered as it pulsed across her shoulders. She knew Abe was coming; something in the wind told her it was so. *He promised that he would find me, wherever I went. This is a good place for him to come out of the forest.*

Layla went inside and added wood to the fire. She planned a simple supper, lentil soup and garlic bread. Then as she did every evening, she would ascend to the loft to write.

The End

Made in the USA
Lexington, KY
31 May 2011